FISHERMAN'S LUCK

Books by Tom Pace
FISHERMAN'S LUCK
THE TREASURE HUNT
AFTERNOON OF A LOSER

FISHERMAN'S LUCK
by Tom Pace

HARPER & ROW, PUBLISHERS

New York, Evanston, San Francisco, London

1817

A JOAN KAHN–HARPER NOVEL OF SUSPENSE

FIRST EDITION

STANDARD BOOK NUMBER: 06–013260–4

LIBRARY OF CONGRESS CATALOG CARD NUMBER: 77–156580

To Tom Holman

CHAPTER 1: Garden stepped up on the seawall and stared at the rush of the tide through the inlet. "It don't look so rough," he said. "No worse than usual." He had to raise his voice above the slap of the water against the seawall. "What was he doing when he fell in?"

"I tole you," Kelley said hoarsely. He jumped up on the wall, not as easily as Garden had. He was as tall as Garden, and a great deal wider. "He was up on the bridge with me," he said. "And it wasn't no rougher than now, just tossing a little."

Garden looked at the swirling water running out swiftly with the tide through the narrow inlet. The water was brown with the tannins of the waterway, too dark to see into. "Was he drunk?" he asked.

"You know better, Ben," Kelley said. "Not on my boat. Not with passengers aboard."

"Sorry," Garden said.

"I guess he just got careless."

"I thought he'd been doing it too long to be careless. How old was he, Tommy?"

"Aw, about twenty-five, twenty-six. Yeah, he's been going in boats for ten, twelve years. Eight years with me." Kelley paused and swallowed. "But that's when they get careless." He spat into the inlet. He put his fists on his hips, his thick shoulders stooped, and stared at the fast brown water.

"Damn it, Ben! When's the county gonna fix this goddam

inlet? Too damn many people get drowned. It ain't wide enough to spit through. Just thirty or forty more feet would calm this run down a whole lot. And that bridge is getting mighty old, anyway." He nodded at the rust streaks on the old-fashioned fixed bridge humped over the inlet.

"Sure," Garden said. "You want to pay for that, Tommy? You and the rest of the boatmen around here?"

"Why should we?" the captain said, scowling. "Don't the fishing bring in tourists? And these damned retired people? Ain't that what the Commission is always saying?"

"Don't tell me," Garden said. He stepped down off the wall, and the captain followed him.

"No, look here, Ben—can't you talk to them? Chief of police and all, they got to listen to you. They—" Kelley stopped, staring out the inlet. He pointed and jumped back on the wall. Garden followed, looking at the small boat surging into sight, coming into the inlet.

"They must have found him," Garden said.

"Already?"

"Sheriff McGee's got some good boys," Garden said. They both watched as the boat wallowed into the inlet, steadying as the deputy at the helm gave it more power, and then came slicing toward them through the turbulent water.

"Yeah, they got him, all right," the captain said sadly.

Garden nodded. As the boat passed below them, close to the seawall, he could see the blanket-wrapped bundle on the floor of the cockpit.

One of Garden's men was in the boat with the deputy and the three divers. He looked up at Garden as they ran past, and made a quick gesture, one finger to the side of his head. Then he pointed to the side, toward the docks, looking urgently at Garden. Garden's eyebrows lifted.

"Pore old Billy," the captain said sadly.

"Yeah! Come on, Tommy." They left the wall and walked

across the parking lot toward the boat docks. At the docks they had to shove through milling groups—the crews from the boats that were in, fishermen and curious watchers. One of the men grabbed the captain by the arm.

"How long are we going to stay here, Captain Kelley?" he asked. "My fish will spoil!"

"Then clean 'em," Kelley said, and tugged his arm away.

"How can I? These people won't let us use their cleaning tables!"

Kelley wheeled and glared at another man. "That so, Henry?"

"That's right, Kelley," the other said. "My facilities are for boats based here. Not for transients."

"Why, you cheap son of—"

"Don't get smart now," Henry said shrilly. "Now don't get smart. Not my fault if your mate fell overboard. Tell you what I'll do—I'll be glad to rent my tables and my hoses to your customers. A dollar a head!"

"What?" Kelley yelled.

"That's fair. That's fair. And I'll even knock five bucks off your docking fee. How's that?"

Kelley was bellowing as Garden pushed away through the last of the fishermen. He nodded at an ambulance attendant and said, "Howdy."

"Hi, Chief." The attendant nodded toward the resuscitation equipment on the planking beside them. "Don't reckon we'll do much good with that. An hour or so he's been in."

"Try it anyway," Garden said. The boat came around the end of the breakwater that extended into the waterway, forming the south side of the inlet. It picked up speed toward the dock.

"Oh, sure," the attendant said.

The boat slowed, and eased into the dock. One of the divers threw a line, and a half dozen hands grabbed for it. The boat bumped against the pilings, and Garden swung forward and

3

down into the boat, balancing his bulk easily as the boat tipped under him. "Howdy, Mack," he said to the deputy. "Okay to come aboard, I hope."

"Yeah," the deputy said. He nodded at the blanket-covered length in the cockpit. "Take a look," he said grimly.

"Eh?" Garden asked. He looked at his man.

Howell rubbed his chin. "We found him about a hundred yards south of the inlet, Chief," he said. "In close to the beach. Yeah, go on, look."

"What's wrong with you two?" Garden asked. He knelt by the body.

"It ain't a simple drowning," Howell said wearily. "Not no more."

"What?" Garden asked. He turned the blanket back. Billy Carter's head was turned to one side. The side of his face showed forth the gray look of death, under the bright hot afternoon sky. The blue hole below his temple was sharp-edged and distinct. The temple bulged a bit more than it should.

"Hell!" Garden said. He let the blanket fall, but not before he'd heard the pattering of clicks from tourist cameras along the dock. He looked up slowly at the wall of astonished avid faces.

"All right," he said wearily to Howell. "All right, then. Tell the ambulance boys they can put away their stuff. And call the coroner. If he says it's okay we can take him out of the boat as soon as we get some photos of our own." He scowled up at the crowd. "And get us a couple more men here. Wonder if you'd give me a hand, Mack," he asked the deputy.

"Sure thing, Chief."

"I got to get as many of these people out of here as I can. And get all the people off Kelley's boat inside for statements."

He stepped up on the gunwale, put his hands lightly on the planking and vaulted up onto his feet on the dock's edge. The crowd lurched away from him, and he looked at them sourly,

4

then looked back across the inlet. Howell jumped up beside him. Mack and the sheriff's divers followed, and began to spread out along the docks, Mack chanting, "Aw right, folks, aw right. Move back now, move back right now. Nothin' to see. Out of the chief's way now."

"First of all, Howell, call the coroner. Then get a car over there. Have them get over to the island." Garden pointed at the narrow spoil-bank island, thickly covered with Australian pines, that stretched out north of the inlet channel. "See if they can locate any kids with a rifle. Or any that heard a shot. It almost had to come from over there." He nodded and Howell shoved away through the crowd. Garden turned to the deputy. "Mack, about lending a hand, could you run over there to the waterway end of the island and go ashore? Sort of watch that end until our people get to the shore end and come through?"

"Sure," Mack said.

Garden took a deep breath, then turned and looked at the crowd. They stared at him from a few feet away, breathless. "Oh, Christ," Garden said, almost to himself. He waited.

Howell dodged back through the mob and said, "Okay, Chief. I got hold of the coroner, and the other guys are coming."

"Coroner say we can move him?"

"No, Chief, he was real positive; not until he gets here."

Garden snorted. "Sure! Right after the reporters get here," he said. "Did Peters round up the people off Kelley's boat?"

"Some of them, Chief. Some of them are cleaning fish and Captain Kelley is about to have a fight with old Henry."

"Fine. Let them fight. Howell, does—did Carter have any family?"

"Couple of brothers, Chief. One in the Army. Don't know where the other is. He had a married sister, up in Georgia, I think. His folks are dead."

"No wife, then?" Garden asked, relieved.

Howell grinned. "Not of his *own*, Chief. I hear he borrowed one, sort of every now and then."

"Oh, yeah?"

"Chief, I can call our other boat," Mack said. "They'll get to the waterway end of the island. I'll tell them you want them to check out anybody leaving."

"Thanks, Mack," Garden said. "Howell, get your notebook and come on. No, wait; before Mack came back in I rounded up a half dozen fishermen who were on the seawall when Carter went in. Some of them even saw him go over. Here's the names." He tore a page out of a small notebook, passed it to Howell. "I told them to come over here and wait. Bring them inside, eh?"

Garden turned and shoved through the people clustered on the pier. They gave way to let him pass and then eased back to stand near the edge, staring intensely and silently at the body with the blanket over it, as though it had a secret to impart if they were just attentive enough to capture it.

CHAPTER 2: Near the entrance to the restaurant, Kelley and Henry stood nose to nose, cursing at each other. A small group of Kelley's passengers goggled nervously at them, hands suspended over half-cleaned fish. Garden growled and shoved between them. Henry fell back a step, but Kelley stood firm, shoving back at Garden.

"All right!" Garden said. "Inside, both of you!"

"He can't pull that crap! This was an emergency, wasn't it?

6

I came in here on account of emergency. I wouldn't dock in this crummy place if I didn't have to," Kelley said, breathlessly furious.

"Crummy—who's saying crummy?" Henry yelled. "Look at that lousy boat! I ought to charge you more'n I said—"

"Shut *up!*" Garden roared. He took an arm of each of them and forced them apart.

"Take it easy now!" Kelley said in anger.

"Listen, Tommy. Your mate's out there dead. Will you for God's sake knock off the clowning?"

"Yeah. Sure, Ben, but this— Listen, they said Billy was shot. What the hell they mean, shot?" They went up on the porch toward the restaurant. Henry went ahead, head twisted toward Garden, stumbling on the step.

"Shot," Garden said, "with a gun. Didn't you hear the shot?"

"Hell, no, I didn't. Before he fell in? No, I didn't."

"Well, he probably didn't get shot after he fell in," Garden said. He stopped in the doorway and looked around the room. It was a bar with the kitchen at one side and an archway into the restaurant at the other. A score of beer drinkers crowded around the bar. "We'll go in the other room, Henry," Garden said. "Too early for you to have anybody eating, isn't it? Tommy, I want you to go out there and round up your passengers. Every damned one of them. Henry, I want you to sit here in the arch. I don't want anybody else in here. Not anybody."

"Suppose somebody *does* want to eat?" Henry asked, anguished. Garden stared at him until he went out reluctantly. Garden pulled out a chair at the center of the longest table and sank into it. It creaked under him. He took off his cap and rubbed his forehead. Howell ushered in a straggle of fishermen, waved them to one side. He came over and sat down at the head of the table, to Garden's right, and opened his notebook, putting two ballpoint pens beside it carefully. He picked one of them up again and carefully dated the page, made a few notes.

7

Garden eyed him. "*You* got any ideas?" he asked.

"Me, Chief? No."

"Anybody mad at Carter? Say, a husband?"

"Maybe," Howell said. "Probably, but—"

"Yeah! If everybody got shot for *that* around this town, we'd have more murder than we could handle. What the hell's keeping Tommy?"

"They're still cleaning their fish," Howell said.

"Oh, for Christ's sake! Go give him a hand," Garden said. Howell left the room, and Garden brooded. It was hot and stuffy and he looked for the switch that would turn on the ceiling fan, couldn't find it, and wished that he could drink a beer. The fishermen stared at him sullenly.

A car tipped sharply down the incline from the beach road and swept past the restaurant, and he recognized the coroner's Cadillac. Right behind it came another, and then a station wagon with a miniature tower mounted on top and the call letters of the local TV station on the side. Garden cursed.

Howell shepherded the captain and his passengers in through the bar. Kelley was grumbling loudly, and there were nervous complaints from the passengers. Most of them were middle-aged men with baseball caps, wrinkles and sunburn, smelling of fish and beer. There were three women, two of them like the men, one a younger woman, undistinguished except for huge breasts under a skimpy jersey, and a gray sick expression. The group in the bar crowded into the archway and stared. Garden glared at Henry, and raised his voice to say, "Nobody else in here. Everybody back at the bar, or I'll close and lock the place until we're through. Got that?"

"All right, all right, everybody back to the bar!" Henry called. "Come on now, you guys! Back to the bar."

"Close those damned doors," Garden said to Howell.

"Okay, Chief. Did you see the coroner?"

"Yeah, and I saw who he brought with him," Garden said.

Howell closed the folding doors across the archway with difficulty. It seemed to get hotter in the room.

"Okay," Garden said, loudly enough to get the crowd's attention. "In case you ladies and gentlemen don't know me, my name is Garden. I'm the chief of police here in Easton. Also in case you don't know, it now appears that a homicide has occurred. We thought Mr. Carter, Captain Kelley's mate, had fallen off the boat. It turns out that he was shot, and I'm going to have to ask you gentlemen—you all to bear with us, while you each describe for us what you saw and heard." There was a flurry of voices.

"Murder!" someone said.

Garden shook his head. "That's unlikely. Probably somebody plinking, and the poor guy got hit by accident."

"Accident!" Kelley snorted. He was leaning on the table staring at Garden. "Accident, hell, Ben! With the boat tossing around in that damned inlet the way it was? And he accidentally got shot right in the head like that?"

"Well, a bullet's got to hit *somewhere*," Garden said. "Sit down, Tommy! And you people, each of you take a chair and relax, please! We'll make this as fast as possible, but we got to have your statements. Siddown, Tommy! Now if you people will sit over there"—he indicated tables near the far wall—"we'll talk to the captain first. Howell, turn that fan on, will you? Switch is over there someplace."

Kelley sat down heavily in a chair by the table, grumbling, while Howell tried a few switches and found the one that turned on the ceiling fan. Its creaking roar filled the room, and Garden noticed with satisfaction that it was as loud as he had remembered. Even the nearer ones leaned forward and strained to hear as he spoke to Kelley.

"All right, Tommy, just tell us what happened, in your own

9

words. Speak toward Howell, but so I can hear it, too, and don't go too fast. He's got to have time to get it down, even in shorthand."

"Well!" Kelley straightened, rubbed his chin, cleared his throat. Garden tapped his fingers on the table. "Well," Kelley said, "it looked like it might rain early this morning, but it was clearing good by the time I got to the docks. No wind, but I knew it would pick up a little. There were—"

"Tommy, I don't give a damn about the weather! I don't even care how many fish you caught!"

"Well, you said—"

"Just tell us about coming in the inlet! Where was Carter, what were you doing, what did you— Ah, hell! Start with coming in the inlet."

"Well, we were coming in the inlet, okay? It wasn't bad, like I told you out there, no worse than I seen it most times. Not as good as it ought to be, of course, if that cheap-ass Commission would get off— Okay, Ben, okay! No other boats in the inlet, so I could bring her in without worrying about running over some dumb bastard in an outboard. Only thing I had to bother me was that guy Ryder blowing off—"

"Who?" Garden asked.

"Ryder. You know, that guy always on the city council's ass about something." Kelley jerked his head at the passengers. "You know him; hell, you ought to—he's the one complained to the council about the budget you put in for last year."

"Yeah," Garden said. "I just didn't notice him."

"He's being quieter than usual. Maybe it shut him up, seeing Billy go over."

"Go on, Tommy. Ryder was up there with you?"

"Yeah. Yeah, I usually don't like a passenger to come up top, but hell, it wasn't too rough, and no other boats going through, you know? Anyway, I'm used to it, he always wants to come up and talk. Shows the other guys what a old hand he is, I guess.

10

So he was jawing about something, and I wasn't listening much, and then Billy swung up on the rail to port, and I looked around and asked him if he had all the rods secured. You know. I knew he had, but just to say something. I guess I was tired of listening to Ryder."

"Go on," Garden said.

"Yeah, well, Billy said something. That he had them all in, or something like that. So he was sitting there straddle of the rail, and Ryder asked me a question, and I turned my head back around to him"—Kelley swung his head to the right elaborately —"and then all a sudden I heard somebody yell, and I looked back, and didn't see nothing, and then I looked for Billy and he was gone." He stopped.

"And then what?"

"What? Oh, well, they kept yelling. I figured one of the damned fools had fell in and I cut the throttles to just hold her there in the run and started yelling for Billy, to find out what was going on. Then one of the passengers started climbing up, yelling that the mate had fallen overboard. I looked back, but I never could see nothing. I wasn't too shook up, Ben. Hell, it happened so quick and anyway, you know how Billy could swim. But it bothered me that I never could see him."

"And then what?"

"Well, I knew we couldn't do nothing there. So I hooked her up and ran around the end of the breakwater and came in here to tie up quick and get people to look for him. Ben, can that son of a bitch get away with charging me that much to tie up? And what he's charging the passengers to use his lousy tables? He hit them each an extra buck to put their fish in his iceboxes, too. He—"

"Not now, Tommy! How long was it from the time you looked away from Billy until you heard somebody yell?"

"Oh, a minute or so. Not long," Kelley said.

"And did you hear a shot? Or anything that *might* have been a shot? The wound looked like a small-caliber slug made it. It might not have been too loud."

"Hell, Ben, no. The engines, and you know how she bangs in that chop. No, I didn't hear nothing."

"And you're sure Carter hadn't been drinking?"

"Ben, I tole you, no! He wasn't even hung over."

"Where were you when you heard the shouts? How far into the inlet? I mean as exactly as you can make it, Tommy."

" 'Bout fifty yards inside the bridge," Kelley said without hesitation. "Near as far in as the restaurant here."

"You sure?"

"Of course I'm sure! I been doing this for twenty-five years, Ben, and—"

"Okay, okay," Garden said. "You got all that, Howell?"

"Yeah, Chief," Howell said.

"All right, Tommy. I'd like to ask you to think about it. If you come up with anything else, let me know. I reckon there'll be an inquest." Garden glanced at the windows and met curious stares from outside. Beyond them he could see the mob, thicker than ever, on the pier and the TV station wagon parked next to the coroner's sedan. "I know damned well there'll be an inquest," Garden said.

"You mean that's all?" Kelley asked.

"That's all unless you think of something else, or I do," Garden said.

"But hell, Ben!"

"All this is about is how he might have gotten killed," Garden said tiredly. "It's not about what kind of guy he was, or how long he'd worked for you. Or anything like that. Not unless it has anything to do with who might have shot him. Okay?"

"I guess," Kelley said.

"I liked him all right, too, Tommy," Garden said.

"Yeah, Ben, yeah. Can I get out of here now?"

"Hadn't you better wait for your passengers?"

12

"Christl!" Kelley said.

"Anyway, I've got to look at the boat," Garden said.

"I can have a beer, can't I? Listen, I'll be on the boat," Kelley said.

"See you later," Garden said. He watched Kelley lumber away from the table, head down, shove the folding doors open and bull his way through the crowd in the bar. "Go shut that damned door, Howell!" Garden said. Howell eased out the few who had spilled in from the bar and closed the doors again.

CHAPTER 3: "All right," Garden said to Howell when he came back to the table. "We might as well tackle Ryder next. Since he was on the bridge. Mr. Ryder! Would you come up here, please?" He and Howell both stared at Ryder.

The man stopped at the table and looked down at them. He was tall and angular, a spare man who had grown a middle-aged paunch. He looked neat and starched, although he wore a sport shirt and shorts, like most of the men grouped against the wall.

"Sit down, Mr. Ryder," Garden said. "Long time since we've talked, isn't it?"

"Yes," Ryder said abruptly. He sat down suddenly, cracking his elbow against the edge of the table.

"You okay?" Garden asked. "Mr. Ryder, we want to ask you a few questions about—"

"He was shot, wasn't he?" Ryder asked. He took a neat handkerchief out of his hip pocket and wiped his face with it. Garden watched him, fascinated. Ryder didn't unfold the handkerchief. The faint sheen on his face remained almost unchanged after he wiped it. "They say he was shot. That he didn't just fall overboard. Is that true?"

"That's right," Garden said gently. "Is something wrong, Mr. Ryder?"

"Wrong? No, of course not." Ryder put the handkerchief away jerkily. He gathered himself, stared at Garden. "Wrong? Considering the circumstances, that's an odd question. Why isn't Sheriff McGee here?"

Garden leaned back in the chair. "Why? I guess maybe he's busy elsewhere. Or maybe because this is in my jurisdiction, Mr. Ryder."

"The inlet belongs to the county, not to the city," Ryder said. "I've worked all these years to get the Commission to do some-thing constructive about improving the inlet. I assure you I know a good bit about it."

"Right," Garden said firmly into Ryder's speech. "Glad to see you feel better. But the seawalls are city, Mr. Ryder. And by old agreement, my department polices it. Outside the inlet, now that's the sheriff's. That's why his boat went out with divers. But this is mine in here. What were you talking to Captain Kelley about when Carter was shot?"

"What— That has nothing to do with it," Ryder said. "Why are we all being held here, Garden? Don't you think you ought to be out looking for that madman?"

"Easy now," Garden said. "Listen, you sure you feel all right?"

"I'm all right," Ryder muttered. "It's just the—the shock. Naturally Mr. Carter was not a close friend. But—"

"Sure. You were talking to Captain Kelley, then. Did you *see* Carter fall from the rail?"

"No! No, I didn't. I was standing near the starboard rail. I was facing the captain, trying to talk to him about—about the local

14

political situation." Ryder gave Garden a thin smile. Some of his color had come back. "Out of deference to your position, I shan't go into any details."

"Well, that's nice of you," Garden drawled. Ryder's smile got a bit glassy. "But couldn't you see Carter from where you stood?"

"No. He was a bit behind me. I was aware of his being there, you understand. He was moving around a bit. I had an impression of motion as though he was climbing down or leaning down. I'm not certain. As I said, I was talking to Captain Kelley. And Captain Kelley is sometimes hard to talk to."

"Especially when he's busy running the inlet?" Garden asked. "Go on."

"Go on? That's all."

"You didn't hear the shot?" Garden asked. Ryder's smile had started to come back. Now it slipped again.

"No. No, I didn't," Ryder muttered. "I just heard some shouting. Then I turned. I saw one of the other passengers. He was shouting to the captain that the mate had fallen overboard. Then the captain cut back the engines. Dangerously so, I thought, considering the conditions in the inlet." Ryder shrugged. "You know all the rest, I believe."

"Yes?" Garden said. "All right. Let's go over it again."

"Is that necessary?"

"I think so," Garden said. Ryder stared at him and Garden returned the stare. "I want to give you every chance to remember things," he said. "Any detail. Let's take it again." He watched, fascinated, for the shadow of fear to flicker across Ryder's face again. It wasn't pleasant to watch. But it was interesting.

"You don't imagine that I'm keeping anything from you, Chief?" Ryder asked unpleasantly.

"Not at all," Garden said. "Let's say I'm just trying to help you remember."

"I see. Of course, you've no reason to spare me any unpleasantness," Ryder said.

"Ryder, I got no reason to spare you or to cause you anything," Garden said. "Just don't imagine anything and then we'll be okay. Right?"

"I don't misunderstand," Ryder said. He glared at Garden in anger and Garden blinked at him, then glanced at Howell.

When he let Ryder go the tall man was deep in a cold indignant fury that Garden remembered from watching him at a few council meetings. He gave Garden a boiling stare and went over against the far wall away from the others. Howell leaned close and said under the cover of the noisy fan, "Chief, you sure got him pissed off!"

"It doesn't seem to be difficult," Garden said.

"I saw. He'll have it in for you now, you know that?"

"Oh, come on! Did you notice how he got shook when I tried to get him to guess how close the shot came to him?"

"That's natural, ain't it?"

"I wonder. Past danger usually don't scare people, especially if it happened so quick they didn't even know it. They even like to talk about it, especially if they're natural talkers, and Ryder sure is. But this spooks him. Curious, ain't it?"

Garden looked at the others in the room and they looked sullenly or anxiously or excitedly back at him. He said, "Okay, let's get on with it." He beckoned at random at another passenger.

Two hours later, Garden leaned back in his chair and stretched, loosening his wrists. He looked at Howell, who was massaging his fingers. "Christ," Garden muttered. "Nothing."

"Like you say, Chief. Nothing."

"Nobody saw him start to fall. Nobody heard a shot. One or two on the seawall saw him in the air. A couple guys on the boat saw him in the water, saw him roll over in the wake. That's all."

16

"It ain't much, is it?" Howell agreed. "We *know* he fell in."

"Yeah, we know that," Garden said. "Who's left?" He looked across the room and beckoned to the one man still sitting against the wall. The man got to his feet wearily and shuffled forward.

" 'Bout time," he grumbled.

"Eh? Oh, hell," Garden said. He nodded at the door. "I forgot about her!" The younger woman stood in the door, one hand on the jamb. She was still gray-faced. A half hour before she had hastily and unsteadily gotten up, stared at Garden and then hurried to the door, holding one hand to her mouth.

"You still wanta talk to me?" she asked tiredly."If you do, let's get it over with." Garden glanced at the last man, who nodded philosophically.

"Figures," he said, and went back to sit down again. Howell held a chair for the woman, and she sank into it. Garden eyed her bust briefly and then carefully kept his eyes on her face.

"I donno what you want me to tell you," she said. "I didn't see nothin'. How could I? I was as sick as a dog. That damned boat. Las' time I'll ever get on a damn boat, you can bet."

"Yes, ma'am," Garden said. "Could you give Officer Howell your name, ma'am?"

"Ellice Felty," she said, in the same complaining whine.

"And your address, Miss Felty?" She spelled that out to Howell.

"Are you a permanent resident here?" Garden asked.

"Since May," she said. "I moved up from Lauderdale. I work at Porky's." Garden nodded. Porky's was one of the more exuberant bars out in the country. Her figure fit Porky's and so did her dull face and listless voice.

"And you say you didn't see the mate fall overboard?" Garden asked her.

"How could I? Laying down there in that cabin, sick as a dog. Somebody tole me, drink a beer or two if you start getting shaky on a boat. And I was fool enough to believe them."

"When was the last time you saw the mate?"

"Him? That wise— I donno. Him and his staring." She straightened indignantly, and pulled up one of the shoulder straps of her jersey. "A person wears comfortable clothes, and every wise guy's got to peek," she said. "Is that fair?" she asked Howell.

"No, ma'am," Howell mumbled, looking down at his shorthand notebook.

"Him and his skinny redhead," she muttered.

"What? Which side of the cabin were you on?" Garden asked.

"I donno. The left side, I guess. I was trying to get to sleep. But the boat kept rocking around and it was hot. . . ." She swallowed carefully. "I tole you. I didn't see nothin'. Can I go? I feel sick again."

"Yes," Garden said hastily. "But if you remember anything else . . ."

"Nothin'," she said, getting up. "That wise guy, peeking down at me. It's too hot in here. . . ." She looked around vaguely.

"That way," Garden said quickly. She clopped flatfooted to the door, bouncing implausibly, grayer in the face than ever. The old man against the wall got up and came over to the table.

"Had a Holstein built like that once," he said. "Gave two gallons a day. Back home in Iowa." He sat down.

"What? Never mind. What's your name and local address?" Garden asked. The man answered and Howell wrote. "Permanent resident, Mr. Issac?" Garden asked.

"Not yet. Left my boy running his place and mine—all beef cattle now, a lot less help needed—and we came down for the summer. Figured it would be cheaper, and me and my wife could see if we like it enough to maybe move down here for good in a year or so. Cheaper? Damned glad I didn't come when it was expensive, if this is cheap."

"How *do* you like it?" Garden asked, in spite of himself.

"Not worth a damn," the old man grunted. "No offense. Nothing really interesting going on, you understand? Thought we might try the Gulf Coast next summer."

"Yeah? Now were you on Captain Kelley's boat, or—"

"On the seawall," Issac said. "Didn't catch anything, either. I usually don't. I hear the fishing used to be good here. What happened to it? And everything else. Man, if you ain't interested in dog-racing, shuffleboard, or girlies, what do you do around here?"

"People manage," Garden said. "Listen, did you see the mate go over?"

"Nope. But I saw him just before he fell in. Not surprised he fell, either. He was hanging onto the rail up top like a monkey."

"What?"

"You know. All hanging down on the side like an idiot. He pulled up once and looked at the captain, I guess he was, the big fat fella standing up there on top, talking to another guy, and then I quit watching. Next thing I know somebody up from me's whooping, and I look, and the boat's slowed down and everybody's jumping around like mad. I finally got the idea somebody fell in, and I figured it was the fella hanging off the rail up top. Looked like he was trying to stand on his head. That lean sunburnt guy in khakis."

"That was Carter," Garden said. "Did you hear a shot? Or anything that might have been a shot?"

"Nope. Didn't hear no shot. . . ." Issac hesitated. "Come to think of it, I *might* have heard something—a crack, sort of. Didn't think nothing of it. Could have been a wave slapping up against the seawall at that. Is that right? Somebody did shoot him?"

"That's right," Garden said. "You didn't *see* anything? Somebody running on the other side of the inlet? Anything like that?" The old man was shaking his head.

"Nope," he said firmly. "I was looking at the boat, trying to

19

figure out what the hell all the fuss was about. I bet everybody else was, too."

"You'd win that bet," Garden said wearily. "All right, Mr. Issac. Let me know if you think of anything else. How much longer are you going to be around?"

"A week or two," Issac said. "Wife's kind of gotten friendly with some people from Ohio we met. Ohio. Either of you know if the snook fishin's any good over around Everglades?"

"Supposed to be," Garden said.

"Supposed to be here, too," Issac said. "Well, I got to say this is more excitement than I've seen since we got here." He got up and grinned at Garden, an old man's cheerful sour grin.

"Thanks," Garden said. "We try not to have this kind of excitement."

"Any kind'll do," Issac said. "If I think of anything I'll call you. But don't hold your breath. Garden? That right? You got any kin in Iowa?"

"No," Garden said firmly.

"Didn't think so. Never heard of anybody named Garden up there." Issac laughed and shuffled away. Garden shook his head and looked wearily at Howell.

"Nothing," Howell said hopelessly.

"Nothing but characters." Garden looked out the window. "Damn, the coroner's gone. And so are the TV people. Let's go see what's going on."

"I'll get Janet to type this stuff up for you before she goes off this evening," Howell said. "If we get back before she leaves."

"Sure. Tell her to put it on my desk. I might get something when I reread it. But like that old man said, don't hold your breath."

CHAPTER 4: Outside, the crowd had dwindled. The ambulance was moving slowly up the slope, and they watched it turn out on the beach road and vanish. Peters came up to them, a tall middle-aged cop, wiping sweat from his neck. "Where they taking him?" Garden asked him.

"Kelley told them what funeral home. He said for them to tell the people he'd pay. I think he's getting drunk, Chief."

"That figures," Garden said. He glanced toward the boat, where Kelley bulked in the cockpit, head down, a can of beer gripped in his fist. "What you got?" Garden asked Peters.

"Let's see. Coroner says death was instantaneous. Small-caliber nonjacketed bullet in the head. Didn't go through. I guess you saw that. He's going over to the funeral home to probe for it. He probed for it here enough to feel some of the pieces."

"Go on."

"Entry path was pretty level. Assuming Carter was upright, that means it came from the island, from the parking lot across the inlet, or from the scrub just the other side of the parking lot. Of course, we don't know that. The boat was tossing around a lot, I expect."

Garden turned and looked across the inlet. The water was bronze, swirling in the late sun. The tide was almost all the way out. Across the inlet the parking lot was nearly vacant. West of it a narrow shallow channel separated the dark green bulk of the pine island from the parking lot. Behind the lot there was a thicket of palmetto and sea grape, sloping up to the high hump of the beach island. A shingled roof rose high atop the hump, over the scrub, masked by palms. Beyond, there were more palms and glimpses of more roofs.

"Nothing?" Garden asked.

"Nothing," Peters said. "No one in the lot. We couldn't turn up anything in the scrub. And we went over the island real good." Peters' voice sounded odd. Garden looked at him.

"What about the island?"

"Nothing that has anything to do with this, Chief. Tell you in a minute." Peters glanced at the people nearby.

"Well, nobody parked up there on the road north of the bridge. And nobody could have come up out of the scrub and driven away."

"No, Chief. There were a couple of people on the bridge fishing off the other side. They didn't know about the drowning. Didn't even hear the yelling. The wind's loud up there, of course." Peters glanced across the inlet, upward. "The gates were locked across the drive at Mr. Wayne's house, too," he said. "Nobody over there now? Locked like that, nobody could have gone down the drive and gotten out in a car."

"No," Garden said. He glanced over and up at the house. "Nobody there now at all." They had moved away from the others. "What about the island?" he asked Peters.

"We went through it real careful, Chief. And some of McGee's boys were watching the other side, on the waterway. We didn't flush out anybody suspicious. There were a few people picnicking on the beach on the other side. They said nobody had come or gone. They didn't hear anything."

"What's eating you?" Garden asked.

"Well, hell. We picked up this couple, Chief."

"Oh?"

"Yeah." Peters looked embarrassed. "In there where the

pines are real thick. They had a blanket, you know."

"Well, what the hell? Why tell me?"

"Well . . ." Peters rubbed his chin. "Actually Arnold found them."

"Oh?" Garden asked.

"Yeah. I walked up right afterwards."

Garden stared at the trees on the island.

"Who are they?" he asked.

"Well, I know the boy," Peters said. "I think I've seen the girl around. Cute kid. They look like twenty-one or twenty-two. You know." He paused. "Arnold knows them."

"He intends to make a report?" Garden said neutrally.

"I believe he might, Chief," Peters said, his voice equally blank. "Since I walked up on them. He hadn't sung out or anything. He was just grinning at them, making a shushing motion, sort of, until he turned around and saw me. And saw I'd seen them."

"Go ahead and say what you want to say."

"Hell, Chief. I think he was going to keep it quiet. And go around and talk to them later."

"Oh?"

"You asked me," Peters said defiantly. "That's what I think."

"A shakedown?" Garden said. "That's what you think?"

"Maybe not for money," Peters said. "I think he'd go around to see the girl, though."

"That's supposed to be *better?*"

"Goddam it, Chief, I'm just telling you, that's what I *think!* You know Arnold better than I do, and he was sure mad when he saw me."

"Where's Arnold?" Garden asked, after a while.

"Over there in the car."

"Okay. Tell him I want his report given to me, personally. Not to anybody else. Tomorrow morning will do. Make him believe it. Tell him to keep his mouth shut until then. Will he?"

"Your guess is as good as mine," Peters said.

"Try and make him believe he'd better. You got those kids' names?"

"You bet I did," Peters said, "when I found out Arnold knew them." He paused. "The girl was crying. She was trying not to let on but she was mad and scared."

"All right," Garden said.

"Yeah," Peters said. "Well, you want the names? We let the kids go after they dressed. They had a car over there in the lot across the inlet. You want the names?"

"No," Garden said. "Tell Arnold you gave them to me, though."

"Yeah!" Peters said. "Yeah, okay."

"Tell Arnold I'm going to talk to them," Garden said. "Tell him I'm going to tell them to call me if they have any kind of trouble. Okay?"

"Okay!" Peters said. "Don't you want to talk to Arnold yourself?"

"Not right now," Garden said. "No, not right now. In the morning. When he gives me his report. Tell him first thing when he comes on duty. All right?"

"All right, Chief."

"Make him believe it now, about keeping his mouth shut. He'd *better* believe it!"

"I'll try," Peters said. "Chief?"

"Go on," Garden said. "Goddam it!"

"All right, Chief. Coroner said he'd send you a copy of his report."

"Good. What else did he say?"

"Well . . ."

"Forget it. Don't forget to *tell* Arnold now."

"Yes, Chief," Peters said happily. Garden walked away scowling.

"What's the matter?" Howell asked him.

"Nothing, goddam it!" Garden snarled. "We finished here?"

"Uh, yeah," Howell said. "Chief, Henry said he wants to see you. I think he's upset about Kelley. . . ."

"Tell Henry he can—" Garden started. "No. Tell Henry I'm going back over with Kelley on the boat."

"All right, Chief," Howell said.

"You'll get that report to Janet so she can type it?"

"Sure."

"I'll see you, then," Garden said, and stalked out on the pier toward Kelley's boat.

CHAPTER 5: He jumped from the pier up to the gunwale and swayed there a second, looking down at Kelley hunkered over the can of beer in his hand. "Hello, you old bastard," he said. "Ready to get out of here?" When he listened he could hear the blowers running, clearing the bilges of gas fumes. He grinned and watched Kelley.

Kelley looked up. "Goddam right," he said. "Goddam right." He raised the can and drained it and tossed it over the side to join a half dozen others bobbing in the dark water near the dock. "I got to go see *Mr.* Henry first," he said. "Something about a docking fee." He stood up massively and Garden stepped down into the cockpit.

"The hell with that," he said cheerfully. "Let's get out of here. You got any beer left?"

"Some," Kelley said. "You think I ought to just leave like that?"

"Sure. Let's take her in. Then we'll go by Smitty's for one or two."

"I really ought to go see him," Kelley muttered. The boat rocked very gently in the dock and Kelley's bulk adjusted to the rocking, minutely and automatically. "Ought not to let him get away with that."

"Hell with it, Tommy," Garden said gently. "Where's my beer?"

"Right here—where you think it is? Right here in the cooler. Hey, ain't you on duty? What you doing drinkin' on duty? What kind of chief of police are you?"

"There's a damned good question," Garden said. He reached up and unpinned his badge, pulled it off his blue shirt and secured the pin. He shoved the badge in his pocket and said, "There—now I'm off duty."

"With that gun still on? Who you joking? Open me one."

"Yeah," Garden said. "This gun." He unbuckled the heavy brass buckle, swung the thick tight weight of the belt away from his hips, the heavy solid bulk of the gun free, dangling from his hand. He looked at it and put it down on the seat nearest him. "Okay, Tommy," he said. "Now I'm off duty. Want me to get the lines? Hell, you get the beer. You're there."

"Yeah," Kelley said.

He walked to Garden, handed him an open beer. "Cheers, Ben." They tipped up the cans and Garden took a long, cold, dusty-room-weary-question-cutting swallow—a long, long swallow.

"God, that's great!" Garden said. "I'll get the lines. Fire this thing up, Tommy!" He went astern, carrying the beer can in one hand, and put it down before he leaned over the side to reach for the stern line. He hoped to hell that Henry would have enough sense to stay indoors until they'd cast off and not come into town to Smitty's tonight.

Kelley walked forward and put his beer down on the ledge

above the wheel, cracked the throttles and put his thumb on the starter. One engine rumbled and belched into life and then the other. Garden shuffled quickly to the bow and cast off the bowline, the boat alive under him. He swung back down into the long-roofed cockpit of the drift boat and sat down on the engine box. "Okay, Tommy," he shouted. "You're free." He raised his beer to his mouth and swayed as Kelley shoved the throttles smoothly forward, so that the big boat lifted and surged ahead, the engines roaring under Garden's butt. He sighed and took another long swallow of beer. Kelley held the throttles hard forward and the boat leaned into it, accelerating, beginning to raise a wash that slapped behind them under Henry's pier. Kelley turned and grinned stiffly over his shoulder at Garden and Garden grinned back and drank from his can. "Watch where the hell you're going," he yelled. The engines vibrated under him. Kelley turned sadly and abstractedly, tipping his head back to drain his beer can.

They moved out into the waterway and Kelley throttled back to a more sedate pace. He looked over his shoulder and snorted, and then looked ahead for the channel markers. Garden finished his beer and went over to the port side of the cockpit and up the steps to the narrow deck that curved around the cabin to the foredeck. He glanced upward and climbed the three steps of the ladder leading to the flying bridge on top of the cabin. He glanced to his right and winked at Kelley, peering through the windshield across the cabin top. Garden rubbed his hands on the rail. So here Billy Carter sat, for his last few minutes alive.

The flying bridge, which was also the top of the cabin, was edged forward and on either side with splashboards, six-inch varnished planks under the rail. From where Kelley stood he could barely see over them and a shorter man would not have been able to see ahead at all. Garden realized why Kelley preferred to run the inlet from up top.

He swung one leg over the rail and rested his weight on it as Carter had. Kelley eyed him glumly through the windshield.

What was it the old man, Issac, had said? Looked like Carter had been trying to stand on his head. Garden grunted. He swung his bulk forward easily, lowering himself down the outside of the rail until he hung below it. He looked around and shrugged. The splashboard was next to his face and the bow wave boiling out to one side, throwing up spray toward his face from the yellow-brown waterway. He shook his head. The only thing he could see from this position was a narrow slice of seat inside the cabin, through the window below his face. He pulled himself back upright on the rail.

Kelley throttled back and stuck his head around the corner of the windshield. "What in the *hell* you doing?" he yelled.

"God knows," Garden yelled back, twisting around precariously on the rail. But why would Carter play games like that? Garden leaned over again, farther down, holding himself above the narrow deck and the churning water with one meaty leg over the rail, one hand clamped onto the varnished wood. The rail creaked.

"Goddam!" Kelley said, around the edge of the windshield.

The blood running to his head, Garden stared down through the window into the cabin. He could see all of the seat and a narrow slice of decking. He grunted and pulled himself upright again, swung his leg back outside the rail and dropped down to the deck. He turned and eased around and down into the cockpit.

"Trying to fall in?" Kelley asked. "Ought to be more beer. Want to get it?"

"Okay," Garden said. "You know you got a mess in the cabin? One of your customers been sick."

"I know," Kelley said. "Likely it was that damned girl. Hell with it, let the boys clean it up. I'm sick of it, you know that?"

Garden found two cans of beer in the cooler and snapped the tops off, tossing the tabs into the waterway. He handed one to Kelley, who moodily watched the thick mangrove creep past them, dark lusterless green above the brown water. "Sick of it," Kelley muttered. "Now Billy's dead, the hell with it. I'm tired a fighting around with these rummies. Gonna sell this thing, maybe get a good cruiser and go charter."

"You had this boat a long time," Garden said.

"Had Billy for a mate a long time, too, Ben."

"Hell with it, Tommy. This is a good boat."

"Sure, what's it good for? Sluts throwing up in the cabin. Bastards like that Ryder pissing in my ear alla time. No, Ben, I'll get a good Lyman, or something like that, and take parties to the Islands. I done that before and I can again."

"Got a mate in mind?" Garden asked resignedly. Kelley glanced at him.

"Sure have. You, Ben."

"Me? You nuts? I got a job."

"Sure you have. Sure! I was thinking, though, Ben."

"Well, don't. I ain't going mate, Tommy. Hell, I just started learning this job."

"Lot of fun, too, ain't it?" Kelley asked. He took a long swallow from his beer and almost absently came back on the throttles, steering with his right elbow as they neared the docks. "Lots of fun. You get to talk to that council pretty often, don't you? And people like Ryder. Hell, here I am feeling sorry for myself. I reckon you get more of it than I know there is."

"Okay," Garden said. Kelley brought the big boat slowly around in the waterway, angling it against the tide without appearing to watch, easing the throttles forward to take it across the flow into the narrow cut next to the docks, still talking.

"Can't tell me you like it, Ben. I know you too well. So why the hell not? This town? Hell with this town. It used to be good.

But it's going to hell. Only part of it's any good now is these damned docks and the boatmen and I reckon they'll run us out one of these days. Don't smell pretty, or something. That what you want to work for, Ben—that kind of town?"

"Aw, knock it off," Garden said wearily. They eased in past the other boats, and boatmen along the pier looked up at them and spoke to each other.

Kelley ignored them. "You think I'm gettin' drunk," he said accusingly to Garden. "Hell, I'm *gonna* get drunk! But not on no couple packs of beer. I mean drunk! You gonna put me in jail?"

"Hell, yes, if you get too bad," Garden said. "If I'm sober enough to do it, that is."

"You will be," Kelley said. "You're the chief of police." He emptied his beer and threw the can, in a long whipping arc, high over the dark water of the dock, to crack and rattle into the cockpit of a cruiser docked at the pier. "Some goddam retired bastard," he muttered. "Let *him* throw it in the garbage! Damn all of them!"

"You take it easy," Garden said.

"*You* take it easy," Kelley bellowed, and used the engines to ease the bulk of the big boat delicately around into the mooring, where a couple of boys waited holding lines, their eyes wide as they stared at Kelley and the chief of police alone on the boat.

They eased in and the boys jumped aboard, snubbing the boat's motion with the lines around pilings, their feet braced against the gunwales. Garden saw them eyeing Kelley sidelong, as though watching a storm cloud from which lightning might strike. Kelley killed the engines and took the key out of the switch. He tossed it in the air and stuck it in his pocket and nodded to the boys.

"Okay, you kids," he rumbled. "Do an extra good job cleaning up, okay? Somebody was sick in the cabin. Sorry I'm so late."

"Captain . . ." one of the boys said.

"Yeah," Kelley said harshly. "Billy's dead. I don't want to talk about it, you hear? Maybe tomorrow. Or sometime. Ben, let's get out of here."

"Right with you," Garden said quietly. He picked up his gun belt and swung it around his waist.

They parked outside of Smitty's and got out of Kelley's ancient wagon, headed in through the fancifully painted side door. It was dark inside. For once the jukebox wasn't blaring, the TV was dark. A score of faces turned to them from the horseshoe bar, in twos and threes. There were two stools vacant and they slid onto them, Kelley ignoring greetings.

Sugar came down the bar to them, holding an open beer and a glass in her hand. She set them in front of Kelley and smiled at Garden. "How you, Ben?" she said. "Where's your badge?"

"I'm not on duty right now," Garden said. He smiled back at her.

"Take that away, Sugar," Kelley rumbled. "Bring me some rum. None of that junk, either. Some of the Añejo."

"Oh? Oh, Lord," Sugar said. "Tommy. About Billy."

"None of that crap, I said," Kelley muttered.

"I'll take the beer, Sugar," Garden said. He slid the bottle away from in front of Kelley and took a long swig from it. "Bring Tommy his rum," he said.

" 'At's right," Kelley said. "Got toasts to drink, eh? You going to stick around, Ben?"

"Going to be a long night, eh?" Sugar asked. She grinned sadly and moved away.

"For a while," Garden said. "Then I got to get back to duty."

"Back on duty? Jesus Christ, Ben!"

"You said it," Garden said.

"Okay," Kelley said. "Hell, I forgot. Besides being chief of police, you're getting married, ain't you? Likely she don't want you hanging around bars, getting drunk with the trash."

"Tommy, you're full of crap," Garden said amiably. "Look,

31

don't shove at me. Here's your rum." Sugar slid a squat glass across the bar, full of ice and amber rum and a slice of lime.

Kelley took it, nodded to her and faced Garden. "Aw right, I'm sorry. But Christ, Ben. Everybody's running out. You are, too."

"Here," Garden said. He held the beer bottle out and Kelley clinked his glass against it.

"First of many," Kelley said, and tipped his glass up. Garden brought up the beer bottle and took a long drink. Everyone in the bar was watching them silently and Garden felt a wry anger. It faded quickly. What the hell.

He finished the beer and drank another and by then the others in the bar were beginning to press around and ask about Billy and Tommy was answering, sullenly, but at least talking; and talking almost warmly, at least to Sugar. Garden put down his empty bottle and touched Kelley's shoulder.

"I'm goin' now, Tommy," he said. "I'll drop in later on. You'll be here?"

"Oh, hell, yes," Kelley said. "I'll be here." He was working on his third rum. Sugar looked worried, but she winked at Garden.

"Fine. Take it easy now," Garden said.

"You, too, Ben," Kelley said sadly.

"Hell, I'll be back."

"Sure you will," Kelley said. He finished his rum. "Sugar!" he called.

Garden left the bar and turned the corner by the liquor store, started through the parking lot in front of the supermarket toward the highway. Halfway through the lot he remembered and stopped to take his badge out of his pocket and pin it back on his shirt front.

32

CHAPTER 6: It was late in the afternoon. The sun was brassy, near the horizon, and the sky was pale and blazing. Garden was soaked with sweat before he'd gotten through the lot. The beers puddled his shirt to his back and he squinted against the glare, crossing the highway to get into the hot shade of the shops on the west side of the street. He had to leave their shelter for the last hundred yards to the police station. The poorly air-conditioned front office felt cold to him. The cop on the desk blinked at him and said, "You walking, Chief? Why didn't you call for a car?"

"God knows," Garden growled.

"Hot out there, eh?"

Garden bit back the first answer that occurred to him. "I get any calls?" he asked.

"Yeah, Chief. That fella Rainey from the local paper came by, said he'd come in later. And somebody from the Miami *Herald* called, want you to call them back. Number's on your desk. The TV station called, too, the news guy. The coroner's office sent down a transcript of his report. And Janet typed up Howell's report. They're both on your desk and there were some other calls. Pete Burke and Miss Harper. They're on your desk, too."

"Thanks, Jimmy," Garden said, mollified. "Where's Howell?"

"He went to grab something to eat, Chief. He'll be back before going off duty, case you want him."

"Okay," Garden said. He went on into his office. The window

air-conditioner made it positively icy. He took off his gun belt and put it on the desk, then stripped off his shirt and went into the washroom off the office. When the phone rang a few minutes later he was back at the desk, wearing a fresh shirt he'd taken from a drawer, reading Howell's record of the interviews at the inlet. He picked up the phone.

"Garden, Police," he said. "Oh, hi, Pete. Damn, I was going to call."

"That's all right," Pete Burke said. "Listen, is it true Tommy Kelley's mate was shot this afternoon?"

"That's right," Garden said.

"Mayor Frieden called me, all in a sweat," Burke said. "He wants a special meeting of the council, an informal one. Told me to tell you to be there, at his house, not at City Hall. Who shot him?"

"I don't know who shot him," Garden said. "Why's Frieden all upset?"

"You know. Remember the stuff in the papers last spring over those killings? Frieden's gun-shy of that kind of publicity. He says that the coroner was posing for TV this afternoon and there's going to be a big deal on the six o'clock news this evening. I can't tell if he's just jealous, or not." Burke chuckled.

"Well, I can't help him. Man gets shot, the news people are going to get interested," Garden said. "What time's this damned meeting? By the way, I thought you weren't supposed to have meetings the public isn't invited to."

"Oh, sure. Perish the thought," Burke said. "Somehow we seem to go on having them. Seven o'clock. At Frieden's house. Okay?"

"Seven, hell. When do I eat?"

"You know Frieden. Five-thirty is dinnertime. Doesn't matter if there's still four hours of daylight left. What do you mean, you don't know who shot Carter?"

"All right, I'll tell you the story," Garden said. He did so.

Burke was silent while Garden talked. "And they found nothing on the island?" he asked when Garden had finished.

"No. Nor in the scrub the other side of the parking lot, north of the inlet. You know how thick it is there below Harper's father's place. But the shot had to come from over there. And if it had come from the south parking lot *somebody* would have seen it fired. Even one of that bunch of dopes we talked to this afternoon."

"I don't know Mack," Burke said. "He's new in McGee's outfit."

"Don't worry about Mack," Garden said. "He's a good man. His boys or mine would have found anybody that—"

"What's wrong?"

"I forgot something," Garden said. "Damn—seven o'clock? That's just an hour. Listen, I'll see you there."

"All right," Pete Burke said. "Cool it this evening, Ben. You been sort of hard to get along with lately, as some of the council see it."

"That's too damned bad."

"Ain't it?" Burke agreed placidly. "Just take it easy tonight."

Garden sat still for a minute with his hand on the phone after Burke had hung up. He glanced at his watch again and, lifting the phone, pushed the button that buzzed the desk man. "Jimmy?" he said. "I want Officer Arnold's personnel record brought in. Yeah. Just pull the whole file and bring it in. Okay? Thanks." He hung up and looked grimly at the wall, then dialed.

When the phone was answered he said immediately, "You were thinking about me and you knew it was me just as soon as the phone rang, right?" He grinned as he heard her thin laugh at the other end of the line.

"All right, Ben. You won't believe it, but I was, and I did."

"Sure, I believe you. I always will believe you," he said. "Are you all right? You sound different."

"Ah, Ben, it's a headache, too much sun. You always know, don't you? And you'll always believe me?"

"It even surprises me," he said. "But it seems to be true. I've got bad news about tonight, though."

"Let me guess," she said. "You're busy being chief of police."

"You couldn't be more right," he said, frowning a little. "You okay?" he asked.

"Oh, Ben, for how long?" The thread of nervous tension echoed in his ear, behind her voice. He still frowned.

"Well. It starts off with a council meeting. Another see-here-Chief-Garden meeting, I suppose. So your guess is as good as mine."

"Oh, well. Jilted for five old men. I don't even have an opportunity to be jealous. Ben, how *do* you put up with it?"

"Not as well as I should, evidently," Garden said. "Burke as much as told me to keep my big mouth shut tonight."

"Oh, Pete Burke's turning into an old man himself," Harper said. "Why *did* he run for the council?"

"He thought he could do a better job than some, I suppose. And he's right, there," Garden said. "I don't know when I'll get through with them, darling. Nor what might happen after that. How about lunch tomorrow?"

"Oh, all right, as long as we can have it over at the beach house," she said. "Unless you want to drive me to Palm Beach."

"I'll settle for the beach house," he said, smiling. "I thought that was closed."

"We're going through some old junk," she said. "One o'clock?"

"Fine. Take care of the headache," he said.

"All right, Ben," she said. "Take care of *your* headache, darling. All these 'darlings'! There ought to be a few alternative words."

"I can think of a few," he said, glancing up as Jimmy opened the door and hesitated, holding a manila folder in his hand.

36

Garden nodded to him to put it down on the desk.

"Now there's someone there, isn't there?" she asked. "I can always tell by the way your voice changes. You sound so businesslike and crackery, Ben. All right, darling, tomorrow. And you don't have to say anything but a nice formal good-bye."

"Good-bye, then," he said formally, and added, "I'll see you tomorrow." He heard her laugh and hang up and he put down the phone and looked severely at Jimmy.

"Here's Arnold's folder, Chief," Jimmy said diffidently.

Garden tried to stop scowling. "Okay. Thanks, Jimmy. Will you remind me, first thing in the morning I'm supposed to see Arnold?"

"Yeah, Chief." Jimmy hesitated and started to turn.

"Anything you want to say, Jimmy?"

"Well, I guess not, Chief." Jimmy went out, closing the door gently, and Garden grunted and opened Arnold's folder. He slowly lost his puzzled frown as he looked at it. He even forgot what had caused the frown.

CHAPTER 7: Mayor Frieden lived in one of the
older houses in town. Two-storied, of frame construction, it had a large yard, with a circular drive and many hibiscus bushes, several palms, mango trees and two avocado trees. There were three cars in the drive when Garden turned into Frieden's street, so he eased his cruiser to the curb in front of the house and got out. He waved at a group of kids on the opposite sidewalk who had stopped playing to stare at him, and started up

the walk. Before he got to the door, Burke swung around the corner and pulled in behind the cruiser. Garden walked back to Burke's car.

"Hi, Ben," Burke said, getting out. Garden grinned at him. Burke wore sport clothes, including what had to be the only tweed sport coat in town. He was brown-faced, gray-haired, and the glasses he wore didn't keep him from being a hell of a good wing shot. He wasn't the only lawyer in town that Garden trusted, but he was the only one he liked.

"Did you see the six o'clock news?" Burke asked him.

"No. I suppose Carter made it."

"In spades. Complete with editorial comment about last spring's violence, and how bad this new murder is for the image of the community." Garden grunted and Burke added, "The coroner came on pretty well. They had a few feet of film with Joel McGee, too."

"What did Sheriff McGee have to say?"

"Said he knew no details of the case, that one of his boats had merely assisted you in recovering the body, that he had the utmost faith that you were bending every effort to apprehend the miscreant. . . ." Burke broke off, laughing. "Word for word, Ben."

"The old bastard."

"And butter wouldn't melt."

"Let's go on in and get it over with," Garden said.

Frieden met them at the door and stared apprehensively past them at the street. "Did you have to wear your uniform?" he complained to Garden. There was a touch of whine in everything Frieden said, as though he continually railed at the fate that not only had let him possess a successful pharmacy that somehow seemed to take more time every year, but also had led him to run for public office that also seemed to consume more time each year, and brought him nothing but complaints from the public; no appreciation, of course not. . . .

"It looked like you two were holding a public meeting right out there in the yard," he said, closing the door behind them. "Come on in the living room, come on. Alice took the girls to the picture and my boy, I guess he's out for the evening again."

"How you getting along, Doc?" Burke asked cheerfully. Frieden glanced back at Burke, opened his mouth and closed it again. There wasn't any point complaining about things to Pete Burke; all he did was laugh at you, and after asking in the first place!

"Come on in," he repeated.

They went into the living room and Burke spoke cheerfully to each of the other council members. Garden nodded to them. Blough, Werner and Delmer. Werner and Blough, like Frieden, were holdovers from the previous council. They both had run real estate offices in town for years. Blough had been the better man, but now his business was close to bankruptcy. Werner and Blough detested each other and kept so close an eye on each other that they were together more than any two other businessmen in town. Werner nodded at Burke. Thin-faced, tight-lipped, he ignored Garden. Blough nodded loosely at both Garden and Burke. He clutched one of Frieden's weak high-balls. Garden noticed his glazed eyes and guessed he'd had a half dozen or so, stronger ones, before getting to the meeting. He wondered if he should quietly call a driver for Blough, after the meeting, and felt a surge of impatient anger.

Werner was looking at Blough's highball as though he tasted something good. Maybe some business he was going to take away from Blough in the morning.

Delmer, Garden thought, now there's a different breed of cat. Not too unusual, around this or maybe any other town, but different from these others. Delmer was Frieden's age, younger than Burke and Blough and Werner; almost as young as Garden. He was thinner, not tall, with a face that would have been honest if he'd been willing to let it look country. It was overlaid with enough inexpensive sophistication so that he looked cheap and obvious. But he wasn't obvious and Garden knew it. Delmer was a lawyer, like Burke. He came from Immokalee, over in the Big Cypress, and he did not practice law exactly as Burke did. But he certainly had a lot of friends for a man who'd been in town for only a couple of years.

Delmer smiled broadly at Garden and asked, "How *you*, Chief Garden? Good to see you!"

"Good to see *you*," Garden said. He dropped into a chair opposite Delmer and smiled widely and innocently at him.

"If we're finished with the polite greetings, maybe we could get to business?" Werner said.

"Certainly. Certainly," Frieden said. "I'll call us to order then and—"

"Knock it off," Werner said impatiently. "We don't even have a clerk. No reason for formality. Garden, what's all this business about a killing at the south inlet today?"

"I guess you know as much as I could tell you, if you saw TV this evening," Garden said. "Somebody shot Billy Carter, Tommy Kelley's mate. Just as Tommy was running the inlet. Mack—a deputy for Sheriff McGee—fished his body out of the surf. So far, I have no idea who shot him. Or why."

"You always got to run to McGee for help?" Werner asked. "He going to take this thing over, too—the way he wiped your nose on them killings last spring?"

"McGee's got the only patrol boats in the county," Garden said. "The waterway and the south inlet are his, even if the seawalls of the south inlet are in the city. If you want to buy me a boat and let me hire a couple extra men to run it, I'll be glad to do my own fishing for bodies."

"Brother! Not on top of your last budget!" Werner said. "But what the hell *are* you doing, then?"

"We're checking on Carter's activities for the last few days," Garden said, "to see if he was in any squabbles with anybody who might have shot him. Personally, I think it was an accidental shot. But we got to check."

"Didn't anybody see it or hear it?"

"Nobody we've talked to," Garden said. "Kelley was busy with the boat, of course. Ryder was right there and he didn't even realize—"

"Ryder! That bastard was there?"

"What? Yeah, Ryder—Charlie Ryder."

"That's the biggest troublemaker in this *town!*" Werner growled. "And he was right there when it happened? Brother!"

"Depends on what you call a troublemaker," Delmer said. "Personally, I've always found Mr. Ryder a very public-spirited citizen."

"Hell, you would," Werner said. "What the hell else you got for bad news, Garden?"

"I think you've heard it all," Garden said.

"Meanwhile, the TV people—" Frieden started to say, shrilly.

Werner finished the sentence. "—are telling everybody we got another murder in town. And I guess the papers will, too."

"I hate to think of the Miami *Herald* tomorrow," Frieden said.

"Aren't you all making too much out of this?" Garden asked. "Don't misunderstand me. I'm not treating it lightly. The man's dead. I want to find out who shot him, accident or not; and by God, I will. I liked Billy Carter, if there wasn't a better reason. But—"

"You would," Blough slurred. He took a long sip at the drink he held. "Yore too friendly with that gang around the docks, Garden. Used to be a fisherman yoreself, didn't you?"

"Yes, I did," Garden said. "I said, if there wasn't any better reason. Damn it, the man's dead. Shot dead."

"Goddam fishermen," Blough muttered. "Give town a bad name. Back when all the tourists wanted to fish, that was one thing. Thing's changed. Think all these retired bastards want to fish? Or to put up with bunch of roughnecks? We ought to close down the city docks."

"I think you'd find out that a lot of people in town wouldn't like the city docks closed," Burke said quietly.

"Yes. Well—" Frieden said.

"Yeah, shut up, John," Werner said, with old weary contempt. Blough finished his drink. "We're off the subject," Werner went on. "Let me be blunt, Garden. If—"

"Do that," Garden muttered.

"What? I say if you don't git off your ass on this killing, if it does turn into another damned war like that mess last spring— well, we ain't going to put up with it. We can get another chief of police damned easy. Yore contract says we got to pay you for a month, lieu of notice. That'll be it."

"You're clear enough," Garden said.

"I agree with Ben," Burke said. "Frank, you're getting too upset, too soon." Werner scowled at Burke, who added, "Any other consideration aside—such as that Ben's a good police chief—don't you realize such drastic action would cause a fair amount of public comment, all by itself?"

"Not likely," Werner said.

"Oh, it might. Especially if it caused a resignation from the council," Burke said. The others stared at him.

"That wouldn't be reasonable," Garden said to Burke.

"Fun, though," Burke said.

"It might even cause two resignations from the council, gentlemen," Delmer said cheerfully. He glanced at Burke, at Garden, "And I think I could guarantee some publicity. How would that sound?"

"Might be worth any stink you could stir up," Werner finally said. "To get you two off the council!" He glared and Burke leaned back and laughed.

"Frank Werner, some ways you're the most honest man I know!" Burke said.

"Look. Look here," Garden said. "This isn't necessary. Mr. Werner, I'd resign before I got to be any sort of embarrassment to the community."

"To this council," Werner said.

"He said to the community," Burke said. "There is a difference, Frank."

"This is ridiculous!" Frieden said. His voice thinned, but he finished the sentence. The others stared at him. Werner started to speak, but Frieden's voice rose above the interruption. "You're getting carried away, Frank. Chief Garden— I don't begin to approve of some of his friends and associates, but he isn't that bad a police chief. And this is just silly. We're worried about something that might not even happen. And what if it does?"

"What if it does?" Werner said. "What if it does! Listen, you stupid— Listen, we ain't playing for pennies around here anymore! You seen those apartments going up down in West Palm? And everywhere else? You got any idea how much building there's been lately? How many people are moving down? Those housing developments we been so proud of, they're nothing, you hear me?"

"Like Spanish Heights?" Burke asked idly.

Werner gave him a stare. "Don't give me any crap, Pete Burke. You know what I'm talking about. Hell, you and your family own some of the best land around here for high-rise apartments. Can't tell me you don't know what I'm talking about. We just can't afford to get tagged as a roughneck town. That was okay in the thirties, when the only people with money that came in here wanted to run over to West End or Bimini, or go out after sailfish. Then it was okay to be wild. Colorful, they called it. Even ten years ago, maybe even five, we could put up with it. Now? Hell, no, man. The people that come here now come from Harrisburg and Evansville and Columbus. They don't go fishing for marlin and then sit around watching the fishermen beat up on each other. They don't want to drink with a bunch of boat bums. All they want to do's move into a nice apartment and bitch about the heat. And there's a lot of them. A *lot* of them. No, sir, I ain't going to let this thing go sour."

All of them looked at Werner. He glared indignantly at Garden, at the others.

"All right," he said. "That's all. We're wasting time sitting around here. Garden. You remember. This has got to be the most peaceful little town in Florida. If you don't make it peaceful, somebody else will. And Frieden, don't be a fool." He stood up. "That's all I got to say," he added. "We through?"

"But—we ought to talk about the sewage plant," Frieden said. "That pollution study—"

"What pollution study?" Werner asked. "How many other towns our size in Florida got pollution studies going on?"

"A few," Burke said.

"Yeah? Good. Let *them* advertise they got polluted water. I don't think we will. Any more crap? If not I'll see you all Monday night, at the regular meeting. This has been a waste of time."

"Oh, maybe not," Delmer drawled.

Werner stopped on his way to the door and looked briefly at Delmer. "Come see me tomorrow," he said unexpectedly.

Delmer grinned at him. "Why don't you come see *me?*" he asked.

Werner snorted in contempt, but he didn't look away from Delmer. "I don't come to you. And I ain't going to have to," he said. "Am I wasting my time talking to you?"

"Maybe I can spare the time," Delmer said casually.

"I sort of think you might," Werner said. He went into the hall and out the front door before Frieden could follow him.

Blough set down his empty glass and said, "I 'clare this meeting adjourned. Frieden, you sure serve lousy liquor." He stood, reasonably well under control. Delmer got up, still smiling, with a touch of abstraction. Frieden looked from one of them to the other, upset.

"Let's get the hell out of here," Garden said to Burke in an undertone.

CHAPTER 8: Outside, Garden took a long breath of air in the still hot evening and asked, "Just why the hell *don't* I go ahead and resign?"

"Your sense of duty and your dedication to your fellowman will not let you desert your post," Burke said. "How about a drink?"

"Yes, sir, Mr. Councilman. And you? Would you really quit if they canned me?"

"It's the best excuse I've found lately," Burke said. "I'll follow you around to your place while you change. Unless you want to go have a drink in uniform. Have you eaten?"

"Yeah, Jimmy sent out for a hamburger."

"You'll get ulcers that way, Ben."

"I'll chance it," Garden said. "Listen, I want to go by the office first. I'll leave the cruiser there."

"All right, Ben," Burke said. "By the way, I know another reason why you won't resign. You want to find out who killed Billy Carter."

"That's right," Garden said.

"And after that it'll be something else you have to get done." They watched Blough move with stately slowness to his car and then lurch, tires scraping, out of Frieden's drive.

"I hope he don't go by Smitty's for his next drink," Garden said. "Not if he's gonna sound off about boatmen like he did in there. Not the way they feel in Smitty's tonight."

"What he'll do is go to the country club and have about ten more drinks. Then one of the busboys will drive him home. Happens every night."

"That far gone, eh?"

"In a year Werner will have *all* his business," Burke said. Garden shrugged and went to his cruiser. Burke slid away from the curb behind him and they turned at the corner toward the center of town, toward police headquarters.

Reynolds, the new night man, looked up as Garden came in. He nodded and got up behind the desk. "Any calls?" Garden asked.

"Well, the newspaper people," Reynolds said awkwardly. "The fella from the town paper came in and the Miami paper called. They all seemed a little bit upset, Chief."

"Son of a gun," Garden said. "Anything else?"

"No, Chief. Nothing."

"How are things? Quiet?"

"Yeah. Well, somebody called in and said they thought there was a fight or something going on at Smitty's. I thought about calling a car to go by, but I figured—you know—so I called there on the phone." He looked uneasy. "Should I have done it that way?"

"Depends on how it turned out. How did it turn out?"

"Well, okay, I guess. Sharkey answered; he's on the bar tonight. He said, hell, no, there wasn't any fight. I had to yell pretty loud for him to hear me on the phone."

"Sounds like that was all right," Garden said. "Was Sharkey polite?"

"Not so you'd notice it," Reynolds said.

"Good. Then there wasn't any trouble. Sharkey's never polite unless he's got some kind of trouble."

"Okay, Chief," Reynolds said, relieved.

"I would have a car drop by there, say, about eleven o'clock," Garden said. "Or before, if you get a real trouble call."

"All right, Chief."

"Tell the guys in the car to be real easygoing."

"Right. What if the newspaper people call back?"

"Tell them to call me in the morning," Garden said. "Not too early in the morning." He went out. Reynolds would be okay. He tried to remember what the boy's rawboned face reminded him of, and then nodded. Reynolds looked like Delmer, but without the layer of sophistication that law school had given Delmer, without the hint of furtive country malice trapped in Delmer's face.

He got into Burke's car and Burke said, "That was quick."

"It's quiet. All the fishermen are busy drinking hard in Smitty's and nobody else seems to be out raising hell. Besides, I wanted to get out before some newspaper calls again."

"You got to talk to them sooner or later, Ben."

"Then make it later. At least tomorrow. Take me home; I want to change." Burke pulled out of the parking lot and paused before turning onto the highway. Garden added, "I was just thinking about Delmer."

"What about Delmer?"

"You know, if Werner was smart he wouldn't ride Delmer too hard. Delmer just might be in a position to remember it someday."

"Yeah," Burke said dryly.

"What do you think of Delmer, Pete?"

"You know damned well what I think of Delmer," Burke said. "He's another cracker going sour. More than his share of ambition. That's all right, but he wants it *now*. He's plenty smart, too. Almost smart enough. He resents everyone he thinks has a better break than he had. That'll ruin him someday."

"I thought you two worked together on the council," Garden

47

said. "The reform candidates, as it were."

"Oh, come off it," Burke said. "Listen, Ben, there are about six thousand people in this town who have lived here all their lives, and their families before them. There are about twenty of us who swing some real weight. I'm one of them. You're another. Delmer knows it."

"So?"

"Well, there are about twelve thousand people here who *don't* remember the big day when the wooden bridge to the beach burned down, and all that. People who have moved here since the war, or their families did. Offhand I'd say that the newcomers have *more* influential people, one way or another, than their proportions would indicate—not less. Maybe two hundred? But most people don't see it that way; the average guy doesn't."

"No?" Garden asked again.

"No. They think, old family, influence, goddam fat cats. Like that, Ben. They don't see any difference between Werner, say, and me, or you."

"Me? Look, Pete. Remember what my old man did? Commercial fisherman. Not a charter boat, a mullet boat. Didn't have a pot to piss in, all his life. Don't give me that fat cat business."

"Oh, no?" Burke steered easily through the light evening traffic. "Look at it, Ben. You're chief of police. You went to college. Hometown boy, old pro ball player—"

"Come on, Pete. One year!"

"Anyway, you're sort of a celebrity."

"I think you're laughing at me, damn you."

"No, Ben. Not at all. And there's another thing, the worst of all." Burke turned off the highway toward the water and pulled up in front of a stuccoed two-story building a half block from the road.

"Go on," Garden said. "Tell me the worst."

"Hell, Ben, you *think*. And it shows. Goddam it, you read books. You even forget to talk cracker, every now and then."

"So what?"

"So you're vulnerable. Even the crackers suspect you. Except the few you're buddies with. And you ain't friendly enough to have many buddies."

"Too damned bad," Garden said.

"Ain't it? And now, with Harper—"

"All right," Garden said. "Leave her out of this."

"You think I can?"

"You're going to. They're going to."

"Sure. You get engaged to the daughter of the richest, meanest old man in the county. Who long ago quit worrying about what anybody thinks of him, be they cracker or Yankee. Who raised his daughter to look at them all the same way he does. He did so good a job of that—" He stopped.

"Go on," Garden said.

"It's not any of my business, Ben."

"It's all right," Garden said. He stared through the windshield. "I knew all about it," he lied.

"And you don't mind me knowing?" Burke asked.

"No," Garden lied again.

"The hell you don't. And I'm a friend of yours. How about the ones that aren't friends?"

"Are *you* trying to talk me into quitting?"

"I'm just reminding you, you're gonna get plenty of rocks thrown at you."

"Let them throw rocks," Garden said.

"Okay, Ben. How does Harper feel? Don't tell me she's in favor of you staying chief of police."

"Right the first time. She isn't," Garden said. He stared out the window.

"And are you going to quit?"

"Nope," Garden said.

"Ah, hell," Burke said. "Go on in. Get changed. Where do you want to go for that drink?"

"It might as well be Smitty's."

"Sure," Burke said. "It might as well be."

Smitty's was only about two-thirds full but the noise made it seem fuller. The jukebox was turned well up and most of the people at the bar were standing, eddying back and forth, shouting at each other. Tommy Kelley was propped against the bar, still drinking dark rum over ice. He turned his head slowly and nodded to Garden and Burke as they came in.

"Howdy, Tommy," Garden said loudly.

"Howdy, howdy," Kelley said, after a while. He'd reached the remote stage. He gestured without looking. "Sharkey!" he bellowed. "Drink for the chief, here. An' for Lawyer Burke."

Sharkey Devlin snarled something from the other end of the dark bar.

"Don't whisper like that," Burke said. He slid into the stool at Kelley's left and Garden sat at Kelley's right. "Don't you want anybody to hear you, Tommy? Speak up, Captain."

Kelley grinned slowly. "Ol' Pete," he said. "Ol' Pete Burke. You tough little bastard. Gimme a shake, Pete." He held out his hand.

"Hell, no," Burke said firmly. "And get my hand busted? I'll buy a drink instead. What you having, Ben?"

"Same as Captain Kelley," Garden said.

"Right. Sharkey! Two of these. And a Scotch and water. Chivas. How's it going, Tommy?"

"Pore," Kelley rumbled. "Pore. My mate got shot, Pete. You knew Billy, didn't you?"

"Sure did," Burke said. "I'm sorry, Tommy. Sure sorry."

"You find out anything, Ben?" Kelley asked, turning his head slowly and massively toward Garden.

"Nothing yet, Tommy."

"Naw. Nothing yet. How was yore meeting at the mayor's house, Ben?"

"Now how the hell do you know about that?" Garden asked. Kelley laughed the sad heavy laugh as Sharkey brought the drinks and slid them onto the polished wood.

"Aw, hell, Ben, everybody knows about the council. Some council. They couldn't pour piss out of a boot. Beg yore pardon, Pete. True, ain't it?"

"'Fraid so," Burke admitted cheerfully. He took his drink and held it up, nodding to the others.

"To Billy," Kelley said, picking up his own drink and nodding as Garden reached for his. "To Billy. Fifteenth drink to Billy." He tipped the glass back and drained it.

Garden and Burke put their half-full glasses down on the bar, while Kelley looked deliberately around. "Don't see none of you bastards drinking," he said, in a voice that carried over the jukebox and the shouted conversations. "Ain't nobody drinking to Billy?" Several of the people in the bar looked at him, some with resentment, some not, as they picked up their drinks. "Better," Kelley growled. "Not good enough. But better."

"Sounds like you're going pretty good, Tommy," Burke said.

"Yeah? I reckon. Going to go around this bar and talk to that Martin after a while, though. He don't look like he's enjoying drinking to Billy. Ain't you found out nothin', Ben?"

"No, I told you," Garden said. "I think it was an accident. Just a stray shot."

"That what the council wants you to think, Ben?"

"It's what *I* think," Garden said.

"I pissed you off, eh?" Kelley observed. "Sorry. Why you ain't looking at some of the people Billy had fights with? And I think he had a new girl friend lately. I tell you that before? You know. He was kind of strutting around, not saying much about it yet. Got to be somebody knows something."

Garden remembered something the girl from the boat had

said. "A redhead?" he asked. "Billy's new girl?"

"Hell, how do I know? I tole you. He wasn't talking yet."

"Ready for another?" Garden asked. "Hell, Tommy, you don't really think anybody'd lay out with a gun and shoot old Billy, do you?"

"Yeah. You must have had some council meeting," Kelley said.

"Now wait a minute," Burke said. "Wait a minute, Tommy. You know Ben better than that." He glanced past Kelley at Garden. Garden slumped back against the bar.

"Do I? Yeah, I reckon," Kelley said. "But hell, Ben!"

"Here," Garden said. "Here, let's have another. Sharkey!"

"Good, let's have another drink. Martin don't drink to Billy this time, I'll go around there and *speak* to him," Kelley said happily, thickly.

"Don't do that, Tommy," Garden said. "Let's just have a quiet drink."

"That's what I mean," Kelley said. "Just a quiet drink, and I'll speak to Martin. I didn't mean nothing, Ben, what I said just now, but hell!"

"Sure," Garden said wearily. "Sharkey!"

CHAPTER 9: Garden was thirty minutes late getting to the office in the morning. He was already sweating when he walked into the outer office. He looked blackly at Jimmy. Jimmy eyed Garden, saw his bruised cheekbone and hastily looked away.

"Got some coffee over there, Chief," he said nervously.

"Fine," Garden said savagely. He went over and poured himself a cup of black coffee and headed for the door of his office. "Bring in that goddam night book!" he said to Jimmy, and went on inside.

Garden settled behind his desk, looked at Arnold's personnel file still lying there and took a sip of coffee. It burned his lips. "Kelley okay?" he asked Jimmy.

"Yeah, Chief. He's asleep. He sure does snore."

"I wish I was asleep. You call his wife?"

"Yeah. She just laughed and said to turn him loose when he woke up. That okay with you?"

"Oh, hell, yes. What about Martin?"

"Well, they wired his jaw up okay at the hospital, according to Reynolds' log." Jimmy hesitated. "I hear he says he's gonna sue Kelley."

"Sure he is," Garden said. "Sure. Well, I might as well get on with it."

"Sir?"

"Where's Arnold?"

"He's out back, Chief. You want to see him now?"

"That's right. I want to see him now."

"You want to look at the book first, Chief?"

Garden looked up at Jimmy. "Why?" he asked.

Jimmy rubbed his head. "Well," he said, "well, Arnold made an arrest last night. You hear about it?"

"Did I hear about it? No, I didn't hear about it. What with Kelley . . . No. What about it? I thought Arnold was off duty."

"Yeah, he was. But he says in his report that he was driving home and this car forced him off the road, so he gave chase. He blocked the car and got out and the driver got out and attacked him—"

"Witnesses?" Garden asked quickly.

"No, Chief. No witnesses."

"He book the driver?"

"No. Not yet. The driver's in the hospital, Chief. Skull fracture."

"Arnold," Garden said. "And he didn't book him. Well? What else? You look like there's something else."

"Yeah," Jimmy muttered. "Yeah. The fellow Arnold hit? It's Mayor Frieden's son. Nick Frieden, you know, that tall kid."

"Yeah. Yeah, I know," Garden said, stunned. He sat there for a minute. "Jesus Christ! Was the kid drunk?"

"Nothing sure. Doctor said no, at the hospital. Arnold says the boy was acting belligerent and irrational. He brought in some pills he says he found in the kid's car. Speed. The doctor identified them this morning."

"I see," Garden said.

"You wanted to see Arnold?"

"Not yet," Garden said. "Leave the book. Anything else?"

"A few drunks." Jimmy shrugged. "And the papers called again. All of them. And Mayor Frieden called twice."

"Yeah." Garden stared at the wall. "Listen, Jimmy, Frieden's boy. Any report that he's been using stuff? Or that he's been a problem?"

"Not that I ever heard," Jimmy said, with emphasis.

Garden nodded. "And you hear, don't you?" he asked.

"I got four kids of my own," Jimmy said, "all girls. Twenty-two down to sixteen, and this is a small town. Yeah, I hear. Because I listen."

"Thank you, Jimmy. Where's Peters?"

"He's off today."

"Get him on the phone for me, will you?"

"Yeah, Chief." Jimmy went out and Garden opened the file he'd left and read with concentration and then read it again, then he sat quietly with his hand on the file on the desk, until the buzzer sounded. He picked up the phone and said, "Garden."

"This is Peters, Chief. You want me?"

"No. No, Peters, just a question. That couple at the inlet yesterday, that Arnold came up on." Garden paused. "Who was the boy?"

"You want to know, eh?" Peters said heavily.

"Goddam it, I asked you!" Garden snarled.

"Yeah. Sure. It was the Frieden kid, Chief. The mayor's son. Surprised?" Peter's voice was sarcastic.

"You've heard, eh?" Garden asked.

"Yeah, I've heard."

"I guess I got to ask who the girl was," Garden said.

"Yes, sir. Her name's Angela Lang. Address?"

"Yeah," Garden said. Peters read off an address and a phone number. Garden copied them down.

"Anything else?" Peters asked.

"No," Garden said.

"Chief, you know what that son of a bitch Arnold did, don't you?"

"Do you *know* that?" Garden asked savagely. "You know it, Peters?"

"To prove, no. But I know it, same as you do. He called that girl and she told the boy and he went after Arnold, blind mad."

"Peters," Garden said. He took a deep breath. "Listen, come on down and make a statement about yesterday at the inlet. Janet'll take it. Get Jimmy to hear it. I want it typed, read and sworn to. Okay?"

"It'll be a pleasure," Peters said. "You seen Arnold?"

"No," Garden said. "No, not yet."

He hung up and went into the outer office. Jimmy looked at him and Howell glanced up from the desk at the side of the room and said, "Hello, Chief."

"Hi," Garden said. He turned to Jimmy. "All right, get Arnold in here."

"I talked to just about everybody in this town that knew Billy

Carter, Chief," Howell said, "and I ain't sure of anything. But he sure cut a swath, you know? When—"

"Later," Garden said.

"We ought to talk to some of—" Howell began.

"I said later." Garden turned and walked back into his office and Jimmy looked at Howell and raised his eyebrows and went out of the front office. Howell sat down, holding his notebook and eyeing Garden's office apprehensively.

Jimmy held the door of Garden's office open and Arnold stopped in the doorway. He wore civilian clothes. Garden raised his head from the desk and said, "Come on in."

"I figure I know what this is all about," Arnold said.

"Do you? Come on in," Garden said. His voice was steady, but Jimmy peered at him with interest.

"Want me to stay, Chief?" he asked.

"No," Garden said. "Go on out and close the door." Arnold edged slowly into the office and Jimmy swung the door shut behind him. Garden looked at Arnold.

"Okay. I busted the mayor's kid," Arnold said. "I had a right. What you going to do, give me the ax?"

"No," Garden said. "Sit down, Arnold. Tell me about it."

"I'll stand," Arnold said. He mopped his face.

"What you sweating about? Tell me about it."

"Look! You don't fool me. Don't act high and mighty," Arnold said. "You going to fire me, fine. We'll see about that. But don't act so snotty, Ben."

"Don't call me Ben," Garden gritted, leaning forward across the desk.

"Well, Jesus—"

"I asked you. Tell me about it. You can call me *Chief* Garden. Why you sweating so, Arnold?"

"I don't have—it's in my report. All in my report. He was high and I busted him."

"After he ran you off the road."

"That's right. You read it, then? He ran me off the road."

"Where?" Garden asked. He had not once looked away from Arnold's face, nor blinked.

"Where? Where'd he run me off the road? On Seaview. He—"

"He was going which way on Seaview?"

"What? West. He was headed west. I tole you, I turned around and chased him."

"You didn't tell me. But it's in your report. You were going home, east on Seaview? That goes to the beach. You live out in Spanish Heights, don't you?"

"You know where I live!" Arnold said. He glared at Garden. "Okay then, I was riding around. But I was heading home. What the hell's the difference?"

"You chased him where?"

"It's in the report."

"Yeah. Tell me again."

"What's all this—" Arnold began furiously. He had to look straight at Garden to yell at him, and his voice wavered whenever he saw Garden's expression.

"Okay," Garden said. "We'll go out there. You can show me." He got up and went into the outer office without looking back at Arnold. "Come on," Garden said to Jimmy. "You better come along."

He said nothing else until they had driven out of town, past the blocklike houses and scruffy yards of the Spanish Heights subdivision, crossed the mossy water of a canal and turned down a narrow road with cracked blacktopping. Jimmy drove and Arnold sat in back. Occasionally Arnold would start talking and subside when Garden did not respond, did not turn his head.

"Right here, eh?" Garden said.

"It's in my report," Arnold said sullenly. Jimmy had eased to a stop. Garden got out of the car and looked at the sparse sandy grass that edged the road. Behind him Arnold got reluctantly out of the car.

"You ran him off the road? I don't see no skid marks."

"Right there," Arnold said.

"Those aren't skid marks. That's where the tow truck turned around when it came out to get his car. Nobody lives on down this road, do they? It peters out in another quarter mile. That why you told the girl to meet you here?"

"You're nuts!" Arnold said. He was sweating.

"Must have shook you up when you saw the kid get out of the car," Garden said. "What did you tell the girl? That you'd charge her and Frieden's kid? Or just talk it around town unless she came across?" Garden turned and looked at Arnold again, and Arnold took a step back. Garden followed him.

Jimmy got out of the car and called, "Listen, Chief—"

"Shut up," Garden said. He took another step toward Arnold and Arnold backed against the car.

"What the hell difference does it make?" he asked shrilly. "What you gettin' so holy about? If she—"

"Yeah," Garden said between his teeth. Arnold stared blindly and then his nerve broke and he shoved his hand suddenly into his right hip pocket. Arnold's fist and the leather blackjack were still knotted in the pocket when Garden caught Arnold's elbow with his left hand and stepped back, yanking. The pocket tore and Arnold was snatched around and toward Garden, off balance. He tried to duck, too late, and the heel of Garden's right hand slammed against Arnold's forehead, snapping his head back. Arnold lurched against the car, his arms down. Garden stepped into him, braced, and let the fury pumping through him find release in his arms. The car rocked with the impact of the blows to Arnold's body, as the squealing grunts Arnold gave at each punch grew thinner.

Arnold hit Garden once with the blackjack, high on the shoulder, more of a reflex than anything else. Garden caught his wrist

58

and the blackjack fell out of Arnold's hand. He hit Arnold three more times in the body, with his right, swinging his shoulder behind each punch.

Jimmy was pulling at him, yelling. Garden stepped back, breathing heavily. Arnold's knees folded and he slid slowly down the side of the police car, sprawling forward into the sand at the edge of the road.

"Christ, Chief!" Jimmy said.

"Yeah. Okay," Garden said. He took long gasping breaths.

"What're you gonna do now?" Jimmy asked.

"We're gonna take him back and book him for assault," Garden said. He bent and picked up the blackjack and handed it to Jimmy. "He assaulted me," Garden said. "Good thing you were a witness."

"Okay," Jimmy said. He stared down at Arnold.

"I'll just see if I can't get him a few things to think about instead of that kid," Garden said.

"Some broke ribs, for a start," Jimmy muttered. "Chief? It ain't any of my business. But you know Arnold's pretty good friends with Mr. Delmer, don't you?"

"I heard."

"I guess we better get him into the back seat," Jimmy said.

"I'll lift him," Garden said. "You get the door."

CHAPTER 10:
They took Arnold to the station and helped him inside. He was at least semiconscious. They booked him and then Jimmy and another patrolman took him

outside and drove him to the hospital.

"He ain't going to go anywhere," Garden said to Howell. "If I thought he was going to run I'd lock him up and ask Doc to come over and look at him here. But he ain't going to run."

"He didn't look so good," Howell said.

"He ain't supposed to," Garden said harshly. He went into his office and Howell followed him in.

"You want to talk about Carter now, Chief?" he asked carefully.

"No," Garden said. "I got to make some calls. To Frieden, first of all. You heard any more about his boy?"

"No," Howell said.

"Hell, I'll go over and see him. Then I got another call to make." Garden took the note with Angela Lang's address off his desk and put it in his shirt pocket. "I oughta kick myself, Howell," he said. "For not getting rid of that guy the first time I had trouble with him. You'd think I'd learn."

"It ain't your fault," Howell said. "Some guys turn sour. That's all."

"The hell it ain't my fault!" Garden said. "That's what I get paid for, ain't it? I'll see you right after lunch. Oh, Christ. Make that about two o'clock."

"All right," Howell said resignedly. Garden went out through the outer office, nodded to Jimmy and left the building.

He had completely forgotten that he was eating lunch with Harper. It seemed strange to think about when he did remember it. He recalled the thin icy tension of her voice in the phone saying gay things not at all gaily, and his frown came back. He could still feel the sweat from the beating in the hot morning sun, still feel the impact of his fists against Arnold's ribs and stomach. He looked at his hands curiously and then closed them tight on the wheel of his car and swung out of the parking lot.

Arriving at Frieden's, he walked back through the shelves cluttered with drugstore junk, to the prescription counter at the rear of the store. The girl at the counter looked at him with hostility. "Where's Mr. Frieden?" Garden asked.

"He's in the office," she said reluctantly.

"I'd like to see him."

"Go on in," she said. He went around the counter and she moved away from him as he passed. He tapped on the closed door of the office and heard Frieden tell him to come in. He went in and closed the door behind him.

Frieden swiveled slowly around and stared across the desk at Garden. He looked more rabbity than ever in his neat white jacket. Garden met Frieden's eyes. He asked, "How's your boy?"

"The doctor says he'll live," Frieden said. "No thanks to your man."

"I'd like you to know that Arnold is suspended," Garden said. "And that charge is dropped, of course."

"That's supposed to make me feel better?" Frieden asked. "Or his mother?"

"No. Of course not," Garden said. "Do you know why it happened?"

"I don't *care* why it happened!" Frieden said. He fumbled aimlessly at some papers on his desk, tossed them away, looked back up at Garden. "Why should I care why it happened? All I know is that my boy almost got killed. And he got dragged into your stinking station with his head broke open and got charged with drug possession. You think I'm going to forget that?"

"No. I wouldn't expect you to," Garden said.

"And because I'm on the council, you slap your officer on the wrist and come around here to tell me all about it. Well, you can go to hell, Garden."

"Listen," Garden said. "Just listen! Arnold didn't get no slap on the wrist. He's over at the hospital himself, right now. And the suspension is a legal formality. What it amounts to, he's off the force. He ain't going to be a policeman anymore, not here, not anywhere else, if I can arrange it."

"You think I care? That doesn't fix my boy's head. Get out of here, Garden. The next time I want to see you is at the council meeting—when we tell you you're fired. Now get out of here!"

"One thing," Garden said. "You could call it a favor." Frieden laughed harshly. "Don't go assuming that I busted Arnold just because you're on the council," Garden said. "You could give me a little more credit than that."

"Go to hell," Frieden said. He looked at Garden, red-eyed. "You got hurt feelings? Get out of here!"

"All right," Garden said. He turned and went to the door, and stopped. He looked back at Frieden and said, "Hell! Doc? Listen, I'm sorry. I'm awful sorry. I don't know what else to say."

Frieden looked at him and Garden saw that the pharmacist had tears in his eyes.

"You want your job awful bad, don't you?" Frieden asked thickly.

"Screw the job! You can *have* the goddam job! I said I'm sorry!"

"Oh, get out!" Frieden said.

"Yeah," Garden said. He went out and closed the office door carefully behind him. The girl behind the counter looked at him, flinched when she saw his expression, and turned away.

Garden stalked out of the drugstore into the midday heat and climbed into his cruiser. He sat there, flexing his fingers on the wheel, staring through the windshield at the glare in the parking lot.

"And I still got to talk to that girl," he said. "Oh, my God!" He started the car.

Some impulse made him go back to his apartment and take off his uniform and shower before calling the Lang girl. He dressed in slacks and a sport shirt and sat down at the long table that he used for a desk at one side of the bedroom. He looked for a second at the stacked novels and lawbooks and texts that went to the ceiling at the back of the desk and then he picked up the phone.

The phone was answered on the third ring. "Miss Lang?" he asked. "Angela Lang?"

"Yes, who is this?" She had a young, pleasant voice, with strain in it.

"This is Ben Garden. I'm the chief of police," he said. There was a silence. "Miss Lang?"

"I see," she said. "What do you want? Or do I need to ask?"

"What? Listen, I'd like to see you. I have to talk to you. Is it convenient for me to come over?"

"Convenient!" she said bitterly. "Are you trying to be funny? Convenient! What choice have I got?"

"Take it easy—" he began.

"Very funny. What is it now? You'll not only keep Arnold quiet but drop that stupid charge against Nicky Frieden, if I cooperate?"

"Listen!" he said.

"So your cop passed me on to you?" she asked. "I suppose he gets brownie points. Well, you can go to hell, Mr. Chief of Police. You can just go to hell. I won't—"

Garden took a deep breath and roared, "Goddam it, shut up and listen! Arnold is off the force, there isn't any charge against the Frieden boy and there isn't going to be any charge against anybody except maybe Arnold! Now shut *up* and listen! I want to *talk* to you about Arnold. I realize that you might not want to talk freely but I assure you it will be held in confidence. Goddam it, can't any of you people give me enough credit to think I might not be on the make? That I might be trying to clean this mess up?" He ran out of breath and stopped.

There was a long silence. He waited, wondering if she was still on the phone. Then she said, "Wow!"

"What?"

"You sure can yell!" There was a long silence. Then she said,

"All right. I'm a fool but come on over. I guess you have the address."

"Yes," he said. "Sorry I yelled but I'm getting a little tired of all this."

"You're not the only one," she said. "If you've got such pure intentions I guess you won't mind if my roommate's here?"

"Hell, no," he said. "Not if you trust her, I don't mind. I'll be right over." He hung up and stared at the phone, shaking his head.

It was nearly twelve. He'd be late for lunch. He grunted and got up, put on his wristwatch, got his wallet and change. Automatically he picked out of his desk the Airweight .38 that he wore with civilian clothes, snug in its holster, and started to clip it to his belt under the sport shirt. Then he stopped, tossed the gun in the air and caught it, then put it gently back in the desk drawer. He got his keys and left the apartment, pulling the door shut behind him, trying the lock. He went down the stairs, feeling odd without the slight weight of the gun at his side.

CHAPTER 11: Angela Lang lived in an older house near the center of town, one that had been cut into apartments before Garden had come back to Easton. There was an entry off the wide front porch. Garden tried to remember who had owned the house originally, and found he couldn't. He knocked and waited.

The girl who opened the door was slender, with thick short black hair. She stared at Garden and said, "All right. Come in."

"Miss Lang, I take it?" Garden said.

She stood back from the door. "Of course. Come on in. Let's get it over with." Garden went inside. A taller blond girl sat on the couch in the living room. She looked at Garden with dislike. Angela said, "Chief Garden, my roommate. Muggs, this is the chief of police. Sit down, Garden."

"Take it easy," Garden said mildly. He sat down in the big chair near the couch and looked around the room. It was clean and freshly painted. The furniture was comfortable. It wasn't Garden's idea of a room furnished by women. "This is a nice place," he said to Angela.

"You didn't come here to talk about our taste." She stood by the couch. "Go ahead."

"What do you think I came here for?" Garden asked.

"To get your cop off the hook," she said stubbornly. "What else?"

"Wrong," Garden said. "I told you that Arnold isn't *my* cop anymore. I've suspended him. I'm going to fire him. But I need some help."

"What kind of help?" Muggs asked suspiciously.

Garden glanced at her. "It'll be his word against Nicky Frieden's, so it'll be hard to hang him for that," he said. "And I can stick him with assault against me, with another one of my men to back it, but that'll look a little funny."

"Assault?" Angela asked.

"He and I had words," Garden said.

"And he got the worst of it?"

"Yes. What I—"

"You mean you beat him up?"

"You could call it that," Garden said.

"Listen, Angie, you don't want to get mixed up in this," Muggs said.

"Just a minute." Angela stared at Garden. "How bad did you beat him up?" she asked curiously.

65

"Not bad," Garden said. He felt uncomfortable. "He had to have some medical attention," he added. "But not like Frieden did. What's the matter, you feel sorry for Arnold? He pulled a blackjack on me."

"You know better," she said. "I'm trying to make up my mind about you, though."

"About me?"

"I'd heard you were rough. But when you came in, I was surprised. Now I don't know."

"Leave me out of it," Garden said.

"I can't. Okay, what do you want from me?"

Garden took a deep breath. "I want a statement," he said. "A statement that Arnold found you and Nicky Frieden over on the island. That he stated, or implied, that he'd keep quiet in return for favors from you."

"She'll do no such *thing!*" Muggs got up and stood by Angela with her arm over the smaller girl's shoulder. "You must think she's crazy!" she said furiously.

"Be quiet, Muggs," Angela said. She folded her arms and looked thoughtfully at Garden.

"He did, didn't he?" Garden asked her.

"And of course I'd have to say what Nick and I were doing," she said. "On paper. Otherwise Arnold wouldn't have had any hold on me, would he?"

"I'm afraid that's right," Garden said.

"And then you'll use that statement as a basis to fire him," she said. "Goody. So you'll be rid of a troublemaker. And then we can read all about it, all about me, in the papers."

"No," Garden said. "Christ, I'm doing this poorly. I won't *use* the statement. I won't even read it. But I want to be able to tell Arnold I have it. If I have to. I want to be able to make him *know* I have enough muscle to fire him and make it stick."

Muggs laughed sarcastically.

"Can't you just fire him? You're the chief," Angela stated.

"We have civil service rules in this town," Garden said.

"You can beat him up, but you can't fire him?" Angela asked. "Can't you just lie to him? Tell him you have such a statement?"

"Sure. And probably make him believe it. But he might have some help. Someone who won't believe me. But that one would be smart enough to know the truth when I tell it."

"No, honey!" Muggs said to Angela. "You can't trust him."

Angela looked at her and back to Garden.

"Yes," Garden said. "It comes down to just that. Whether you can trust me or not. Doesn't it?"

"Yes," she said. "How many people will hear that you have such a statement?"

"Just Arnold and his lawyer if he gets one. I won't even tell Nick Frieden."

"Why should I care whether Nicky knows?" she asked.

"Well, I thought you might—" Garden started to say, and then he shut up. Angela smiled, surprised.

"No, I'm not in love with Nicky," she said. "He's nice but he's a kid."

"I see," Garden said.

Angela looked at him narrowly. "My God! I think I've shocked you." She laughed, a little angrily. "Muggs, I've shocked the chief of police. How about that?"

"All right," Garden said.

"Why don't you just leave?" Muggs asked him. She tightened the arm about Angela's shoulders.

"Be quiet, Muggs," Angela said thoughtfully. "Let go. Let me think a minute."

Muggs took her arm away and sat down on the couch, staring her distrust at Garden. Garden smiled at her in as trustworthy a manner as he could manage, feeling that it was probably a leer. He watched Angela.

He had expected someone quite different. She was both more intelligent and less pretty than he had imagined she would be.

She didn't fit any image he might have had of a girl who would have been making love over on the island in the middle of the afternoon. And she had completely disabused him of any idea of romance with Frieden. He blinked at her.

"And don't look at me like that!" she said.

"Sorry. I didn't realize I was looking at you any particular way," he said.

"Oh? Come off it, Mr. Chief of Police. You're thinking the same way everybody else does."

"Everybody over thirty?" he asked gently.

"Yes, as a matter of fact!" she said, and now she *was* angry. She turned away and sat on the couch with her arms folded. Her roommate soothed her and looked darkly at Garden.

I don't know, Garden thought. She *isn't* a tramp. But they sure do think different these days. No wonder a dumb bastard like Arnold got confused. When you have to tell the tramps from the nice girls not by what they do, but how they think about what they do . . . He cleared his throat.

"How's this?" he asked. "I don't give a damn about your private life. Not one way or the other. The only thing I'm interested in is the practical result. Can we look at it like that?"

"Why not?" she asked. "But you're shocked, just the same."

"If it pleases you," he said. "Arnold did call you, right?"

"That is right."

"And he was, let's say, dirty-minded? Take it easy now. We're being practical, remember? He assumed that because you'd been intimate with one man, you'd be willing to do the same with another. Especially to buy his silence. Right?"

To Garden's astonishment, a slow thick bright blush suffused her face.

"Well?" he asked.

"That's right," she said, looking away.

"*Would* you sign a statement to that effect?"

"Why *should* I do that?"

"You know you're blushing?" Garden asked. "Why should you do that? I've told you."

"It's none of your business if I'm blushing," she said furiously.

"Right. I just commented on it. Like I might point out that it's raining, or something," he said. "How about it?"

After a while she said, "I don't want to sign a statement."

"But why not?" he asked reasonably. "What Arnold did was plenty dirty. I want to nail him for it and I want to have that good-sized club if I have to have it, to threaten him with."

"You beat him up. Isn't that enough?"

"No. Not if he can walk out of here and be a policeman again, somewhere else," he said. "Or even be a policeman here again, if I should lose my job."

"So it's still trust you or not," she said.

"Right," he agreed. "I can't do anything but give you my word."

"Your word!" She twisted around and stared at him.

"Yeah," he said. "Funny, we both got bad habits. Bad if you're trying to be tough and all that. Trying to be with it. You blush. I give my word and I stick to it. I can't help it any more than you can help blushing."

"Well, I'll be damned," she muttered.

"What's so funny about it? You want me to give you my respect. No, don't interrupt. Well, you've got it. I can't prove that, you just have to accept it or not. But if you do, looks like you'd take my word, too."

"Oh, for God's *sake!*" she said.

"I'm over thirty," he said. "Well over. Far enough over so I'm pretty square. Who else but a square would ask you to take his word about something?"

"You're a cute one, you know that?" she asked. "And a police-man, for heaven's sake. I must be out of my mind to trust a policeman."

"But you do, don't you?" He grinned at her.

"Yes, I guess I do," she said slowly.

Her roommate groaned. "Don't do it, Angie! Suppose he *has* to use it to charge that other cop? If he fights being fired, or something?"

"I'll tear the statement up," he said to Muggs. "Rather, I'll give it back to Angela. That's all."

"I don't believe you!" the roommate said. She put her hand back on Angela's shoulder, glaring at Garden. "Don't give it to him!"

"Well?" Garden asked.

"All right," Angela muttered. "Good Lord. Muggs, bring me a pen and some paper. Why not? You have to trust somebody *sometime.*"

"That's exactly right," Garden said.

"But if you're lying; if you spread this all over town . . ."

"In order to get rid of Arnold?" Garden asked. "If I'm no better than Arnold, that is? Then what, Angie?"

"I guess I wouldn't trust anybody for a long time," the girl said softly.

"Yeah," Garden said. He cleared his throat.

"All right," she said. "Where's that paper, honey?"

"On the desk," the roommate said. "You damned fool!"

"She isn't being a damned fool," Garden said. "She's trusting me."

"*I* don't," Muggs said furiously.

"Sure you do," Garden said gently.

Muggs looked narrowly at Garden and then looked away quickly. Angela was watching them both. She smiled nervously and said, "He's got good sharp eyes, Muggs. Let's trust him, okay?" She was once again stained with the slow dark blush.

Garden stood up, off the couch, and stared through a front window of the apartment, hoping he'd moved quickly enough so that she'd think he hadn't seen her color this time. He didn't want to meet Muggs' eyes, either. Garden was a little shocked and he cursed himself. It was one thing to be over thirty, with what that was supposed to imply. But he *liked* both these girls and he didn't enjoy embarrassing them.

Angela brought him three sheets of paper folded over once and handed them to him. He smiled at her and said, "Have Muggs sign it as witness and date it. Then seal it in an envelope. I told you I won't use this."

"I hope you won't," she said, turning away. "My folks live in Orlando," she added.

"Right. And they read the papers," he said. "I'll be careful."

"You'd better be." She handed him the envelope and held the door for him. "You certainly aren't what I expected," she said thoughtfully.

"What did you expect?" Garden said.

"Oh, you know. Fat, with a leer."

"I've been called fat."

"Oh? But you aren't, really. How old *are* you?"

"Over thirty," he said. "Remember?"

"I guess I better think about that, too," she said. "You aren't married?"

"I was," he said. "Once, a while ago."

"Damn it, I don't know about you," she said.

"Let me know what you decide," he said, smiling.

"Maybe I will," she said, and there was the hint of the blush. He grinned at it and she said, "Go on now!" and the red deepened. He found he was still grinning, in the car, as he locked the sealed envelope in the glove compartment.

"There's such a thing as good glands," he said aloud. "She isn't trying. It's just there." He shook his head and started the engine. He was going to be late for lunch. But he felt good for the first time all day. He could think about Doc Frieden without shame.

71

CHAPTER 12: He drove through town and out across the waterway and turned south down the beach road. It went past the good houses and through what was scrub not so long ago and was motels now, between the oaks on the beachside and the dredged-out mangrove along the waterway. Then the road turned toward the ocean and climbed a low ridge and ran along past the few really good houses, sitting high above the beach, among their palms. They were nearly all old, built in the twenties and thirties, with one or two that dated from the prosperity of the boom after the war.

This was different from the rest of the beach. The houses sat each in its own wide expanse of sea grape and palms and green lawn. They had a solid settled look, up on the ridge, overlooking the waterway behind and the Atlantic in front, half shielded by their trees. Even the casual shabbiness of some of the houses was impressive; like a very rich man wearing blue jeans. It made Garden remember what someone had once told him about Manalapan: that Vanderbilt and the others had settled Manalapan when Palm Beach got too common for them. This part of Easton wasn't quite Manalapan, nor Hobe Sound, but it didn't miss them by very much.

To the left was a row of palms and the steep slope down to the beach. The ocean glittered under the early-afternoon sun, surging lightly, green over the brown-shadowed shallow rocks near the beach. The arch of the bridge was ahead of him and the jetties of the inlet sticking out into the ocean. Brown water from the inlet stained the green ocean, spreading out to the south in a wide dark fan as the tide ran out. He slowed and turned in through a gap in a high dark green hedge. A heavy wooden gate stood open in the gap. His tires crunched on the graveled drive and he drove down the turning slope, slowing and stopping as the drive fanned out before the garages.

An ancient highly polished Buick sedan sat inside one of the opened garage doors and Harper's Jag sat outside, under the shade of the wide veranda above that encircled the house. Garden made sure he was clear so that the Buick could back out, and left his car. He glanced up at the massively timbered veranda, at the silvery cypress siding, and followed a brick path around to the front of the house, through the thick and raggedly overgrown clumps of hibiscus and jasmine.

The ground sloped up so that the veranda was only six feet above the ground at the front of the house. The path widened into a bricked terrace and he climbed the broad timber steps to the veranda. French doors spread out to the left and right, with heavy louvered shutters on either side that could be folded across and locked shut against hurricanes. Garden knocked on the front door and it moved under his hand after the second knock.

"Hello, Andros," he said. "Is Miss Harper in?"

The massive, straight-backed Negro looked down his nose at Garden and said, "Certainly, sir." His Bahamas accent was as strong as ever, just as his hair was no grayer than Garden remembered it from the first time he'd seen him, perhaps twenty-five years before. "Come in," Andros said, and stepped out of the way, holding the door open. "You'll find Miss Harper in the kitchen, making a salad," he added coldly. Garden understood that Andros disapproved. He grinned at the tall Negro and went into the dark hall. It smelled stale and close when the door eased shut behind him and cut off the breeze from the ocean.

"Garden? Come in here!" Harper's father called.

Garden glanced at Andros, who nodded silently to the right. Garden hesitated and then turned and went through the door.

Harper's father swiveled in a chair behind a cluttered desk and stared at him. "Thought that was you," he said. His voice was years younger than his splotched heavy face. "Nobody but you and Andros make those boards creak that way. Have a drink."

"I'm already late for lunch with your daughter," Garden said. "Mr. Wayne, you trying to get me in more trouble?"

Harper's father grunted. "Any time you set out to please a woman, you're already in trouble," he said acidly. "Set down. Andros?"

"Sir," Andros said. He went over and took a large crystal decanter from a sideboard, brought it to the desk with two glasses.

"Get some ice," Wayne said. "I ain't as young as I was," he added to Garden. "Need something to soften the liquor." Andros disappeared and the older man said, "He'll tell her you're here. How've you been?"

"Pretty good," Garden said. He sank into a generous leather chair and admired the glasses.

"That's Waterford," the old man said. "Old Waterford. I understand they're making it again now. What the hell do you mean, pretty good? They fire you or something?"

"Not yet," Garden said.

"Then you're still chief of police? Hell of a note. Why do you waste your time that way?"

"There's worse ways," Garden said.

"Tell me something, Garden. Would you have turned down working for me if you weren't seeing Harper?"

"Would you have offered me the job if I *wasn't* seeing Harper?" Garden asked. "I don't know a damned thing about ranching."

74

"That ain't what Pete Burke says," the old man said. He stared at Garden. "All right, you stubborn bastard. No, I probably wouldn't have. Because I probably wouldn't have got to know you. Just another fisherman's boy around town."

"All right, then," Garden said.

"Be that as it may, I don't like you sitting around this town, chief of police. Hell, I'd rather you were running a charter boat, if you don't want to work for me."

"I like being chief," Garden said. He grinned at the old man. "I'm a good one. I like police work."

"Bullshit!" Wayne said angrily. "Working for those damned puny two-bit bastards on the town council? Out picking up drunks out of the gutter? You ought to be able to do better than that."

"Burke's on the council," Garden said. "You respect Burke, don't you?"

"Less than I used to, before he went into politics," the old man said. "Ah, hell, you're as bad as he is. Pete's the stubbornest Burke I ever met and God knows his daddy was stubborn enough." He glanced at the door. "Christ, Andros, I thought you'd gone to Miami for the ice."

"No, sir," Andros said. "Can't you wait? Seeing you're not supposed to be drinking." He gestured with the ice bucket in his hand and then used the tongs to put two cubes in each of the tumblers.

Wayne stared at Andros, grinning. "About time I shipped you back to the goddam Islands," he said. "You getting as bad as the doctor, bad as Harper, even." Andros poured a good four fingers of bourbon into each glass and Garden sighed. He picked up his glass as Andros left and the old man stared at him.

"Come to think of it, you look like you need a drink. Your health, sir."

"And yours," Garden said, and drank. "Wow. Yeah, I need one. I went to a wake last night."

75

"How's that?" Wayne asked, lowering his glass.

"A friend of a friend got killed yesterday. Right over there at the inlet, in fact." Garden nodded toward the south.

"Oh? I guess I did hear Andros say something about that," the old man said without interest. "Who killed him?"

"I don't know," Garden said. He sipped from his glass again. "Yet," he added.

"Christ. Fishermen's killings. That's what I mean, Garden. You intend to spend the rest of your life mopping up after Saturday night brawls?"

"Funny thing," Garden said, and laughed. "Most people in town seem to think that I got this job, and keep it, *because* of you. That's about all I've heard lately. I wish they could hear you on the subject. How about giving me a statement? Sort of an antitestimonial?"

"They think that, do they?" the old man growled. "Hell, ain't that what I've been telling you? You're wasting your time looking after this town. I wish you'd get out of it." He took another drink.

"Sorry," Garden said after a pause. "But I got a few things to do. I'm not saying I want the job forever. But . . ."

"I thought Burke was planning to run you for sheriff," Wayne said. "What happened to that?"

"That's out," Garden said. "Joel McGee can have that job as long as he wants it."

"Joel does pretty good," the old man agreed, "for such a lazy bastard. Now that job counts for something. But this town? It used to be some good. Now . . ." He looked as if he wanted to spit.

"It ain't that bad," Garden said.

"It ain't worth a damn!" Wayne said savagely. He gestured at the mass of paper, old envelopes, old clippings, drifted across the desk. "What you think I'm doing?" he said. "Cleaning all this up. So I don't need to come back here. This house. When

Harper's mother was young . . . Now, the hell with it. Don't intend to leave the ranch any more'n I can help." He glared at Garden. "Anyway, not for this pesthole," he said.

Garden sighed and finished his drink. "All right," he said wearily. "So I'm wasting my time."

"Makes me wonder if I was wrong about you," the old man said.

Garden met Wayne's cold speculative gaze and grinned. "Look, just don't worry about it," he said. "In fact, I'd appreciate it if you'd get off my back. You know I'm not going to change my mind, don't you? Then why not forget it?"

"Well, Jesus Christ. Hell of a way to talk to your prospective father-in-law." Wayne smiled at Garden. It was a pretty furious smile.

"Ain't it?" Garden agreed. He got up. "I better go have lunch. Before she comes in here and gives us both hell. You got any more advice for me?"

"Oh, go to hell," Wayne growled. Garden left the room and the old man's grin faded as he leaned over his unfinished drink, staring across the desk at the wall.

CHAPTER 13: Garden stopped in the door of the morning room—at least that was what Harper usually called it—and smiled in at her. "I'm late," he observed.

"How unusual!" she said acidly, but then she smiled in return. Garden walked into the room. "Not only the whole town do I have to worry about," she went on, "but then even my father waylays you. Have a good drink? I was going to give you a martini."

"I'll take it," Garden said. "Even on top of bourbon. Why should I be the only nondrunk in town?" She stood up and started to turn toward the sideboard and he said, "Hey, just a minute there."

"What?"

"Come here first."

"Before lunch?" she asked, and laughed and walked around the table toward him.

"The hell with that," he said. She was the only woman Garden had ever gone with who could stand flatfooted and look level in his eyes. He looked back at her brooding stare, her slight smile, and he put his hands on her shoulders. "Before lunch. Or after. Or any time," he said. Striking. Garden had seen her a dozen times before he'd realized, why, she's beautiful! It was that sort of beauty; imperious and arrogant and often angry.

She had a lean dark almost Indian face. Her dark glossy long hair framed the face but didn't soften it. Neither did her astonishing long full body. Garden took a deep breath. He didn't have to pull her to him.

"All right," he said, after a while. "Lunch?"

"You'll have to let go of me first," she said.

"And you'll have to let go of me," he said.

She laughed. "I hope you're hungry," she said.

"You mean for food? Oh, yeah. I suppose."

"Stop that. You'll shock Andros, if he comes in. Avocado and crab meat? And a steak. The steak will be all right. I told Andros to wait until you were through with Dad before he put them on. Stop it!"

"All that?" He released her partially, reluctantly. "My God, Harper. How am I going to work this afternoon?"

"Oh, nonsense. I thought you might drive to Palm Beach with me. I want to shop."

78

"I'd love to. But not today."

"Hell, Ben!"

"I told you, I have to work. I've already got Howell about up the wall."

She freed herself the rest of the way and went to the sideboard. "Oh, Lord," she said. "Police work." Her tone wasn't pleasant.

"That's what I do," he said. He watched her mix the martinis.

She handed him his glass and said, "I wish we'd met before you took that damned job."

"Sometimes I do, too," he said. He sipped at his drink. "This is fine. Not even too dry. But we didn't."

"No, we didn't. Why *didn't* we meet a long time ago, Ben? We could have."

"Sure," he said. "Well, you know why." He nodded toward the French windows. Through them, the veranda looked out through the palms, over the inlet. "I was right down there, working on the boats. It's a long way up here, Harper."

"Is it?" she asked. "I knew some fishermen." He decided to change the subject.

"Or in high school?" she continued. "You were in high school here, when I was. Before I went to Switzerland."

"All right," he said.

"Poor Ben," she said, and laughed, this time brightly and coldly. "All right. I won't embarrass you. But I wish we had met before Switzerland."

"I'm glad we didn't," he said, and drank.

"Yes, there's that, isn't it? If we'd met then, as we *would* have met, then—"

"Harper!" he said harshly.

"Oh, don't be touchy, Ben. You know that I liked you before I even loved you? It was because you were so damned vulnerable."

"Vulnerable! Me?"

"I'm an expert on vulnerability," she said.

"Let's eat," he said.

"Let's. Ben? Have you had many fights because of me?"

"Not one," he said wearily.

"Oh? Is that because you're so adult? Or because they're so afraid of you? You mean no one has elbowed you in the ribs and told you about—"

"Goddam it!" he said. "How would you like a whipping? A good hard one?"

"You mean that, don't you?"

"You're damned right I do!" he said. "Here. Fix me another martini!"

"All right," she said. He sat down, pulling a chair out from the table, and she came over and took his glass out of his hand. She looked down at him and then leaned over and kissed him, very hard and very long.

"There," she said, and touched his lips with the tip of her tongue. "Now eat your salad. Then I'll ring for Andros and the steak."

"Harper—" he started.

"Quiet. I'll go to Palm Beach and shop by myself. But I'll be home early. You *will* be free this evening, won't you?"

"God, I hope so. Yes," he said.

"Fine," she said. "I'll call." She went away toward the sideboard and he stared after her, not smiling. The icy edge to her voice was still there, still in his ear after she stopped talking.

The lunch would have been too much for appetites less than Garden's and Harper's. Garden was glad of the food after the three drinks. He thought of Howell waiting for him and firmly refused wine. He and Harper made idle conversation, mostly about her shopping trip to Palm Beach. Her face was perfectly controlled. He would have thought her angry, if he hadn't known her. Still, there was the tension and the electric gaiety that bothered him.

"Take it easy on the turnpike," he said, as they sipped coffee.

"I always do," she said, smiling.

"Sure. How many tickets have you had this year? Somehow I wish your old man didn't have so many hired hands in Tallahassee. I'd feel better if you *didn't* have a license."

She stared at him and laughed, her loud clear laugh as free as any man's. He felt relieved to hear it. "Hell, Ben, I don't have a license! Never bothered to get one," she said. She laughed again at his expression.

"Okay. Okay. Just don't tell me any more. And me the chief of police," he said bitterly, grinning.

"You know how good a driver I am," she said.

"Sure, sure." He looked at his watch and then looked across the table at her.

"Damn the time," she said.

"I do damn it," he said. "But I have to go."

"And you want to," she said.

"I can't want just one thing, Harper," he said gently.

"Oh, I know."

"How long do you think you'd want me if I took a job working for your old man?"

"All right." They stood up and she smiled stiffly at him. "You're right," she said. "If there's anything I don't need it's another slave."

"How about if I take a week of vacation soon?" he said. "As soon as I can work it out? I'll even give in and let you fly us to Jamaica. You've been talking about that for six months."

"My God. You mean I've finally seduced you into the honeymoon before the honeymoon?" she asked. "Fine. It sounds fine."

"Dress rehearsal, call it."

"Wonderful," she said. Suddenly she came around the table and reached for him, and he held her, wondering at the strength in her arms, wondering at his own worry.

Harper let him go into the hall alone and Andros appeared silently, from Wayne's office, closing the door behind him. The huge Negro nodded majestically to Garden and opened the front door for him.

"Thank you, Andros," Garden said. He paused and looked curiously at the man.

"How is he, Andros?" he asked. "Really?" He had almost asked Andros about Harper and had changed his mind at the last minute.

"Mr. Wayne is quite well, sir," Andros said briskly.

"Yes, but something is bothering him. Is it something I can do anything about?"

"I know of nothing," Andros said.

"Of nothing bothering him? Or of nothing I can do?"

"Neither, sir." Andros looked at him opaquely.

"And you have nothing to tell me, either, do you?"

"I have nothing to tell *anybody*, sir," Andros said.

"Okay," Garden said. He started across the veranda and paused. "Andros, look after Harper, will you?"

"I have looked after the Waynes for thirty-five years, Mr. Garden," Andros said. "I shall continue to do so." He nodded politely and swung the door smoothly and silently closed.

CHAPTER 14: Howell was waiting in the outer office when Garden entered. Garden looked at the clock and said, "My God, three o'clock! Come on in." Howell followed him into his office.

"Anything new?" Garden asked him.

"Nothing much," Howell said. "You want to talk about Carter now?"

"Yeah," Garden said. "Sit down." He slid into the chair behind his desk and Howell sat down opposite him and pulled out his notes. He went through them carefully and Garden listened and asked questions, from time to time forcing himself not to yawn. He cursed himself for the lunch and took satisfaction in poring over Howell's notes with him.

"Porky's," he said. "You keep mentioning that place. Billy did spend a lot of time out there, then?"

"Well, that's what I understand," Howell said. "From a couple of his buddies."

"But they didn't know much about him at Porky's?"

"They claimed not to," Howell said. "The bartender said he never heard of him. Porky was smarter. He knew Bill, all right. Said he hadn't been in in a long time."

"Porky's is outside town," Garden said. "You check with McGee's office?"

"Sure," Howell said. "I talked to the sheriff. He said he didn't have anything much on them, yet. He said you ought to call him, by the way."

"Yeah, I haven't talked to Joel in a while," Garden said. He thought for a minute. "You think Porky knows something about Billy?"

"I think Porky knows something about everybody that ever went in his place," Howell said.

"Yeah, and that girl, on the boat. She works out there. *She'd* remember Carter. Hell, she said something." Garden rubbed his forehead. "Something about a redhead. And Carter. Carter had a redheaded girl friend?"

"Probably lots of them," Howell said gloomily.

"Yeah," Garden said.

"Want to go out there?"

"Hell, yes," Garden said. The box on his desk buzzed and Garden stared at it and touched the key. "Yeah?"

"Chief, it's that guy from the newspaper again," Jimmy said. "On the phone."

"You tell him I'm here?"

"No. Told him I thought you were out, but I'd check. Then I put him on hold. You here?"

"Nope," Garden said. "Tell him I've gone to see Sheriff McGee, tell him he can catch me at Joel's office." He closed the key and said to Howell, "Come on. Let's get the hell out of here."

On the way out of town, to Porky's, he asked Howell, "Did McGee have anything on Billy Carter?"

"No, Chief. His people picked Billy up a time or two, of course. Fights, drunken driving one time, you know. Nothing in connection with Porky's, either."

"What *did* he say about Porky's?" Garden asked.

Howell grinned. "He tole me we shouldn't make too many waves. Said he was biding his time on Porky's. I reckon he's going to give him a little rope and then hang him."

"Porky getting that rough?" Garden asked.

"Ah, you know. A little gambling. A little this, a little that," Howell said. He paused. "I reckon he's using those cabins out back. Late at night."

"Getting pretty careless," Garden said. "He ought to know Joel McGee better than that."

"Porky ain't really smart."

"He'll get educated," Garden said. They were moving along down the two-lane blacktop road through the back country, the deadly stretch that ran straight as a string. Howell drove smoothly and fast and Garden relaxed and watched the bright green pastures and the clumps of punk trees alternating with stretches of tomato fields edged with Australian pine wind-

84

breaks. "There it is," he said. "Not many cars out front."

"Too early," Howell said.

The building was large and rectangular, with a steeply pitched roof of galvanized iron. Its real name was Porky's Tin Roof Tavern, but nobody called it anything except Porky's. Once it had been a farm machinery sales and service place, but that business had gone broke, proving rare business incapacity in its owners, in this intensive farming area. Porky had bought the building and grounds and had made significant changes. Howell slowed and turned into the potholed lot in front of the building.

The neon sign across the front of the building had letters four feet high that spelled PORKYS. Under the sign, against the dirty white of the concrete block, was painted TIN ROOF TAV-ERN, in smaller black letters. Under that it said *NO HABLA ESPAÑOL*. Spotlights were mounted at either end of the dis-claimer, turned to shine on it at night. Garden looked at it wryly. Porky believed in giving fair notice to Mexican and Puerto Rican farmworkers. He'd sell them bottles, sell them drinks at the bar. As long as they paid cash and were cleaner and neater and quieter than his Anglo customers. But in any dispute, they would be wrong. Porky's didn't speak Spanish. They weren't going to.

The huge barroom was gloomy, with the lights on only in the center over the big horseshoe of the bar. A few early-evening drinkers sat at the bar, a few more back in the dark booths near the walls. They all looked at Garden and Howell as they moved over to the bar to stand there for a minute or so while the bartender at the far end eyed them. Finally the man walked sullenly toward them.

"Looking for something?" he asked.

"For Porky," Garden said.

The bartender shrugged. "He's in," he said. "Go on back."

"No, tell him to come out here."

"He's busy," the bartender said indifferently, and started to turn away.

"He'll be busier if I have to go back there," Garden said softly.

"All right!" the bartender snarled. He plodded back down the bar toward the door to the back.

"Thanks," Garden called after him.

"There's an old acquaintance," Howell observed, nodding toward a table at the rear of the room. "The gal on Tommy's boat."

"Yeah," Garden said. "What was her name?"

"Felty," Howell said. "The first name was a funny one. Lisa? No—Ellice."

"Let's say hello," Garden said. He walked back toward the rear table. The girl warily watched them come.

"Howdy," Garden said cheerfully. "Mind if we sit?"

"I guess not," she said unhappily. "I got to take care of the customers, though. I don't wanna get fired."

"Maybe we're customers," Garden said. He and Howell sat down.

"No you ain't," she muttered. "What you want? I told you I didn't know nothing about that mate." Garden smiled at her. She had on a peekaboo jersey blouse of shiny material in a violent pink, so tight that it was obvious she wore no bra. When she nervously uncrossed and recrossed her legs, Garden saw that what there was of her skirt was an equally glaring green. The combination was unfortunate.

"Enjoying the view?" she asked venomously.

"Just admiring." Garden smiled at her. "While we wait for your boss."

"Listen, Porky won't like me sitting here. I better get on."

"Not yet. When did you say was the last time you saw Billy Carter in here?"

"Who?" she asked. "Oh, him. I never did say I seen him in here."

"But you *did*, didn't you?"

"Well, yeah. Once in a while. I got to go."

"Did he bring the redhead in here?" Garden asked.

"Naw. Not in the—" She stopped abruptly. "I got to go!" she said again. "Fellow up there needs a beer."

"Not in the what?" Garden asked. "Not in the bar? Where, then?"

"*I* never seen him with no girl!" she said uneasily. Garden stared at her and she got up and hurried toward the front of the bar, teetering in her rhinestoned heels.

"Lots of help!" Howell said.

"Maybe she was," Garden said. "Not in the bar? Where, then? In the cabins out back?"

"There's Porky," Howell said. The bar owner came out of the back room into the bar and lifted a wooden flap to come out by their table. The bartender stayed behind the bar.

"Well, howdy, howdy!" Porky yelled jovially. "How you, men? Chief Garden, how you doin'? Don't see you near as much as I'd like." He pumped Ben's hand vigorously, nodded to Howell and sat down heavily at the table. "What you like?" he roared, looking at Ben with unwinking cold small eyes.

"Nothing for Howell, he's in uniform," Garden said cheerfully. "But I'll have a Coke, since you're offering."

"A *Coke!* Christ on a raft, Chief!"

"A Coke," Garden repeated.

"Hellalmighty! Whitey!" Porky bellowed, turning his head.

"I hear," the bartender said.

"Bring the chief a *Coke*. He's on the wagon or something." Porky chortled and the table jiggled. "And bring me a Miller's."

"Coming up," Whitey said.

"Now what can I do for you, Chief? Besides give you a Coke.

And let you look at my pretty waitress."

"Yeah," Garden said. "Billy Carter used to hang out here, didn't he?"

"Who? Oh, yeah, that fisherman got killed yesterday. I told your man here, I knew who Carter was, that's all. You found out yet who done it?"

"When was the last time he was in here?"

"Hell, I don't know. Those fishermen mostly hang out in town, don't they? Too rough out here in the country." Porky grinned at Garden. "You used to be a fisherman, didn't you, Chief? You know how it is."

"I know how it is," Garden said. Whitey brought the beer and the Coke and clunked the bottles onto the table.

"Get a glass for the chief, you slob!" Porky shouted.

"No glass," Garden said. He picked up the Coke. "When was the last time Billy shacked up in one of your cabins?" he asked.

Porky stared at him. "What kind of place you think I'm running?"

"I know what kind of place you run. Answer my question."

"Let's see," Porky said. His voice was suddenly soft, inaudible ten feet away. His lips didn't move. "We're four miles out of town. Last I noticed, you didn't have any business out here anyway. So you come in trying to start trouble. Why don't I just sling your ass out of here?"

"Because it'd bounce," Garden said. "Bounce right back in. Assuming you could do it in the first place. Come on, be sensible. All I want to know is who Billy's girl was. His new girl."

"I wouldn't tell you nothing," Porky said, still softly. "If I knew anything to tell, I mean. Beat it. I don't have to have you in my place."

Garden noticed the way Porky's fist gripped the beer bottle.

"Hey!" Whitey said suddenly. They glanced at him. He was staring through the door into the back room. "Nobody but employees supposed to be back there!" He gave Porky an urgent look.

Joel McGee came through the door into the bar, with a young deputy behind him. "Relax," he said to Whitey. He picked up the flap and came through it. "Howdy," he said to the table in general. "Porky, old buddy! Ben, what you doing out here? Howell, glad to see you."

CHAPTER 15: "What the hell you come in through the kitchen for?" Porky asked. He glared at McGee and tried hard to make his face welcoming.

"Oh, you know. Just curious," McGee said. He pulled the fourth chair out from the table and sank into it with a sigh, as his deputy leaned against the bar. McGee looked at Garden and grinned. Garden grinned back at him, not without relief.

"Customers usually come in the front door," Porky said.

"I ain't a customer," McGee said. "Hot out there. Ben, what in the name of God you drinking?"

"A Coke," Garden said.

"What'll you have, Shurf?" Porky said. His voice was loud again, hollowed.

"Nothing, fella. A Coke! Got religion, Ben? Porky, how long's it been since you scrubbed out that kitchen? Like to of made me sick walking through there."

"I didn't know you was on the board of health," Porky said.

"Oh, I'm not. But I just might talk to them. Really, you got to do something about that." Porky looked around desperately.

Everyone in the room was staring at their table, fascinated.

"For God's sake, keep it down!" Porky said. "Don't you fellows want *nothing* to drink?"

"Not right now," McGee said.

"Whitey, bring me a shot," Porky said over his shoulder. "McGee, why you leaning on me? I got troubles with the help, you know that. Everybody's got troubles keeping good help."

"I see you do," McGee said. Two other girls had entered the bar, had felt the strained interest and had gone to sit in a front booth with the Felty girl. They looked and dressed as alike as sisters. "Where'd you get those pigs, Porky?" McGee asked.

"What the hell gives you the right to talk like that?" Porky said furiously. Whitey came from the bar and handed him a full shot glass.

"Take it easy," McGee said.

"Shurf, those are damned nice, pretty girls," Porky said, still angry. "You got no right to talk that way!" He tipped his head back and tossed the whiskey into his mouth.

"Consider that I've apologized," McGee said. He looked at Porky with amusement. "I reckon you mean it, too." He turned to Garden. "You share Porky's taste, Ben?"

"Not too much," Garden said. "I like redheads better. Skinny redheads, like Billy Carter's girl. That Porky was just going to tell us about. Weren't you, Porky?"

Porky looked down at the table and took a long breath. "I swear," he said complainingly. "I swear to God. You guys won't leave a man alone. Always on him about his kitchen and I don't know what all." His voice was full of whining self-pity.

"All right," Garden said wearily.

"Chief, if I could help, I swear—"

"Oh, knock it off. You know we'll find her sooner or later. What the hell's wrong with you giving us a little cooperation?"

"Listen to the chief, Porky," McGee said.

"Shurf, if I knew anything, why, I'd be the first man to speak up. But I don't know nothing about no redhead. And I can't really remember when I last seen Carter. What you want from me?"

"Nothing," McGee said with distaste. "Ben, you want anything else?"

"Lots," Garden said. He glanced at McGee, who moved his head slightly sideways. Porky sat staring sullenly at the tabletop, wearing a long-suffering expression. "But I guess I ain't going to get it," Garden said. He looked at his half-empty Coke, pushed it away and got up. Howell rose with him and McGee got up heavily.

"Remember, you ought to do something about that kitchen," McGee said. "Getting where you can smell it all the way to the courthouse."

"I sure will, Shurf. I sure will," Porky said, standing up. "Chief, nice of you to come by." He looked unwinkingly at Garden. "Glad to see all of you, any time," he boomed.

"Sure," Garden said.

McGee stood there, his fat bulk somehow not ridiculous, any more than his placid moon face was stupid. He looked at Porky and smiled wearily, not tolerantly. Porky looked somberly back at McGee.

"See you, Porky," McGee said. "One of these days."

"Shurf," Porky said.

Near the front door, Garden looked idly at one of the booths and said, "I'll be damned." He turned and walked toward the booth. McGee and Howell stopped at the door and watched him.

"Howdy," Garden said to the man in the booth. "Mr. Issac, isn't it?"

"You remember," Issac said. He cupped his beer in his hand and stared at Garden. "Thought you worked in town."

"Oh, I do," Garden said. "Mind if I sit down? What you doing way out here?"

"Just passing the time," Issac said.

"You're a tourist," Garden said. "I guess you want to see the sights. But if you don't mind advice? This place isn't one of the best."

"What're you, a tour guide?" Issac said. "Don't worry about me."

Garden sighed. He sat down in the booth next to Issac. "You were the one complaining about nothing to do around here, weren't you?" he asked. "This what you picked to keep from getting bored?"

"By God, I never seen such a thing," Issac said. "Maybe you're a chaplain, too? Man, I'm over twenty-one. Go on!"

"Okay," Garden said. He shoved himself back out of the booth, stood up.

"Hell," Issac said. "Now you're pissed off."

"Not really. Just tired of—just tired," Garden said.

Issac looked up at him and made a puckered grimace. "Son, my wife's out living it up with some other fat—some other ladies from up home. Really cutting up. They probably got to the lemonade by now. Lord God, I spent all my life in Iowa. You trying to tell me this ain't Miami Beach? You know, I figured that out for myself. But what the hell? It's lively and the beer's cheap. And the entertainment's free."

"If you like it," Garden said.

"It'll do," Issac said. "How you coming on that murder?"

"Yeah, that murder."

"You know, I been thinking. I might have seen that guy in here last Saturday," Issac said.

"What guy? Carter?" Garden stared alertly at Issac. "You sure?"

"Hell, no, I ain't sure. I just got that one look at him at the inlet. I told you. But anyway it was a tall guy, heavy sunburnt, in khaki clothes. He came in around midnight. Reason I noticed him, he was barefoot."

"Barefoot?"

"And his clothes, you know, like he'd dressed sort of casual. Shirttail out."

"Keep talking," Garden said. "Was anybody with him?"

"Not in here. He walked in, like I said. I think he had a drink at the bar. Wasn't watching. Then he walked in there." Issac nodded toward the door to the package goods store. "I wasn't really paying much attention, anyway. But then when I went outside I saw him come out and get in a car." Issac grinned happily. "Car was parked over in the shadow, but when he pulled around to the back they went through some light. Looked like a right pretty girl."

"A redhead?"

"Yeah," Issac said. "You know?"

"Just a little," Garden said. "You'd know her again?"

"I might," Issac said. "Might not."

"Around back, you said?"

"Yeah." Issac grinned. "I hear there's cabins out back?"

"Don't find out," Garden said. "You pretty sure it was Carter?"

"That his name? Tole you, no. Just, it could have been. You interested, eh?"

"Maybe," Garden said. "Saturday night, around midnight? What the hell you doing out here that late?"

Issac made a sour face. "There you go again. Those friends of my wife's threw a square dance, that's what."

"Ever see him here before or since?" Garden asked.

"Can't say I did."

"If you saw some pictures of Carter, you think it might help you decide if it was him or not?"

"Might. Might not. Willing to try," Issac said. "I take it you think he got shot over that woman?"

"Now what makes you think that?" Garden asked.

"Well. He just sort of had that look, you know?"

"Thought you weren't paying much attention."

"Didn't have to pay much attention," Issac said. "He walked sort of swaggering, as I remember. This is the place for it, all right." He was looking past Garden, with a bright interested stare, and Garden didn't have to turn to know what he was looking at.

Garden sighed. "All right," he said. "You mind coming by sometime tomorrow and giving us a statement on this? Something you can sign and we'll have witnessed? They'll show you some pictures of Carter first."

"Why you want me to make a statement?"

"Just in case we do turn up something. And want to try to place him here."

"What I think I remember ain't no proof of anything."

"That's right, but it might help. And don't worry, I'm not going to tell your wife you were out here until midnight."

"A hell of a lot she'd worry," Issac said. "I don't know. I might come in."

"Why don't you?" Garden asked. "Who knows? We might tell you all about it."

Issac looked at him alertly and then snorted at Garden's smile. "Okay, wise guy," he said. "I need another beer. Want one?"

"No, thanks. See you," Garden said. McGee and Howell and the deputy had gone outside. He went out and saw them standing by his car across the lot.

"Who was that?" McGee asked.

"Just an old bastard down enjoying our tourist attractions," Garden said. "I'm sure glad I don't live in his home town. He thinks he might have seen Carter in here last Saturday night. Looking like he just came in to buy a bottle on the way to bed, with a redhead."

"Oh, yeah?" McGee asked. "Bed out back, eh? Yeah, I see. A redhead, eh? How'd our man know Carter?"

"Not sure he does," Garden said. "But he was over at the inlet. Matter of fact, he probably came closest to seeing Billy get shot off the boat. What the hell you doing out here, Joel, coming in with that big fat surprise business?"

McGee chortled. "Just keeping you out of trouble, Ben. Anyway, I didn't want you to rile Porky any, not right now. I thought I'd drop in, after Howell called."

"Come on, you old bastard. You're up to something."

"Sure," McGee said happily. The sun was down behind the building and it was cooler and a few more cars were parked around them. McGee glanced around casually and smiled at Garden.

"Porky," he said. "I understand that old boy. Not too smart, you know that? He's figuring, ol' McGee, out here throwing his weight around. He's cursing me, but he ain't too unhappy. Because he figures that if I was really about to hit him, I'd tiptoe around for a week or a month or more, to throw him off. Oh, Porky's shrewd." McGee grinned. "He's inside right now, thinking about how shrewd he is. Figuring he better keep an eye on me, but that right now is the time to swing a little, before I get ready to come in. Shrewd."

"When you going to raid him?" Garden asked.

"About eleven, midnight. I'll bring in as many boys as I can manage without making too much fuss, try and go in the front and the back and cover them cabins out back, all at once."

"What do you think you'll get?"

"Oh, this and that. Ought to get a few games, from what I hear. Might embarrass some people, too." McGee scowled. "Jesus Christ. I don't care who lays who, Ben. I doubt if the people who elect me do, either. But Porky's getting a little raunchy, from what I hear. I'll see exactly how raunchy."

"Sure he won't get tipped?"

"Sure as I can be. Judge Adams is giving me the warrants. At his house. My *good* people know. The rest think I'm expecting a riot at the diamond ball game in niggertown tonight and that's why they're on alert."

"If you catch Porky far enough off base, you reckon you could ask him a few questions about Billy Carter and who Billy might have been buying a bottle for and taking back to those cabins? Last Saturday night?"

"You know, I wouldn't be surprised?" McGee said. "Carey, you want to get the car?" The young deputy nodded and went away toward the corner of the building. "Good boy," McGee said, looking after him. "Not as good as Marty Hart was. Might get there, though, someday."

"Yeah. You still don't have a chief deputy?"

"No, Ben. I'm still holding the job for you."

"I still got a job."

"Good luck with it," McGee murmured.

"You old bastard," Garden said.

CHAPTER 16: The quick dusk was thickening the light in the street when Howell and Garden got out of the car and entered the station. Garden went into his office and glanced at the papers on his desk and sighed. "I guess I better get at this stuff," he said to Howell. "Why don't you go on home? Let's get together in the morning."

"All right," Howell said. "I don't really know what we're going to get together on, Chief. Unless that redhead . . ."

"Yeah," Garden said. "Well. I guess I can't ask you to go talk to every redhead in the county, ask them if they knew Carter. Howell, you got any idea?"

"No. When McGee brings in those people at Porky's . . ."

"Yeah, I hope," Garden said. "Christ. Go on home." After Howell left, Garden sat down at his desk and took a deep breath and picked up the first piece of paper on top of the pile. He looked at it and then tossed it down and keyed the outer desk. "Anything going on, Jimmy?" he asked hopefully.

"Not much, Chief," Jimmy said. "Quiet tonight. Those people from the papers are getting pretty upset, you know?"

"Are they? Well," Garden said. "Well, I'll be in here for a while. How's Frieden's boy?"

"He's okay. Doc says he'll be in the hospital for a day or so longer, but he looks pretty good." Jimmy paused. "They let Arnold out, too."

"Good," Garden said. "Well, I'm going to get at this paper work."

"Okay, Chief," Jimmy said.

"Yeah," Garden said, and keyed off. He looked at the papers and grunted and picked up the top piece again. It took him the better part of a half hour to get into the middle of the work and then he worked on easily through it, making notes on things he wanted Janet to type up, or routine matters that Howell or Jimmy should see to. After a couple of hours the in basket was empty. He blinked at it and looked at the sorted piles of paper and the few sheets of notes on his desk.

He was tired and his head hurt. For not the first time, he cursed the paper work, and then wondered why it bothered him so much. He used to be able to tolerate it, at least. He went into the washroom off his office and washed his face, looked at the dark window and glanced at his watch. It was well after eight. He grimaced and went back into the office, to the desk, and picked up the phone.

Harper answered on the fifth ring. "Hello!" he said.

97

"I thought you were going to call."

"Hello, Ben," she said.

He frowned at her tone. "How was the shopping trip?"

"Hectic," she said listlessly. "You know how the traffic is."

"Yes," he said. "Hon, you feel all right? You sound tired."

"I *am* tired," she said. "I told you. Ben, could we call it off tonight?"

"Sure," he said. "I understand. Lunch again, tomorrow?"

"Fine," she said. "In the Grill?"

"Sure. Did you close the beach house today?"

"No," she said. "Not yet."

He frowned again. "I'll meet you there around one, then? At the Grill."

"If you don't get tied up."

"I won't," he promised. She laughed shortly, but at least she laughed. They talked quietly for a few minutes, and Garden was smiling when he hung up. The smile faded as he sat looking at the phone.

"Up and down," he said to himself. "Dammit!" He picked up the phone and called Pete Burke.

"Howdy," he said. "What you doing tonight?"

"I'm going to another council meeting," Burke said with resignation. "A late one. Ten o'clock, at Werner's office. Can you guess what it's about?"

Garden nodded slowly. "They're going to bounce me, eh?" he asked.

"I think so, Ben. Blough will do whatever Werner bullies him to do. And Frieden—well, you know."

"I've talked to him," Garden said. "So that leaves you and Delmer. Three to two."

"I suppose," Burke said. "I'm going to try to get a compromise, Ben. Suspension, not firing. You got *anything* yet on Carter's shooting?"

"Nothing solid," Garden said. "McGee might dig up something tonight. But I doubt it."

"McGee?"

"Yeah. I'll tell you about it. Hell, you had dinner?"

"No."

"Pick me up at my place. I'll change quick and we'll go somewhere quiet and grab something to eat. Okay?"

"Okay," Burke said, with exasperation. "Goddam it, I'm never going to get a good meal again."

"Skinny fellow like you," Garden said. "How do you do it? When you're always thinking about eating. Half hour, okay?" After he hung up, he looked around the office. The shabby room wasn't really much to look at. He tried to analyze how he felt, and muttered and got up. He looked at the neat piles of paper on his desk, took off his badge and left the office.

"See you tomorrow, Jimmy," he said, as he went through the outer office. "Anyone wants me, I'm having dinner with Pete Burke. Probably at the Cattle Car, but call around if I ain't there. All right?"

"Sure, Chief," Jimmy said. He looked sadly after Garden. One of the day men had told him Arnold had been bragging in the bars that Garden would be out of a job in a day or so. Jimmy wondered if he should have told Garden. Garden could take care of himself. But it made Jimmy angry.

Garden was standing in front of his house when Burke turned into the block. Garden wore a polo shirt and a fresh pair of slacks. Once again he had left the snubnosed pistol in his desk drawer. He was surprised at himself; this time he had done it almost without thought. He shook his head, and opened the door of Burke's car when the lawyer stopped next to him.

"Howdy," Burke said. "Where you want to eat?"

"I told Jimmy I'd probably be at the Cattle Car. Okay with you?"

"I guess. Don't you ever eat anything but steak?"

"Seafood's fine with me, too," Garden said. Burke slid away from the curb. "I guess I might be lucky to be able to afford mullet I net myself," Garden added. "If I get laid off tonight."

"I don't think you'll starve," Burke said. "What's McGee got?"

"He's hitting Porky's tonight. Among other things, he's going to push Porky a little on Carter. We think Carter'd been meeting a new girl out there. You know. If he had to take her to Porky's cabins, there must have been a reason. Old Billy would just as soon have done it on U.S. 1 at noon, if it had been just up to him."

"A married woman, then?" Burke asked. "Where'd you get this?"

"Not out of any Bible," Garden said, and told him.

"Not much."

"Better than nothing," Garden said. "It figures, though. Tommy Kelley said Carter had a new girl that he wasn't talking about. And Howell couldn't dig up anything on her. That's rare, for a guy like Carter. And this Issac—he's a dirty old man, all right, and that helps. He looks close."

"Not much to hang your job on," Burke said. "Even if Carter *was* meeting somebody's wife. So what?"

"I told you. Better than nothing. And the hell with my job. Somebody shot Billy, remember?"

"Sure, I remember," Burke said. "You're not going to find out who did it if we fire you."

"I'll worry about that when it happens," Garden said. "I'm hungry. Let's get on." Burke turned onto the state highway and headed for the Cattle Car.

They had settled into a corner table in the big room, spoken to several people, joked with the waitress, asked for and received martinis, and ordered dinner—Garden a porterhouse, to Burke's groan, Burke a small filet—before Garden eyed Burke and asked, "Who'll take over if they do fire me?"

"Who do you want? Howell?"

"Sure. He don't *want* the job. But he'd do it okay for a while. Maybe longer than a while."

"Fine. I can swing that. The rest of them won't care." Burke hesitated. "Suppose it goes all the way, though? They won't want to give the permanent job to Howell."

"No?" Garden said. "I guess then it'll be somebody's pet. Or somebody's cousin."

"Ben, don't take this wrong," Burke said. "But have you thought about—"

"No. I won't call old man Wayne," Garden said. "Hell, Pete."

"All right," Burke said.

"Besides. What the hell does he have to do with town anymore? I doubt if he's said jump to Werner or Blough in five years," Garden said. "And he barely knows Frieden's alive. He *doesn't* know Delmer's alive." He reached a stalk of celery from the relish tray.

"That might be a mistake," Burke said. "Ignoring Delmer. He worries me, Ben."

"Oh, come on. He's a country boy on the make. Since when did they worry you?"

"I know. I've seen them come and go. But Delmer." Burke shook his head. "He's too goddam intense. Like he's going to get there, or else. And it might be a big or else. Besides that, he's smart."

"Pass the salt," Garden said.

"Speak of the devil." Burke stared past Garden. "Here's your salt. And guess who the devil's got with him."

"I give up," Garden said.

"Howdy, Delmer," Burke said, past Garden. "*And* Mr. Ryder. How are you all? Ben, you know Mr. Ryder, of course." Garden sighed and turned in his chair. The two men hesitated and then stopped by their table.

"Mr. Delmer," Garden said. "Mr. Ryder."

"Well," Delmer said cheerfully. "How you all?" Garden looked at the amusement in Delmer's eyes.

"Just fine," Pete Burke said easily.

Ryder cleared his throat. "I take it you two are planning your strategy," he said. "Well, good luck with it."

Garden stared at him. "Not exactly. As a matter of fact, we're just having dinner."

"Oh, yes?" Ryder asked in disbelief.

"I guess I'll see you at Frieden's," Burke said to Delmer.

Delmer glanced away from Garden. "Certainly you will," he said.

"I'd like to say that I'm sorry, Chief Garden," Ryder said in a rapid voice. He didn't sound sorry. He beamed genially at Garden and smoothed his hair. "But when it is for the good of the community . . ."

Delmer took Ryder's arm. "I think our table's ready, Mr. Ryder."

"There was never anything personal," Ryder went on to Garden, in his hurried precise voice. He smiled broadly. "Never. But when one has the public interest at heart . . ."

"I understand," Garden said. "Sure I do." He stared at Ryder.

"One has to do what is best for the community," Ryder said proudly. "I'm happy to help, myself. All I *ask* is a chance to help." His eyes glittered.

"That's all," Garden said.

"And thanks to Mr. Delmer, I have that chance," Ryder said. "I take it you have other employment in mind?"

"I'll see you later, Burke," Delmer said. "Garden."

"Sure," Burke said. "Have a good dinner." The two men went away, Delmer towing Ryder.

"Ryder doesn't sound like he's got any doubt," Garden said. "And I reckon he got his information from Delmer. You sure you can count on Delmer to vote with you?"

"Now I'm not sure of anything," Burke muttered. "Hell, Ben."

"Oh, well," Garden said. "That's sure a funny combination. Delmer and Ryder. What are *they* up to?"

"I guess I'll find out," Burke said. "For God's sake, let's have another drink."

"Sure," Garden said, and looked for the waitress.

CHAPTER 17: The phone rang. Garden laid down the book he held and rubbed the back of his hand across his eyes. He glanced at his watch, leaned forward across his desk and took the receiver off the base.

"Hello?" he said. "Hi, Pete. Well, how'd it go?"

"You got a drink at your place?" Burke asked.

"I might find one," Garden said. "I take it I'm fired."

"You're right," Burke said grimly. "Three to one. Funny, Frieden didn't vote against you. He abstained."

"You didn't quit?"

"No, Ben. Hell."

"That's good," Garden said. "That would have been stupid. What were the grounds?"

"Well, pretty vague. You understand. Inadequate performance. Low morale in the department. What they mean is, Carter's killing in the papers and Frieden's kid."

"Sure," Garden said.

"Yeah. Listen, there was something funny. I didn't really understand what he was driving at. But when we were breaking up, Delmer told me he was interested in Arnold's suspension. He wouldn't explain. Does that make any sense?"

"It might," Garden said. "Arnold's got a lot of slob friends around town. Voters. Anyway, don't worry about Arnold. I can keep Delmer from following that up."

"How?"

"Never mind," Garden said. "I can turn him off Arnold, though. Him or any other lawyer. Where are you?"

"At the office," Burke said. "I got something to drink here. Come on down."

"Let's go to Smitty's."

"Oh, hell, no," Burke said. "Come on down."

"I don't exactly feel like a party."

"Will you for Christ's sake get yore ass down here?" Burke said tiredly. "*I* want a drink. I don't want to have one alone. Now come on."

"You heard from McGee?"

"No, I haven't heard from McGee. They're probably still flushing people out of the bushes back of Porky's."

"I'll be over," Garden said.

He parked in front of Burke's office. The light was on in the front office as it always was. He tried the door and found it unlocked and went inside. "Howdy!" he called.

"In here. Where else?" Burke called. Garden went into the back office. The room was twenty by twenty, with file cabinets and bookshelves around the walls and two desks made out of slabs of cypress with Pete's swivel chair between them. A door at one side opened into a narrow side room with a sink and a refrigerator in it, and doors opened off that room to a toilet and a shower and to the parking area out back. Pete was out of sight and Garden heard ice hitting glass. He pulled a comfortable leather chair next to the front desk and sank into it, looking at the Harold Newton paintings above the bookshelves on three of the walls, Indian River scenes and beach scenes. Burke came into the room carrying two large glasses and a bottle under one arm. Garden said, "You need an office boy?"

"What do you think *I* do around here?" Burke asked, and handed him a glass. "There isn't any water in that," he added.

"Good, good," Garden said. "Hell, I'd work cheap."

"Ah, shut up." Burke sank into his heavy chair, creaked it back and put his feet on his desk. He stared at Garden, shoved back gray hair with his free hand and said tiredly, "Hell, Ben! Here's to you."

"Thanks," Garden said. They drank.

"Ah," Burke said. "You know, I must be getting old. This surprised me, tonight."

"What's so surprising about it?"

"I thought Werner was the trouble. And he doesn't like you much, sure. And Frieden's still pissed off. But it was Delmer, Ben. Delmer. I thought up to this evening, when we met him and Ryder, he might be with me. But he'd been at Werner already, I could see that. They still don't like each other, but they had it all set up. What's Delmer got against you?"

"Nothing that I know of," Garden said.

"Oh? Maybe. Maybe. But at the end—maybe I just don't like him. But he acted way too triumphant to suit me. Out of proportion. Does he have anything to gain by booting you?"

"I don't know." Garden sipped at the drink. "Few more of these and I won't care," he added.

"Well, *I* care," Burke said. "Not just because you got fired, either. I don't like a slimy character like Delmer being up to something I don't understand. Especially when he's leading an old horse like Werner around by the nose."

"Don't worry about them," Garden said.

"I got to worry. I live here," Burke said.

"So do I," Garden said. He slid farther down in the chair and put his feet up, too. "You know I might get used to the idea of being fired? In fact, I might like it okay. What do you think of that?"

Burke peered past his glass at Garden. "Well, I guess it'll make Wayne happy. And Harper, from what you say."

"That, too," Garden agreed.

"But what about Billy Carter?"

"That's Howell's problem now," Garden said. "You *did* give the job to Howell, didn't you?"

"Sure. Temporary. We're all supposed to suggest candidates for the job at the next regular meeting." Burke snorted. "Who do you suggest I recommend?"

"Tommy Kelley," Garden said, and laughed.

"Well, he'd liven things up some," Burke said. "Listen, that Delmer has me worried. He's got something else up his sleeve."

"Oh, God." Garden finished his drink. "Shove me the bottle," he said. "Twelve-year-old Scotch? My God, Pete."

Burke leaned forward and pushed the bottle toward Garden. "Got plenty of ice?" he asked. "What do you think about Ryder tagging around with him?"

"Who can figure out a guy like Ryder?" Garden asked. "Yeah, I got plenty of ice." He poured his drink. "Ryder," he said reflectively. "I don't know that you'd say he's got a chip on his shoulder. That isn't exactly it. It's more like he goes around looking for someone to slap him down, expecting it. Almost happy when it happens."

"Yeah, and he's so civic-minded and all," Burke said. He blinked at Garden.

"Civic-minded, hell. Ryder-minded. He really wants to be a hero," Garden said.

"Yeah," Burke said. "Yeah! And what kind of hero?"

"What's eating you?"

"I think I just begin to see," Burke said. "Ryder. Since he's been here, with all his hooraw about helping the public, I've seen him weasel out of a dozen jobs that might have done some good, but would have been dog work. You know. That park committee thing. Like that. But he keeps coming back. Like you say. He wants to be a hero. And how does a guy like that get to be a hero? In his own eyes?"

"By finding some dirt," Garden said. He yawned.

"And what has Delmer got to offer him?"

"Ain't you got anything better to worry about?"

"Not really," Burke said. "Listen, Delmer talked all around it, but there *was* something else. He was asking some questions about the Waynes. Does that mean anything to you?"

"No," Garden said.

"Nothing definite," Burke said. "And I was too sore to pay much attention. But he had that sort of lip-smacking look he gets."

"He better stay away from old man Wayne," Garden said.

"Yeah?" Burke muttered. "Ben, I don't think Delmer is afraid of old man Wayne."

"Then he's stupid."

"Maybe, but stupid men can raise a lot of hell." Burke paused. "He did say one thing straight out. He'd like to talk to you."

"Would he? Well, he can find me."

"I think it might be worthwhile," Burke said.

"Ah, hell, Pete! Why should I talk to him?"

"To see what he's up to, maybe. To find out what's eating him. You want your job back? It might help if we knew why he decided to take it away from you."

"I ain't sure I want it back," Garden said, and drank.

"Okay, then. *I* want you to have it back. And what about Billy Carter?"

"Let Howell find out who killed him."

"Sure. Will you go see Delmer in the morning?"

"Oh, hell, I guess so," Garden said. "To shut you up. Listen, what did he ask you about the Waynes?"

"Nothing definite. I told you."

"About Harper? Or just her father?"

"Well, the family," Burke said.

"Listen, Pete, if he's trying to drag Harper into politics—"

"Calm down!" Burke looked at Garden and Garden watched Burke without seeming to, as he reached the bottle and poured himself a light drink. "Get some more ice," Burke said. Garden got up and went out to the refrigerator and got a cube of ice. He padded back into the office and saw Burke slumped back in his chair staring at the wall.

"You look tired, Pete," Garden said.

"I am tired," Burke said. "Damn this council. Ben, we got to do something about this Carter business. Then, too, when a day or so have gone by, Werner and Frieden will be cooler. They'll listen to me."

"Okay," Garden said. "I ain't so sure they'll listen to you but you can try. And maybe McGee can get us something on Carter. And maybe not. And maybe I want the job back and maybe not."

"But you don't like being fired from it, do you?"

"Go to hell. You going to tell me what Delmer had to say about Harper?"

"No, I'm not."

"Okay!"

"Damn it, Ben! It wasn't anything like that. I just don't feel it's important enough to muddy up the water. He's only curious. Delmer wants power so bad he can taste it. The old man was —is—the big stick around here. Delmer's got to be curious about that family."

"All right," Garden said.

"Damn it, if you're going to pry anything out of Delmer you can't go in ready to swing on him!" Burke said.

"I'm not going to hit him, Pete," Garden said. "I'm not going to kiss his behind, either. But I'll take it easy."

"All right." Burke hefted his glass. "It's too late to have another drink," he said. "Ain't it? You want one? Damn it, Ben. You're a good chief of police."

"I was. At least, I hope I was. I ain't been too sure lately."

"Finish up," Burke said. "I'll fix us another."

CHAPTER 18: Garden let himself have an extra hour's sleep in the morning. He got up and showered and dressed in civilian clothes and once again left the gun at home. He ate breakfast downtown, ignoring stares and meeting the counterman's invitations to conversation with easy chatter about fishing. The news hadn't taken any time at all to get around town.

Jimmy looked at him sorrowfully when he walked into the outer office, and Garden grinned at the desk cop. "Gonna be a lot tougher around here now," he told him. "Howell's gonna work your butt off, Jimmy. He in?"

"Sure is, Chief," Jimmy said. "Go on in," he added awkwardly.

Howell sat on the end of the desk in Garden's office. He looked at Garden accusingly. "Chief, why in hell did you let them do this?" he asked.

Garden laughed. "It's their job, Howell. I was just using it awhile."

"All right. They ain't serious, are they?"

"I reckon they are," Garden said. "There ought to be a letter or something here for me."

"Right there," Howell said. He nodded at the desk. "Girl from over at City Hall was here with it at a quarter after eight."

"Not wasting any time," Garden said. "You get one?"

"Yeah. Hell, Chief!"

"Relax," Garden said. "Take care of things. You'll do okay."

"When will you be back in?" Howell asked him.

"Don't count on it," Garden said. He picked up the envelope and looked at it and went behind his desk and sank into his chair. He tore open the envelope and read the brief letter, while Howell watched him, brooding.

"Short and sweet," Garden said. "Yeah." He folded the single sheet and put it in his shirt pocket, tossed the envelope into the wastebasket.

"McGee get anything?" he asked Howell.

"Well, he called. Said we ought to come over and see him," Howell said. "I told him you were fired."

"What did he say?"

"He said, bullshit, and come over anyway." Howell grinned. "I guess he don't believe you're gonna stay fired, either."

"Anybody'd think you don't want the job, Howell," Garden said. "Well. I guess I can go talk to Joel, chief of police or not. After I get this mess cleaned out." He scowled at the desk. The buzzer sounded as he pulled out the center drawer. "Get that, Howell," Garden said.

Howell keyed and said, "Yeah?"

"Howell? The guys from the paper are here," Jimmy said through the intercom. "They want to see Chief Garden."

"*Ex*-Chief Garden," Garden said. He swore softly. "Well, I guess I might as well. Sit in with me, Howell!"

"If you say so," Howell said.

"Take it easy. Just don't get shook when you read the paper and find out what they *say* you said."

"Okay," Howell muttered.

"Get them in here, then," Garden said.

110

An hour later, as Garden and Howell were leaving the office, Garden glanced at Howell and said, "You understand about the papers now?"

"Yeah," Howell said. "Listen. That one guy—"

"Don't worry about him," Garden said. "You read his paper? We're police, that's all. That's all he needs to know. He *knows* we've been up to no good. He just wants a little general background to use in his story about how much we've been up to no good. Christ, don't worry about him."

"The others were all right."

"Yeah. The others are pros," Garden said. "Howell?"

"What?"

"That guy. He was thinking about Arnold. About cops like Arnold. That's what we pay for the Arnolds. We just have to take it."

"I don't have to like it," Howell said.

"No, you don't have to like it," Garden said. "Drive me to McGee's."

"Listen, Chief," Howell said. "Arnold's been talking some, you know?"

"Talking about what?"

"Well, about coming back. You knew he'd hired a lawyer?"

"No," Garden said. "Who?"

"Delmer," Howell said.

Garden looked startled and then he laughed. "All right," he said. "Drive me to McGee's."

Joel McGee looked across his desk at them and snorted. "Ben, damn you!" he said. "Lettin' yoreself get fired. Howell, I hope you ain't such a fool."

"Come on," Garden said. "What did you find out?"

"Well, not much about Carter," McGee said. "Maybe a little. Say, we did pretty good there, though. Really caught old Porky with his pants down. For real. That Felty girl shore is beefy,

111

ain't she? Plus one poker game, just old boys off the farms. I chewed them out; Judge fined them a little and let them go. Damn it, they want to play cards, they ought to have sense enough to do it at home. Plus some other gals, with customers. And we got some illegal liquor. *And* some dope."

"Porky's dumber than I thought," Garden said.

"Ain't he? Funny. The stuff we got, why, if you buy it across the counter with a prescription, it's just pep pills. I think they even advertise them on television. Ain't that great? But without a prescription it's dope, and I can haul them in. Wish I could haul the *legal* users in, get them off the road and whatnot."

"Hey," Garden said. "Howell?"

"Yeah," Howell said. "The stuff Arnold had. That he said he took off Frieden's kid. I wondered."

"Arnold ever go out to Porky's?" Garden said.

"Don't know," McGee said. "I reckon you can find out, though, if you want to ask Porky. I reckon he'll tell you anything you want to know, about now."

"Why, Joel! You leaning on Porky?"

"Leaning, hell. The whole world's leaning on Porky. He just didn't know it."

"Can we have him in?" Garden asked.

"Why not?" McGee pushed at a button and said, "Carey, you want to bring ole Porky in here? I reckon he's asleep now. Rise him and shine him. His lawyer show up yet?"

"No, Sheriff," Carey said through the intercom. "I guess the lawyer he called bowed out. We offered to let him call another one, but he sort of wanted to think it over. I'll bring him in."

"Thanks, Carey." McGee switched off and grinned at Garden.

"What lawyer did Porky call?" Garden said.

"Why, he called yore friend," McGee said. "Mr. Delmer, that's who he called. I gather Mr. Delmer ain't gonna take Porky's business."

112

"Mr. Delmer's getting respectable," Garden said.

"I hear," McGee said. "Mr. Delmer's sort of down on the bad element, ain't he? Porky and you."

"All right," Garden said.

"Ah, hell, Ben. Hey, here's Porky. Mornin', Porky."

Porky cursed them blearily, and slumped into a chair. Carey leaned against the door and McGee regarded Porky.

"Now that ain't nice! Just when we called you in to tell you about yore good luck," McGee said.

Porky answered briefly and obscenely.

"And here's Chief Garden, come in here to give you a chance to make a few points. Not too many, you understand. Just some." McGee looked at Porky. The amusement on his broad face faded into sudden chill. "It might be the last time anybody offers you any points, buddy," he said. "Any at all. You listening?"

"I don't have to talk to you bastards," Porky muttered. "Not without my lawyer."

"Yeah, yore lawyer. Looks like yore lawyer done decided you ain't worth the paper work, buddy. Don't take my word for it. Call him again. Be my guest. There's the phone." McGee shoved the desk phone toward Porky. Porky put his hand on the phone and looked at them.

"Call him," McGee said.

"McGee, don't shit me. Did Delmer call back?"

"No, Porky. But I say, call him."

"All right, " Porky said. He stared at the phone.

"Hell. You want a lawyer? We'll give you one, you know that. You heard what Carey read you when we busted you. You know yore rights."

"That son of a bitch," Porky said. His full face was waxy.

"Well? You want another lawyer?" McGee asked.

"I don't want nothing."

"Aw, hell," McGee said. "Sure you do. You want a lot of

things, like most people. You want out of here, don't you? You want some way out of the ten and fifteen years I can get you. You want a lawyer, Porky?"

"Damn you, McGee!"

"Damn me, nothing. Start talking, buddy. You want some consideration, let's have some out of you. *I* don't need nothing from you, you know that? Chief Garden here, he *might* be interested, could you tell him something. Or he might not be. What you got to say, Porky?"

"Nothing to you," Porky said.

"It ain't going to hurt you any," Garden said. "What if Billy Carter used to bring his girl out there to your place? Hell, Porky. What difference does it make to you? And it might help us some."

Porky stared at Garden, with an odd expression. "Never mind," he said slowly.

"A redhead. That's what your fat girl friend told us, Porky. Which redhead?" Garden asked. "All you got to do is have a friendly little chat with us. Might not help you any, but it sure as hell won't hurt. How about it?"

"Go to hell," Porky said.

"You need a lawyer," McGee said. "We got to give you one, Porky, you know that. Who you want? I can get you a good one over here from the public defender's office, all bright-eyed and bushy-tailed, three months out of law school." McGee grinned. "He'll be hot to go, Porky. Shall I call for you?"

"Go screw!" Porky said. "I wanna make a phone call."

"You already had yore phone call," McGee said.

"That's right. You going to give me another? Or do I just shut up and then start hollering later?"

"You can holler all you want. And you can call all you want. Who you want to call this time?"

"That's my business."

"Okay," McGee said. "All a sudden, you sound like you got

114

something going. You sure you're okay?"

"Don't worry about me," Porky said, viciously and happily.

"I wouldn't think of it," McGee said. "Who you want to call this time?"

"Screw you!" Porky said. "I want it private."

McGee stared at him. "All you mean is, you want us to get out?"

"That's right."

"You know something?" McGee said. "Gall like yours, you ought to get away with it. Okay, Porky. We'll get out, and you make yore phone call. Christ." He got up and Garden and Howell reluctantly stood up after him. McGee stared at Porky.

"Make it good, buddy," he said. He turned and left the office. Garden and Howell followed him.

"Hell, Joel!" Garden said.

"Okay," McGee said. "So maybe he'd talk. If we pressured him to talk to us before he called another lawyer, we wouldn't have a chance. Judge would turn him loose and apologize to him for our bad manners."

"Damn it!" Howell said.

"Might as well get used to it," McGee said. "Anyway, we'll know who he's calling. I got a tape on my phone. And no beeper."

"How illegal can you get?" Garden asked.

"Can't use it for evidence, but I get some nice information that way. You men want a cup of coffee?"

Garden looked at his watch. "Hell!" he said. "Listen. I got a date for lunch. And I still got to clean out my desk. You're not going to get anything out of Porky, but I'll call back and find out, anyway." He nodded to Howell.

"Damn it, stick around!" McGee said. "I sort of wanted to talk to you. You need a job now, don't you?"

"Ah, no," Garden said. "No you don't. Talk about getting out of a frying pan into a fire."

"Hell, I was looking forward to teaching you something about police work," McGee said. "Think about it."

"I will," Garden said. "But not too hard."

"What you gonna do? Go to work for old man Wayne?"

"Hell, no. He's worse than *you*," Garden said. "How in hell am I going to get back to the station?"

"There ought to be a deputy sitting on his butt in the front," McGee said resignedly. "If I'm lucky there ain't but one. Tell him I said to run you over. I guess the county can stand it."

"Thanks," Garden said. "Howell, I'll see you." He went out and McGee sighed. He looked at Howell.

"Seem to you like Ben ran out of interest?" he asked.

"I don't think that's it."

"Right," McGee said approvingly. "He just remembered you're acting chief. And he don't want to cramp you."

"I wouldn't mind," Howell said.

"He knows that, too. Howell, they going to give him back the job?"

"You probably know more about that than I do," Howell said unhappily. McGee grunted.

CHAPTER 19: When Garden had finished with his desk, all his personal belongings didn't quite fill the one cardboard carton that Jimmy had found for him. Garden carried it out and put it on the back seat of his car and then went into the station again.

Jimmy looked at him. "Is that everything, Chief?"

"I reckon." Garden stared around the room. "Oh, yeah," he said. "Here." He took his badge out of his pocket and handed it to Jimmy.

"You could at least let all this go for a while," Jimmy said. "Maybe things will change."

Garden grinned at him. "I doubt it," he said. "Well, I'll be around. Take it easy now."

"Take it easy, Chief," Jimmy said unhappily. Garden went out into the sunlight and got in his car. He started the engine and switched on the air-conditioning and drove out of the parking lot onto U.S. 1, turning toward the beach road. He left the window open until the hot air in the car had a chance to mix with the slightly cooler breeze. It was a hell of a summer.

He drove into the lot at the Grill at exactly one o'clock. There weren't many cars and he spotted Harper's Jaguar near the building. There was a new and expensive-looking dent in the left rear fender. He scowled at the car, walked past it to the Grill. How in hell he would pay for her tastes on any salary he could earn was more than he could guess. Of course, she'd still have her money. Garden felt he could cope with that. But it bothered him a little, that he felt he'd have to cope.

The front bar was cool and shadowed, the green light from the waves that slapped the beach throwing trembling glittering reflections on the beamed ceiling. Garden blinked and looked through the bar toward the dining room, and then he saw Harper smiling at him from one of the booths. He nodded to the bartender and went over to her.

"See?" he said. "Right on time. I'm improving."

"Being fired doesn't have anything to do with that, does it?" She was smiling thinly. She put one hand on his arm. "Go ahead," she said. "Curse. If you want to."

"I don't want to," Garden said. He smiled at her. "Hello, you."

117

She tightened her fingers, very hard, and then let go. "Let's have none of your celebrated public displays of affection," she said, and laughed. She nodded at the bartender, who came alertly around the end of the bar.

"What are you drinking?" Garden asked.

"A spritzer," she said. " *Very* temperate, am I not? Have one."

"Hell, no," he said. "How are you, Al?" he asked the bartender. "Bring me a Pauli Girl, eh? Harper, you ready for another of those?"

"Absolutely," she said, and drained the tall glass. "Thank you, Al."

"You sound a lot better than you did yesterday," he said, as soon as Al had gone. "You must have been tired."

"I was."

"Palm Beach still that active? It ought to be pretty dead by now."

"There's still a lot of traffic around," she said absently. "Ben? Shut me up if you want to. But have you thought about Dad's offer?"

"Sure," he said, and smiled at her. "It still goes, Harper. I shouldn't be working for your father."

"Ah, hell!" she said.

"You said it yourself. You don't need another slave."

"You wouldn't be working for me. You'd be working for Dad."

"And everything that's his is yours. Everything he does is done for you. You know that."

She looked away again. "Yes," she muttered. "And I've sure been appreciative, haven't I?"

"What are we having for lunch?" Garden asked.

"*I'm* having lobster salad," she said. She looked at him and smiled swiftly, brilliantly. "And I *won't* be moody," she added.

Garden took her hand. "Lobster salad sounds good to me," he

118

said. "Hey, good. Thanks, Al." He took the drinks from the bartender. "How about a menu?"

"We don't need a menu," Harper said. She ordered and Al nodded gravely as he listened and then went to find a waitress.

"He's got a twenty-drink-order memory," Harper said. "But he'll make sure the waitress writes it down. Now give me back your hand."

"With pleasure," Garden said. "What are we doing after lunch?"

"I can't get used to it," she said. "Your not having to rush off somewhere in a police car. To a shooting in niggertown, or something."

"Or at the docks," he said. "That's one thing I regret," he added. "I *really* regret. I wanted to find out who shot Billy Carter."

"I suppose someone will," she said absently.

"I hope so. I thought it was an accident. That's still the only thing that really makes sense. But I got a feeling. . . ."

Harper was looking down at her drink. "What sort of feeling?" she finally asked.

"Oh, nothing. Something strange. I keep thinking there's something I ought to remember, something having to do with Carter and his girl friends. One of them, anyway." He shook his head. "If I remember, I'll call Howell. Then I'll try not to think about it again. I promise."

She squeezed his hand. "I think I've thought of something to do this afternoon."

"What's that?"

"You'll see," she said. "Here comes our lunch."

"Already?" He still had half his beer left.

"They aren't too busy right now," she said. "Doesn't it look good?"

"Our joint grocery bill is going to be something, all right," he said. She laughed.

119

It was nearly three when they left the Grill and the heat in the lot was painful. "Where are we going?" Garden asked. Out in the sun he felt the two beers he'd had.

"Let's drop your car off at your place," she said. He held the door of the Jag for her and she slid into the seat, careless of her skirt, pulled it up impatiently to free her legs and winked up at him when she saw where he was looking. "Nice to know I have your interest," she said.

"I'd say you do," he said. "I'll be right behind you. Take it easy." He closed the door of the coupé and she started the engine and was out of the lot before he got to his car. He shook his head and slid behind the wheel, grunting when he sat on the hot upholstery.

She slowed, so that he was right behind her when they got to his apartment. She got out of the Jaguar before he reached her and stood there smiling. He took her arm and said, "Well?"

"Let's go up," she said. Her voice sounded tense. "I haven't seen your place lately." He looked at her narrowly. She looked steadily at him and took a sudden deep breath.

"All right," he said. His throat felt dry.

They climbed the stairs and she watched impassively as he unlocked the door and held it open. She went inside. The apartment was hot and she went immediately to the windows and started the air-conditioner, closing the windows. She glanced back to where he stood by the door and turned and drew the blinds. He swung the door shut.

Harper walked rapidly toward him, the look on her face almost angry. She stopped just short of touching him and reached past him and he heard the latch click on the door. She turned away abruptly, before he could speak, and went across the room into his bedroom. He heard the window unit in the bedroom start and heard the windows closing. He walked across the living room and stood in the door to the bedroom.

She glanced back at him and then drew those blinds. Then

she turned and looked at him through the afternoon shade of the room.

"It's hot," she said harshly. "Come unzip me." She turned and he walked slowly to her and unfastened the hook at the top of her dress and took hold of the zipper. He saw that she was shaking.

"Nervous?" he asked. His voice was strange to his own ear.

"Damn it, go ahead!" she said savagely.

At one time she moaned at him, near incoherence. "Don't go away, don't leave please don't leave me—"

"I won't leave you," he panted.

"Ah don't leave me I can't bear to be left alone now—"

"I won't leave. I'm not leaving."

She became wordless again.

He must have been asleep, because he suddenly saw her standing looking down at him, drying her face with a towel. The room was shadowed and he sat up and asked, "What time is it?"

"It's nearly seven," she said, and laughed. The tense Indian look was gone. She smiled at him.

"You and your plans for the afternoon," he said huskily.

"I told you. I'm a good planner." She draped the towel over his head and he pulled it aside and reached for her and she chuckled, evading him.

"What do you plan for tonight?" he asked.

"Would you believe that Dad has three old friends from Tallahassee coming for dinner? A sort of a state dinner. I guess they're going to fire the governor, or something. And I'm hostess, of course. Dad's meeting them at the airport, but I've got to be at the house."

"Hostess, hell," he said.

"I've got to," she said calmly. "That is, I want to. Not forever. When we're married, the hell with it. But right now it's still my duty."

121

"What time's the dinner?"

"Ten," she said. She put her hands on her hips. "By nine o'clock I have to look like a duchess. Instead of somebody's doxy. Look at me!"

"What the hell do you think I'm looking at!" he asked. "Ah, Harper!"

"Yes," she said. His lower lip swelled as she looked at him. "It *was,* wasn't it? Damn it, Ben, don't you touch me! I couldn't stand it. And I *have* to go."

"All right. Then for God's sake step away, or turn around, or put some clothes on, or something. So I can get up without running into—"

She laughed and turned away. "All right. I can take a hint," she said over her shoulder. He leaned toward her and she fled toward the bathroom, grabbing her dress from a chair as she went. Garden stood up and stared after her, grinning, feeling like a fool, and enjoying the feeling.

He had put on a pair of slacks and was pulling on a shirt when she stuck her head out of the bathroom and said, "Where in God's name is my purse? I must have left it in the car. Ben, would you? I can use your comb and brush, but you're short of lipstick."

"All right, all right," he said. He pulled down the polo shirt, roughed his hair into place with his hand and shoved his feet into zoris. He went out and down the outside stairs, meeting his landlady at the bottom. She was watering her plants. Garden smiled and spoke to her, not without apprehension. She was in her sixties, widowed and very active in church work, and her apartment was under Garden's. He was still wondering uneasily just how loud Harper had been; when Mrs. Hickley turned to look at him, and gave him a broad, conspiratorial, completely lascivious wink.

"Tired, Chief?" she asked loudly, and Garden mumbled and

fled toward Harper's car, blushing, with the old lady cackling behind him.

Wondering if he could sneak around to the back stairs to avoid passing Mrs. Hickley again, he opened the Jaguar and looked for Harper's purse. It was on the floor by the driver's seat; he leaned across the seats, reaching past the gearshift, and picked it up. Absently, as he started to straighten up, he picked up a crumpled piece of paper from the floor, half hidden under the edge of the right seat. He looked at it casually as he turned away from the car, and started to wad it up in his hand. Then he stopped and, holding the purse under his arm, straightened out the paper until he saw what it was.

He stood there for a minute, frowning. Then he shoved the paper into his pocket and walked back to the stairs. Mrs. Hickley had turned off her hose and she cackled at him again from the door of her apartment. He gave her a broad abashed grin and went on up the stairs.

"Good!" Harper said. She grabbed the purse and retreated to the bathroom. "My God. I *have* got to move. At least I can get respectable enough to go out in public. Who was that I heard talking?"

"Just the landlady."

"Oh God, Ben!" she laughed.

"Don't worry!"

She came back out of the bathroom, straightening her dress, tossing her hair back. "Do I pass hasty inspection?"

"More than hasty," he said. "Come here."

"Certainly. The hell with the lipstick, then," she said. She kissed him hard and broke away. "Now. I've got one hour and thirty minutes to drive to the ranch, shower, dress and make up fit to kill, find out what Andros has laid on for dinner, and organize the drinks. That's not half long enough. But I'll make it. Lunch tomorrow?"

123

"Yes."

"Ah," she said. "Same time? Same place? And how about the same dessert?"

"Oh, yeah," he said. She kissed him again and spun away, laughing, and went through the door. He walked out and watched her swing down the stairs, dip into the Jaguar, wave to him and leave the curb with a quick hard chirp from the tires. He sighed and went back inside.

He took the piece of paper from his pocket and straightened it, frowning. It was a Miami traffic ticket, issued the day before.

But she had been in Palm Beach.

She might have gone down to Miami from there.

Then why hadn't she mentioned it? He tossed the ticket onto his desk and went into the bathroom to brush his teeth, scowling to himself.

CHAPTER 20: "All right," he said to Burke.

They sat in Burke's study and Garden had his third drink since dinner in his hand, and he was beginning to be aware of being tired. "All right, Pete, I hear all you say. But you know damned well Werner and Delmer aren't going to take me back!"

"Aren't they?" Burke asked. "Do you *want* the job back? You don't sound like you do. I've asked before."

"I don't know," Garden admitted. "I just don't know."

"Well, that just isn't any help," Burke said tiredly.

"I don't want you to waste your time."

"It isn't being wasted, unless you really don't want the job,"

Burke said. He ran one hand through his gray hair and poured himself another drink.

"I just hate to leave loose ends," Garden said slowly, "especially one like Carter."

"All right," Burke said, "Carter. Want to put it on that?"

"What do you mean?"

"Carter. Let's see what we can do on that, with McGee and Howell. If you help straighten that one out and the fuss in the papers dies down, I think you might have a chance at the job back. Might get it back, hell—I know you would. Frieden's no fool; he doesn't blame you now that he's cooled down a little. And Werner"—Burke shrugged—"he's getting pretty wary of Delmer."

"Why is he getting wary of Delmer?"

"Well," Burke said, "there's something not too kosher about Delmer."

Garden laughed. "There never was."

"No, not that he's crooked. I guess. He's just too much of a hustler. He's under a lot of strain. The kind of strain that makes you leery of a man." Burke sipped at his drink. "Werner and I had a little talk with him this afternoon," he said. "About some city stuff. Delmer acted as though he was hardly even in the room with us. Spooked."

"Spooked at what? He wasn't spooked the other night. Intense, yeah, but not up the wall."

"I don't know, Ben. But something's getting to him."

"That's interesting," Garden said slowly.

"Isn't it! And then Werner found out about the business with Ryder, and he blew up, and Delmer went completely blank on us."

"What business is that?" Garden asked.

"Didn't I tell you? Hell, Delmer went back into the city files and dug out a lot of stuff—official correspondence, bills, meeting notes, all sorts of stuff. Archives, I guess you'd call them. Except

125

nobody ever tried to sort them out. Stuff going back at least twenty years, maybe back before the war. He turned all this mess over to Ryder a few weeks ago, says he wants Ryder to look it over, maybe work up an official history of the town."

"Ryder? My God, Pete!"

"Yeah, sounded funny to me, too. You know Ryder, but then what sort of dirt could he dig up out of all that crap? But Werner blew up. One of the clerks mentioned something to him about it today, and it was worrying him all evening. Then Delmer asked, 'So what?' Werner really boiled over."

"What makes Delmer think Ryder could write a town history?" Garden asked.

"God knows. He was some sort of accountant before he retired, or a tax man, something like that."

"And why's Werner so broke up about it?"

"Well, I don't know," Burke said. "Maybe there are more skeletons in the closets than I'd thought. But . . . hmm." He leaned back, thinking.

"What're you brooding about?" Garden asked. "Anything I ought to know?"

"I doubt it," Burke said shortly. Garden looked at him, but Burke was staring at the wall behind him. A minute or so later the phone broke the silence and Burke started and picked it up.

"Burke," he said. "Oh, howdy, Joel. Yeah, he's here." He handed the phone to Garden, saying, "McGee."

"Hi, Joel," Garden said into the phone.

"Howdy," McGee said. "You ain't very easy to get hold of, are you? I finally figured out you'd be with Burke. Didn't you want to hear about your buddy Porky?"

"What about Porky?"

"Why don't you run over here?" McGee asked. "You might want to hear something. I been looking for you since before dinner."

126

"Hear what?" Garden asked. "Oh, that tape? Okay. Where's Howell?"

"He's right here," McGee said impatiently. "Come on over."

"We'll be there."

"Yeah," McGee said, "bring Burke. Might be good to have somebody off the city council here, and he's the only one I trust. Might be good to have a lawyer, too."

"Like that, eh?" Garden said. "Okay, we'll be there in a few minutes." He hung up.

"Where will we be?" Burke asked. Garden told him and told him why.

"That tape isn't worth two cents as evidence," Burke said.

"McGee doesn't want it for evidence," Garden said. "It's more like a pry bar. Wonder what he's got."

"I notice he didn't want to talk about it on the phone," Burke said.

"So he didn't. Let's go."

McGee ushered them into his office and closed the door firmly. Howell sat by the desk, tapping his notebook on his knee. Young Carey lounged against the wall and nodded pleasantly at Garden and Burke. "Sit down," McGee told them. He went around and eased his bulk into his chair. "All right," he said, "just listen to this." He examined the tape machine and touched a key. "In case you don't remember, this is Porky's phone call," McGee said. "When I let him have my office, private, just before he shut up on us."

They heard the buzz that represented a phone ringing and the clack of the receiver lifting. "Hello?" a voice said. Garden raised his eyebrows. Even on the poor tape, the voice was recognizable, Delmer's.

"Hello yoreself, you son of a bitch," Porky's voice said harshly. "How come you running out on me?"

"Running out on you? I didn't know I had any obligation to you," Delmer's voice said.

"I need a lawyer," Porky's voice said. "You picking and choosing your clients? I need somebody to get me out of this place."

"There isn't anything I can do for you," Delmer's voice said. "There are plenty of lawyers around."

Porky's voice laughed unpleasantly. "I want you, though," he said.

"I don't believe there's any point in carrying on this conversation."

"Wait! Jes' wait." Porky's voice cut in quickly. "Don't hang up, don't you hang up. I finally figured it out. Don't you hang up on me, you son of a bitch."

"Who the hell do you—"

"Yore wife," Porky's voice said harshly, triumphantly. "I finally put it together. Yore wife. That redhead! *She's* the one been coming out to my place with that Carter. *You* knew, eh? Now I know, Mr. Lawyer. Mr. Politician. I need help. I reckon I'll get it."

"I'll be goddamed!" Garden said.

"Quiet!" McGee said. There was silence on the tape.

"Shut up, you damned fool," Delmer's voice said finally. It was all but unrecognizable; harsh, automatic.

Porky's voice laughed, softly. "I'll shut up," it said. "Sure I will, long as I get help. Long as I get bailed out, get some help to get this bastard sheriff off my back. If I don't, why then I got to look after myself, don't I?"

There was a silence. "Well?" Porky's voice spoke again.

"I'll be over," Delmer's voice said. It was a bit more controlled. "You haven't said anything to anybody? Don't answer that. Don't say anything else, you fool."

"You'll be over," Porky's voice said triumphantly.

"I'll be over," Delmer's voice repeated. The phones clacked twice on the hissing tape.

McGee reached forward and shut it off. "Nothing else on there," he said. "How about that?"

"Yeah!" Garden said. "For Christ's sake."

"You know it figures?" McGee said. "I seen her a time or two. Yeah!"

"Did Delmer come over?"

"Oh, yeah. He bailed Porky out, made the big fuss about what did they say to you, did they tell you yore rights, all of that, and took him out, grinning all the way. I wasn't there, damn it. I would love to have been there looking on."

"Hell!" Burke said. "What do you think, Joel?"

"Well, I think Delmer's pure sweating, anyway," McGee said happily. "That pore son of a bitch."

"Yes," Garden said.

"I wonder if Porky's got sense enough to worry," Howell said.

"What?" Garden asked.

"Hell, Chief, *somebody* shot Carter."

"Oh, hell," Garden said softly.

"Yeah," McGee said. "What say we wander out and talk to Delmer? Anybody got any real good excuse for it?"

"Ben could go out and beg him for his job back," Burke said, "except I don't think he will. My God, Howell, you don't really think Delmer shot Billy Carter? McGee?"

"I done quit trying to guess what people will do over a woman," McGee said. "All I know is that tape ain't worth nothing in court, but I take it no one minds going out and leaning on Delmer a little? He lives outside town, so I got an excuse."

"Leave me out," Burke said. "I'm going home. I ought to stay out of this part of it."

"Lead on," Garden said.

"Let's mount then," McGee said.

Driving out through town, Garden asked McGee, "How do you know Delmer will be home?"

129

"I don't, but maybe his wife will be. We can at least get a look at her, eh? Where you reckon we can get a picture of her? To show that girl from Porky's."

"She had her picture in the paper," Howell said. "Some woman thing or another. They ought to have a copy."

"Good enough," McGee said. "You want to see about that picture?"

"I'll get one in the morning," Howell said. He blinked at the street signs going by under the lights. "Delmer live way out here?"

"That's right. Next turn, Carey," McGee said.

The house sat well back from the street on a deep lot thick with oaks. Traffic sounds were muted into the silence as they got out of the car in the glare of an ornate electric carriage light beside the carport.

Garden eyed the carport and the one car there. "I doubt if Delmer's here," he said.

"Okay," McGee said. "Hell, three of us is enough to barge in. Carey, you want to stay out here?"

"Okay. Pretty neighborhood, ain't it?"

"I suppose," McGee said. "I like houses you can't look at from the street, though. These are made just to look pretty and expensive."

"And they are expensive," Garden said. "You'd be surprised how many of the people out here are behind in their mortgage payments. Has anybody figured out my legal standing in this? I expect Delmer will want to know."

"You're a special deputy now," McGee said, "helping me on a case or two. Okay?"

"Just don't expect to make it permanent," Garden said. He and McGee and Howell got out of the sheriff's car and approached the house, McGee leading.

McGee thumbed the doorbell and they stood under the soft glow from overhead, listening to the chimes. They waited for a while and then McGee grunted and tried the bell again.

"Lights are on," Howell said.

"Don't they have a maid?" McGee said, somewhat sarcastically.

"Day maid, probably," Garden said. "Live-in, no."

"Somebody's coming," Howell said.

The door clicked and they heard the rattle of a chain and then it swung open into the light on the steps.

"Well, my goodness," the woman said. "Look at all this."

Garden looked carefully at Mrs. Delmer. He remembered seeing her at a distance around town a time or two, but he had remembered only red hair and a vague impression of leanness and sullenness. Now he looked more closely. Her hair was longer than he'd remembered and it fell forward over her shoulders. Her face was slender and she wasn't lush, but there was no impression of scrawniness. She had on what might have been called a jump suit, made of yellow satin, and when she turned to gesture them in her figure was obvious.

McGee was saying, "Sure hate to bother you, ma'am, but we need pretty bad to talk to Mr. Delmer—"

"Oh, come in," she said impatiently. "The mosquitoes, terrible! I don't know where Johnny is right now. But if you could tell me?" They went in and she ushered them into a living room that would have been beautiful with one or two less colors.

They took chairs, protesting, and she said brightly, "How about drinks?"

"I'd just admire that, ma'am," McGee said, "but we're all on duty, you understand."

"I'm not," Garden said, and grinned at McGee. "I'm a civilian, remember? I'll join you, Miz Delmer."

She studied him coolly and picked up a tall glass from the coffee table by the huge couch. "Come show me how you like it," she said. "Sheriff, would you like coffee, then?"

"No, thanks, ma'am," McGee said patiently. Garden followed

her into the kitchen. She wasn't tall. Her heels, too high for her costume, made her walk interesting.

In the kitchen, she gestured toward one of the cabinets and said, "See what you like." She opened the freezer and added a handful of ice to her glass. The gin bottle and a bottle of fruit mix were open on the counter. Garden found Scotch and a squat glass and poured a short drink. She indicated the freezer and he opened it and got his ice while she leaned against the counter, stirring her drink.

He swirled the ice with his finger, tasted the drink and smiled at her. "Thank you," he said. She looked at him broodingly. He decided that she wasn't drunk, just a little reckless. He eyed her openly and waited for her to say something. She was standing so that all the roundnesses and the tight yellow-sheathed wideness between her thighs were visible, and she wasn't smiling.

She had green eyes, and freckles under the smooth makeup. She wasn't quite old enough for her face to be hard between the tight wings of auburn hair, but that wouldn't take long.

Her voice turned pure cracker. "So yore that cop," she said. "Johnny said yore fat. I couldn't remember jes what you look like. How come you never around when Johnny was running for council?"

"I don't hang around politics much."

"I wouldn't if I didn't have to," she said. "Don't you have to? What you want with me?"

"We came to see your husband," Garden said, "remember?"

"Yeah, but I figure yore just as happy he's not here. Why is that?" She stared at Garden. It was not a friendly stare.

"When did you last see Billy Carter?" Garden asked her.

She looked at him expressionlessly. "You ain't chief of police anymore," she said. "Johnny tole me that, and you can go to hell."

"That doesn't help any," Garden said.

"I got no idea of helpin'," she said. "Goddam you, come on."

She turned and headed for the living room.

"I'm not the only one who knows," Garden said to her back. She stopped and glanced over her shoulder. She looked a little scared, not much.

"You ain't dumb enough to think you can use it to push Johnny around," she said. Near the door to the living room her cracker accent had diminished. "He's goin' to run this town pretty soon, you know that. He'll run more than that someday." Her mouth twisted. "Seems funny, don't it? Little Johnny. But he will, all right. You don't want him down on you."

"Maybe I don't care," Garden said.

"You think he'd thank you?" she asked. "Think again. He'd give me hell, but he'd get you for it, for knowin'. You better care." She went on into the living room and Garden took another sip of Scotch and followed her. It was very good Scotch.

CHAPTER 21: The interview didn't go very
well. Back in the living room, she sat with her legs under her on the couch and played the bright suburban housewife after one or two drinks too many. The cracker occasionally showed through the careful layering of sophistication, and when it did she appeared shallow, without any of the sullen depths Garden had glimpsed during the brief talk in the kitchen. He wondered if she wasn't at her best in the dingy back cabins at Porky's.

She couldn't tell them where Johnny was, he'd been working so hard lately, what with politics on top of his law business. Then he had so many law clients, two new ones just today. She looked innocently at Garden and McGee, ignoring Howell.

McGee, with greater subtlety than most people would have expected, brought up the Carter killing. She looked blank, but interested.

Garden asked her about Ryder. Oh, that old man Johnny talked to every now and then? She shook her head, and Garden found himself agreeing with her that Ryder was really very dull.

She did it well. Finally, McGee sighed and got up, a good bit more easily than his bulk would make one expect. "You will have Mr. Delmer call me, won't you?" he asked. "I just believe we can settle up a thing or two if we could get together."

"Why, I surely will!" She got up quickly. Her glass was empty and had been for some time, and she had been turning it around in her hands. She went ahead of them toward the door and Garden sipped the last of his Scotch and put the glass down on the varnished surface of the coffee table and followed them.

They went through a last round of "I'll surely tell him, and good night now, you all," and McGee and Howell moved off the steps.

Garden turned to her. "I could come back," he said quietly.

"Lak hell," she said, just as quietly. She gestured with the empty glass and moistened her lips. "Beat it."

"We could have an interesting talk."

"Go on," she said. "Talk! Screw you, mister. Jes' keep away."

"I liked Billy Carter," Garden said. "I want to find out who killed him."

"Oh, sure." She eyed him stonily. "Do yoreself a favor. *Don't* come back."

He looked at her deliberately. "I'm not after that," he said. "It looks mighty good, but I don't want that. I'm telling you the truth."

"Don' care what you want," she said viciously. "Whatever, you ain't getting it from me." She closed the door in his face, almost slammed it. He followed McGee and Howell out to the car.

"Damn, these mosquitoes are bad," McGee said. "Let's get on, Carey."

"You're telling me," Carey said wearily. He slapped his neck and started the car.

McGee turned heavily, looking over the seat back at Garden and Howell. "You get anything, Ben?"

"No," Garden said, "and I don't think I could. Just in case that was what you meant."

McGee laughed. "All right now. What do you think?"

"She's likely, all right," Garden said. "Playing a part, and damned tired of it. Drinking too much. Dressing fancy and talking fancy, and not enough to do. Bet her maid knows *some* stories."

"So you think it might be right. She was Carter's girl?"

"I know she was," Garden said. "Or somebody's, because Delmer knew she was. Remember? Porky didn't hardly have to push him any."

"That's right," McGee said. "Hell, this is gonna be touchy."

"Yeah," Garden replied. "Glad it's you guys, not me."

"Don't be that way."

"I'm out, friend," Garden said. "Tomorrow I got to start looking for a job."

"Hell, Ben!"

They were coming back into town. "Swing by my place and drop me," Garden said. "I'm getting pretty sleepy. Come on, Joel, face facts. I'm out."

"You might not have to stay out," McGee said.

Howell nodded. "That's right, Chief."

"Okay," Garden said. "Either of you guys think I might *want* to be out? Man can get tired of a job, you know."

"Horseshit!" McGee said.

"Well, he can," Garden said. "Next place, Carey. Those apartments. I thank you, men."

"Come see me tomorrow," McGee said.

"Soon as I finish job-hunting," Garden said cheerfully. McGee cursed.

Garden stood on the walk until the car rounded the corner and then he turned and glanced up at his apartment. He was tired. But hell. He walked to his car parked at the curb, fumbling for his keys.

Delmer's offices were in one of the fancier new office buildings, near downtown, built on a lot that had held an ancient hardware store, one of the oldest buildings in town. The cypress framing and tin roof were gone and the new building had a flashy tile front that gleamed in the street lights. There were the normal bright night lights in the front windows. Garden drove slowly around the block and glanced through the alley toward the back of Delmer's building. There were a couple of cars there, and one of them was Delmer's maroon Cadillac. He drove on and parked in front of the shiny building.

He thought about going to the main door and decided against it. If Delmer didn't want to open up he wouldn't, and if whoever was with Delmer didn't want to be seen he could be gone before Garden could get around back. He walked between the building and the drugstore next door, down the thinly asphalted alley. It opened into a broader space behind the building and Garden glanced at the car beside Delmer's. It was a Rambler, several years old. He continued past it to the back door of Delmer's office and gently felt the knob. It was locked. He knocked on the door. Very loudly.

There was a long enough time after he knocked so that he was about to knock again. Then the knob turned and the door opened a short distance and stopped against a chain.

"All right," Delmer said. "What do you want, Garden?"

136

"How'd you know it was me?"

"I looked out the window," Delmer said impatiently. "I asked you what you want."

Garden looked at the only window, onto the back lot, a high window bespeaking a toilet, and his eyebrows rose. "Being cautious as all hell, aren't you?"

"I asked you what you wanted."

"Want to come in and talk," Garden said.

"We got nothing to talk about, Mr. Garden. If you need legal advice—"

"If I needed legal advice I'd look for it in daylight," Garden said. "And somewhere else. Let me in."

"I'm busy right now," Delmer said impatiently.

"Listen, I want to talk about you defending Porky," Garden said. "And why you're defending him. Come on, Delmer, open up. I know all about it."

There was a silence, and then the chain rattled and the door opened. Delmer looked out at Garden, the dim light behind him leaving his face dark. "Just what the hell do you think yore doing?" Delmer asked. As with his wife, the cracker showed through, and not pleasantly.

"You know what I'm doing," Garden said. "I want to talk to you."

"I got a client with me."

"Fine. I'll wait till he leaves. Who is it—Porky? Or Arnold?"

"Wait outside," Delmer growled.

"I'll wait inside."

"Damn it, you can't—"

"You think McGee can't make Porky talk about your wife?" Garden asked harshly. "Come on, Delmer. Let's do this right."

Delmer stared at him. "You jes' might pay for this, Garden," he said thinly.

"I just might." Garden moved forward and Delmer held the door open. Garden walked through the dim hallway and went into the main office, hearing the latch click and then Delmer's footsteps behind him. Ryder blinked at Garden from the chair in front of the desk.

"Well, well," Garden said.

"What do you—you—what's he doing here?" Ryder asked, looking past Garden to Delmer.

Delmer sat down behind the desk. He looked strained. "We can finish this up tomorrow," he said to Ryder.

Ryder stared at him. He shut his mouth tightly. "I don't understand this," he said finally. "I don't care for this, Mr. Delmer."

"There's nothing to understand," Delmer said. "Something else just came up. We can finish our discussion in the morning." He smiled at Ryder. The smile was paper-thin.

Ryder looked from Garden to Delmer. "Exactly what business do you have with *Mr.* Garden?" he asked Delmer suspiciously. "You can't expect me to accept this with no explanation, you know."

"I have *no* business with Garden," Delmer said through clenched teeth. They both looked at Garden. "He thinks he has some with me. He's mistaken, but it might take a while. So if you would . . ."

"I don't like this," Ryder said icily. "I don't like it at all. Why, this is the very thing we've been talking about, Mr. Delmer. The very thing that's wrong with this town. I certainly hope I haven't misplaced my trust in you, Mr. Delmer."

"For God's— Look, who gave you— Ryder, will you just relax?" Delmer asked. Garden peered at him closely and Delmer avoided Garden's eyes, concentrated on Ryder. "Don't worry, for God's sake!" he said. "Just take it easy. We'll get together first thing in the morning and finish this up, and I'll explain then. Okay?"

Ryder looked back and forth between the two of them and then got angularly to his feet. He was beginning to assume the expression Garden was familiar with from council meetings: long suffering, sure of martyrdom, triumphantly relishing dissension.

"I shall certainly be interested in your explanation," Ryder said stiffly to Delmer. "I certainly shall." He picked up a cheap briefcase from the desk in front of Delmer and shoved a few sheets of paper back into it.

"You can leave all that here overnight," Delmer said easily.

Ryder gave him a long stare. "I think not," he said.

"Oh, for God's sake, Ryder!" Delmer said.

Ryder looked down his nose at him. "I am more than ever sure that my original plan was correct," he said.

"Think that over," Delmer said tightly. "Think about it."

"I shall, very carefully." Ryder hugged the briefcase under his arm.

"Don't make any mistake," Delmer said.

"I don't believe I will," Ryder said. He skirted around Garden, turned at the door and gave them both a bright proud stare, suspicious and disdainful.

"I'll see you out," Delmer said, getting up quickly.

"That's not necessary."

"Oh, no trouble, no trouble!" Delmer hurried over to Ryder and they went out into the hall, Ryder giving Garden one last look. Garden listened to the mutter of voices by the back door. He couldn't make out words, but the tones were interesting.

Delmer came back into the office, his face gleaming in the soft lighting. He returned to his desk and sat down.

"I interrupt something?" Garden asked politely.

"You son of a bitch! Garden, I don't have to take anything from you. I don't have to take this."

"Your smooth is slipping," Garden said. "What did I interrupt?"

"I don't have to answer any of your questions!"

"Not even why did you decide to take Porky as a client?

That's a rhetorical question, Delmer. I know the answer. You're going to lose that one both ways, you know. You can't get Porky off a couple of the charges McGee has on him, and you can't make him shut up. Especially after you don't get him off."

Delmer looked at Garden with cold hate. "I'll worry about my own affairs," he said.

"Your wife is your own affair," Garden agreed, "but I'm curious. What you think you can do for Porky? It would take an awful lot of pull to get him off, and you haven't got it."

"I'll worry about my business," Delmer said sharply.

Garden tried to identify the new note in his voice, the new light in his eye. "Oh? Do that, then. I don't really give much of a damn about that, Delmer. I don't care about your wife, either. That *is* your business. Except you got to know she might have something to say about Carter. I'm sorry, and you can believe that or not. But I got to say it, and somebody *did* shoot Billy."

"That son of a bitch," Delmer whispered.

Garden blinked. "I said I was sorry," he said, "but not sorry enough to forget about a murder."

"It isn't any of yore business. You ain't chief no more."

"What the hell difference you think that makes?"

"You can't drag me in. Me or my wife."

"Your wife dragged herself in."

"You," Delmer said. The vein in his forehead pulsed. Looking at him, Garden suddenly realized he'd underestimated Delmer's temper. He watched him grasp for control. "You," Delmer repeated viciously. Garden watched him in fascination. "What you got to say?" Delmer asked frantically. "Who're you to criticize? You, and that slut of yores? That rich slut, and all of them, that walk around like they owned it all. They can get away with murder, like she did. They could get away with anything. But not no more. Not no more. That's where that fool Ryder is right. He don't know just how much he's right."

"That's enough!" Garden said, louder than he intended.

"What the hell do you—" He stopped.

Delmer leaned back in his chair. He had an exhausted look, suddenly frightened as he caught himself in the clutch of fury. He licked his lips. "Get the hell out of here, Garden," he said.

"Let's hear a little more about that getting away with murder!" Garden said.

"You know. You know all about it. High and mighty, ain't they, all those people? You know, sucking around like you do. But they'll pay. They'll see, and then you won't have to worry about how much pull *I* got. All you'll have to worry about is staying out of my way." Delmer stopped and took a long shaking breath.

"You don't make much sense," Garden said.

Delmer sank back in his chair and glared at him. "You'll see, that's all."

Garden looked at Delmer for a while and then stood up. "You said a lot," he said. "Either too much or not enough. Let's hear some more."

"Screw you. Get out!" Delmer said.

"One, you're being blackmailed into taking on Porky, when you know you ain't got a chance. Two, there's some foolishness with Ryder. Whatever you two are cooking up, you got a chance of getting burnt. Hell, man, can't you tell what kind of loser Ryder is?"

"I'll worry about Ryder," Delmer said tightly.

"Oh, yeah? And then you're going to have to tell me more about this crack you just made, about getting away with murder. Sooner or later, Delmer. You weren't just talking in general, you *meant* something. I don't think I like it." Garden put his hands on the desk and leaned forward.

"You don't scare me, Garden," Delmer said. "None of you dumb bastards do!"

"I'm not *trying* to scare you," Garden said gently. "Oh, yeah, this business with Arnold. You really going to represent him?"

141

"You know it," Delmer said. "He's going to get his job back."

"You fool!" Garden said. "You believe what he told you?"

"I believe you beat him up, and you fired him out of prejudice. So will a jury."

"I got a statement," Garden said.

"What kind of statement?"

"Oh, one that gives Arnold a motive for hitting Frieden's kid. That a good scrappy solicitor might use to charge Arnold with extortion. One that would make a fair fool out of you in court. One that would put Arnold ass deep in trouble, if you take this up."

"You're lying," Delmer said.

"No, I'm not," Garden said. "You know I'm not."

Delmer stared at him, then he shrugged slightly.

"Like that, eh?" Garden said slowly, after a minute.

"I don't know what you mean," Delmer said. He looked at his watch. He was slowly reclothing himself in his smooth professional attitude, with only the tatters of his anger still showing on his sweating face.

"Like that? The hell with what happens to Arnold? But what do you— Oh. All his buddies around town. All those votes. And all of them will remember you done your best for Arnold. They'll think so. You dirty bastard!"

Delmer shrugged again.

"I could tell them different," Garden said.

Delmer grinned at him arrogantly. "Take your statement and shove it." He got up. "Now I got work to do, Garden. You can go out the front way."

"You're pretty close to the edge," Garden said. "You know that?"

"Don't give me any crap," Delmer said.

"I don't have to. Think about it. Porky. Arnold. Ryder. Your wife."

Delmer's face twitched when Garden mentioned Arnold,

and clenched in anger again at the words "Your wife." "Get off
—shut up about my wife, Garden. Shut up. I'm going to make
you sorry you ever mixed into— You. You'll find out. When her
old man had to send her right out of the country to keep her
from—" He turned abruptly and stared at the wall.

Garden looked at him. "I keep telling you, you're going to
have to make yourself clear to me," Garden said. "You keep
hinting. I'm getting tired of it."

"Get out of here," Delmer said. He sounded close to hysteria.
Garden looked at him and then he turned and left the office.

CHAPTER 22: Garden walked to the corner and
back and paused in front of Delmer's office. He felt an irrational
desire to go knock on the door again. He was still furious. He'd
lost the game of temper, in spite of Delmer's flares of fury and
his own outward calm. Delmer's threats, the hints about Harper
. . . He cursed himself.

Behind the building he heard the faint rich growl of a large
engine. He got in his car and drove around the block, but
Delmer's Cadillac was already out of sight. Garden cruised aim-
lessly along the street and then turned onto the highway again.
He found himself heading toward the shopping center, and
Smitty's. No point in trying to sleep, the way he felt.

He parked near Smitty's and started to get out of the car and
then remembered something and slid back into the seat. He
unlocked the glove compartment and took out the sealed envelope that held Angela's statement. He looked at it. He was

still too angry to be amused at how wrong he had guessed Delmer's reaction. Well, he would return it to her in the morning. He put the envelope back into the compartment and locked it again, then got out of the car, still thinking about the small girl and her odd blend of sexuality and fastidious distaste for his violence against Arnold.

Smitty's was nearly empty but Tommy Kelley was still propped against the bar, bellowing jovially across it at someone in the shadow of the far side. Sugar smiled at Garden and he grinned back and walked toward Kelley. Garden clapped Tommy on the shoulder and the captain twisted his bulk around.

"Well, goddam!" he boomed. "If it ain't the unemployed police chief! What the hell, Ben, you want a job? See me at the docks. Have a drink." He waved at Sugar and turned toward Garden, knocking over his bar stool as he moved.

"Work for you? Hell, you old bastard," Garden said, "I'll starve first. How you, Tommy?"

"Same as I was yesterday," Kelly said. "Sugar, how about that drink? What you drinking, Ben?"

"Bourbon, I guess," Garden said to Sugar. "Tommy, who the hell's that hidin' behind you?"

The man next to Kelley uncoiled himself and extended his hand past Kelley's breadth. "How you, Chief?" It was Martin. His voice still wasn't clear, due to the wire in his jaw.

Garden blinked at him and shook his hand. "Don't know about that," he said. "You guys got a pretty good head start, don't you?"

"Damned right," Kelley said loudly. He slung one massive arm around Martin's shoulders. "Me and my buddy, we been doing some thinkin', Ben. I reckon we got something to tell you. Later, you know, not where every son of a bitch in town can hear. How's yore drink, buddy?" he asked Martin. "Don't want to run out."

144

"It's okay," Martin said fuzzily. He slouched back against the bar and grinned happily at Kelley and at Garden. Garden grinned back and picked up the drink Sugar brought him.

An hour or so later the bar was mostly clear and Sugar was yawning on her stool by the cash register. Martin had gone to sleep in the corner booth and Kelley leaned over the bar next to Garden, his voice far gone into an inaudible growl.

"Tommy," Garden said. "Hey! What the hell was that you were going to tell me?"

"'Bout what?" Kelley mumbled. "Lissen, *when* they gone give you yore job back? I tell you—"

"Never mind that," Garden said. He yawned. "Damn, Tommy, I'm pretty beat. You going to tell me your secret?"

Kelley turned his head ponderously, looking up and down the bar. "Aw right," he said finally. "Let's go outside."

"Outside, hell. Nobody's listening."

"Outside," Kelly insisted.

"All right." Garden drained the last of his drink and nodded to Sugar, who nodded back sleepily. Garden made a check-writing gesture and, patting Kelley on the shoulder, got down from the bar. Kelley followed, moving heavily toward the door.

Outside, the cold air of after midnight washed over them. Garden looked at his wristwatch in the yellow street light. "My God, Tommy," he said. "Okay, what's the story?"

Kelley came close to him, lurching a little. "Ben," he said, "you know who killed Billy?"

"Hell, no. Who you think did it?"

"I *know*," Kelley said. He looked solemnly at Garden. "Me and Martin figured it out this afternoon. We can't prove it, but it shore makes sense."

"Okay," Garden said, and yawned. "Who killed him?"

Kelley looked around again. "Yore buddy Delmer did, that's who," he said heavily.

"Tommy, what in the hell are you talking about?"

"Aw, Ben. Listen now. I know he's a wheel around town, and he's one of those candy-ass guys that you don't think would really get up to anything. But listen—the woman, Billy's girl. Martin ran into them once, down at the drive-in south of town. I guess when they first started, before they got smart enough to stay out of sight. And he recognized her. That skinny redhead Delmer's married to, you know. You seen her? She used to come in here in the afternoon, before her husband got out of his office, to have a couple drinks. I used to see her looking around the bar, looking at the men. That sort of lean bad-tempered look some girls get, you know, Ben."

"I know what you mean," Garden said.

"Dressed in those whore clothes," Kelley said. "Expensive, but whore clothes just the same. I figured then, look out, a lawyer husband in politics and her sitting around in the bar, looking for it. But then she quit coming in. Just quit, entirely. Was about that time Billy started swaggering around, too. It figures, Ben."

"It figures," Garden said tiredly. "So you think her husband must have killed him? Oh, hell, Tommy! I hope you ain't been talking this around."

"I ain't exactly stupid," Kelley said. "I *know* we can't prove it, but who else would have wanted to kill Billy?"

"Look, just don't worry about it," Garden said, "and for God's sake keep quiet about that."

"I wouldn't kill nobody over a woman like that," Kelley rumbled, "but some men would. You seen her, Ben?"

"I've seen her," Garden said. "You hear me? Keep quiet. Delmer's a lawyer, remember? He'd cut you up bad."

Kelley blinked at him. "I don't cut up too easy, Ben. You forgot, or something? But yore right. I'll take it easy. But Ben, hell! You figger I'm right, don't you?"

"Well, you're right about her and Billy, but the other? I can't see Delmer doing that."

146

"Men have, Ben."

"Sure they have, but they weren't politicians. Christ, what he'd do is try like hell to make sure nobody found out, while he arranged to railroad Carter for something. And he might slap hell out of her, but shoot *him,* from ambush? Not Delmer."

"Goddam it, *somebody* shot him!"

"That's right, somebody shot him."

"What you going to do then?"

"Damned if I know. Hell, I'll talk to Howell in the morning. And to Joel."

"Aw, hell, you know they can't do nothing. If you were still chief—"

"I ain't," Garden said.

"Shit!" Kelley said. He leaned heavily against the wall of the building.

"That's the way it is," Garden said.

"Yeah," Kelley said. "Hey, look there."

"Joel and Howell will do what they can," Garden said. "Look where?"

"Yore buddy," Kelley said. He nodded and Garden followed the gesture to watch a thick man getting laboriously out of a car up the block from them, moving around to the sidewalk and walking toward the bar entrance.

"I do reckon that's yore buddy Arnold," Kelley said.

"Okay," Garden said, "so he wants a drink."

"He's been doing a lot of talking around town," Kelley said. "I reckon we ought to see what he says now."

"Don't get eager," Garden said.

"Aw, come on, Ben. Man looking for it, you ought to let him have it." Kelley shoved himself forward on the sidewalk. "Hey!" he yelled.

"Tommy, for God's sake!" Garden said.

"Hell, sooner or later," Kelley said. "You got to land on him someday. Hey! You, Arnold!"

Arnold stopped near the door to the bar, swaying. He walked slowly toward them. "Well," he slurred. "Chief Garden, the great Chief Garden. Only you ain't so goddam great anymore, eh?"

"Listen to that!" Kelley said. "Drunk enough to be brave, huh? What you think of that, Ben?"

"Don't give me no hard time, Cap'n Kelley," Arnold said arrogantly. "I'm gonna be back in uniform before long. More'n yore buddy here can say, and then we'll see, you give me a hard time now."

Kelley eyed him. "I damn if you ain't drunker than I thought," he said, in a dangerously gentle rumble. "Else you gone out of yore mind. But I can wait. I figure right now yore butt is Ben's. Eh, Ben?"

"Tommy, I hope I ain't around when you grow up!" Garden said. "You're going to be dangerous. Arnold, just get the hell out of here."

Arnold cursed and Kelley laughed at him. "You heard him, pup," he said. "Git! Ben, ain't you going to hit him once, anyway?"

"Shut up," Garden said. "Go get your drink, Arnold."

A couple of people walking toward the bar turned their heads and hesitated, hearing the men's voices. Arnold glanced over his shoulder and saw them. He raised his voice. "You mighty big, ain't you?" he said to Garden. "Still walking around like you ran things. I reckon you'll get shown. You and yore slut and yore rich friends. It's caught up with you, ain't it?"

"Well, well," Garden said hollowly. "That sounds familiar." He found he'd taken a step toward Arnold.

"All right," Arnold said loudly. He glanced quickly back toward the couple. "All right. If you want, might as well get it over with."

"That's what *I* said," Kelley said. "Cute, ain't he, Ben? All set to holler lawyer. All right, you gents step around the corner here. Okay with you, Arnold?"

Arnold glanced again at the audience. "You ain't scaring me!" he said. He swaggered forward, walking just a little drunkenly, past Garden, toward the corner and around it into the dim-lit asphalted parking area.

Kelley turned quickly. "All right!" he said. He waddled away, toward the two who had started to follow Arnold, intercepting them with spread arms. "How you all?" he asked. "Come on, let's go inside. Drinks on me. Let's get in out of the night. How about it?"

"What are they—" one of the others started to ask, and Kelley cut him off.

"Nothin' at all," he boomed, "nothin' at all. Right this way to the drinks. 'Night, buddy," he said over his shoulder to Garden. He hustled the two toward the door with booming laughter.

"Goddam you, Tommy," Garden said softly. He went around the corner. Arnold had turned to face him.

"Where'd they go?" Arnold asked.

"Where'd who go? Nobody here but us," Garden said. He stood with his hands dangling at his sides, ten feet from Arnold. He saw Arnold swallow.

"What's the matter?" Garden asked him. Arnold took a step back. "Don't want to talk to me without witnesses?" Garden asked gently. "Why's that? Somebody to pull me off? Somebody to talk to Delmer, after? Or you think I'd go easy, with someone watching, is that it?" He began to move toward Arnold.

"I been drinking," Arnold muttered. "We can talk this over in the morning, Chief."

"No we can't," Garden said. He took another step and Arnold looked around desperately.

"Nobody here," Garden repeated. "Just you, me and your mouth. Let's hear those things again."

"I don't know what you mean," Arnold said.

"About my rich—about my rich friends. What about it?"

He caught a gleam from Arnold's eye. "Yore too touchy, Chief," Arnold said nervously.

"Yeah," Garden said. He took another step forward. Arnold backed up suddenly and his shoulders bumped the wall of the building. He stood against it and looked at Garden in front of him in the shadows. Arnold's mouth sagged open. Garden could smell his drunken fear.

Past the corner of the wall he could see the rear of his car. He heard Arnold's fast shallow breathing and thought of Angela's statement in the glove compartment and her look of fascinated revulsion when he told her he'd beaten Arnold.

Here he was, in a dark alley again. Feeling the tension in his forearms, his quickening breath, the knotted readiness. Familiar, too damned familiar.

Arnold sagged against the wall, waiting.

"All right," Garden said. He took a long deep breath and felt dizzy. He stepped back. "Go on," he said. "Beat it!" Arnold stood there.

"I said, go on," Garden said impatiently. Arnold still didn't move. "Hell!" Garden said. He turned and walked around the corner, down the sidewalk toward his car.

As he backed out and drove away, he saw Arnold standing at the corner, arms hanging at his sides, staring after him.

"I wonder how he'll tell that around town," Garden said aloud. Christ, he thought. Am I worried about what *Arnold* says about me?

When he reached his house, he took out Angela's statement and locked the car. In his apartment he tossed the envelope on the desk and stared at it. He cursed, slowly and bitterly.

He had the phone in his hand and was trying to recall Angela's number, when he stopped, surprised at himself, and looked at the clock. He swore and put the phone down and then grinned, suddenly. He wondered what she would have said, half awake, to his call. Next to the envelope was the wadded traffic ticket he'd found in Harper's car. He looked at it, the rueful amusement gradually draining from his face, and then he snapped off the light and went to bed.

CHAPTER 23: Late the next morning, Garden drove across the causeway to the beach, his eyes slitted against the glare of the hot sun on the waterway. He followed the beach road south, up onto the dune, past the rich houses, and he turned into the drive of Wayne's beach house. Harper's Jag was alone before the closed garage. Garden got out and went around to the front.

He knocked on the broad door and waited, and knocked again, but got no answer. He tried the knob and it turned, and he swung the door open and called, "Howdy!" He heard Harper answer and he closed the door behind him and went down the hall.

He paused and looked in the morning room and went through it and out onto the veranda. Harper lay back in a wicker lounge. She sipped from the tall glass in her hand and smiled at him, her ravaged smile.

"I knew you'd find me," she said. "Morning, darling."

"I called the ranch and Andros said you'd come over here," Garden said. He looked through the palms down to the flicker of sun on the water swirling in the inlet.

"Come here and kiss me," she said imperiously. Garden went

over and bent down to her in the lounge.

When he straightened, Harper looked up at him. "Well!" she said. "You seem distracted. Not like yesterday, Ben. When I left you."

"No," he said. "Sorry. I'm still half asleep." He moved her legs over and sat on the lounge. "How was the dinner?" he asked.

"Dull. A lot of talk about old times."

"Doesn't sound like your father," he said.

"No! I guess it doesn't. Perhaps he's getting old. Get yourself a drink, Ben, and get me another . . ."

He took her glass and got up. "What is it?"

"Just limeade," she said, and laughed. "Isn't that funny? I feel temperate this morning."

"I'll get a beer," Garden said. "I wound up with Tommy Kelley last night. Tommy's company is hard on a man, especially the next day."

"I haven't seen Kelley in ten years," she said. "Not to speak to. He's getting fat, isn't he?"

"Always was," Garden said.

"Not that fat," she said. "Ben? Want to put a little light rum in that limeade? We ought to have some Puerto Rican in the bar."

"Fine," he said, and went inside. When he came back with the drinks she was standing at the rail of the veranda, staring down through the screen at the inlet.

"Here," he said, handing her the drink.

"Thank you, darling."

"What were you looking at?"

"A nice big cruiser that just went through," she said gaily, restlessly. "Ben? After we're married, you'd like to have a boat, wouldn't you?"

He took a swallow of his beer. "I can't exactly afford a nice big cruiser," he said.

152

"*We* can," she said. "No, wait. Remember what we agreed? The necessities you pay for. I agree. We'll live where your job can pay the rent, we'll eat on your salary, but luxuries *I'll* pay for."

"So we live in a hundred-dollar-a-month trailer and go fishing on our forty-foot Rybovich," he said. "Seems strange."

"The hell with seeming strange. Strange to whom?" she asked. "It seems awfully attractive to me."

"Hell, we could live on the cruiser," he said.

She shook her head. "Oh, no. That would violate the agreement." He threw back his head and laughed and she put down her glass and came over to him, hugged him suddenly and violently and he kissed her, a long kiss, holding his can of beer away from her side.

She broke away and said, "Damn a beer drinker, anyway! You're supposed to use *both* hands. How about lunch?"

He took a deep breath. "Okay," he said, "in a minute. Harper, we got to talk."

"Talk? All right, Ben."

"Let go," he said. She laughed and let go and he stepped away and took a swallow of beer.

She looked at him, still smiling. "You look serious," she said. "What is it?"

"I guess nothing," he said. "I thought I never would ask. I've shut you up every time you tried to talk about it, but now I want to ask you."

"Ask me about what?"

"Switzerland," he said.

She looked at him. "Oh," she said. She turned and looked down at the inlet.

"Okay," he said, "I'm a bastard. But I want to know."

"Who have you been listening to?" she asked.

"I haven't been listening to anyone," he said. "I wouldn't even listen to you."

"Well, there has to be a reason why you want to know now," she said.

"Yes, there is."

"What?"

"It doesn't matter. I'd tell you, but it doesn't matter. You tell me about it."

"I just want to know, so I'll know what I'm fighting," she said. She tipped her head forward a little, thinking. "But I guess I know. What else? So you want to know what sort of wild one you're marrying after all, Ben? What you have to look out for? I wouldn't have thought it would bother you. Certainly not after yesterday."

He went over and put his palm flat between her shoulder blades. She didn't look up or look around.

"I'm not worried," he said. "Not at all. Not about you, Harper. But I told you, I got to ask."

"You don't really have to," she said flatly. "You know. All right, I was pregnant."

"I figured that," he said.

"Nineteen," she said. "Can you guess what it felt like?"

"I can guess," he said.

"Well, guess again," she said, and burst out laughing, a short harsh laugh. "Mostly, I felt outraged. You know. How *dare* this happen to me?" She finally looked around. "All right," she said, "I was pretty spoiled. And now you want to know who did it?" She stared at him.

"No," he said, "not at all. Not now, or ever."

"You don't? My! Suppose I told you I wouldn't know who it was?"

"I'd slap you flat," he said between his teeth. "What are you trying to make me think? I know you better than that."

"Do you?" she asked. "Well, you're right about that. I knew who it was, all right." She turned away again and added, "He's long since gone away, though. You don't have to worry about him."

"I hadn't planned to," he said.

"You brought this up, remember."

"I know," he said.

"You're crumpling that beer can," she said calmly, looking back at him. "You'll get beer all over." He set the can down on the wicker table by her drink. "You've got the strongest hands of any man I've ever known, Ben. 'Even stronger than Tommy Kelley's."

"All right," he said.

"Do you want to know something else about Switzerland?"

"If you want to tell me."

"After it was over, I went into a private school there. It was a pretty good one, if you wanted it to be, and I found out I was pretty smart. It surprised me, a little. I even took a physics course once." She laughed. "I made an A. I've forgotten most of it, but one thing I remember. We were studying the very light gases and I remember how hard they are to keep in a container. They leak right out of anything you try to keep them in. Isn't that funny? I used to imagine a mason jar full of hydrogen. A mason jar, like Dad and his friends used to buy moonshine in, for the hell of it, at the hunting camps out in the Glades. Did you know I used to go out there? When I was twelve or so. I'd make Dad's pilot fly me there in the Howard, when he took out some steaks to fill out the venison and turkey. If there weren't any call girls from Miami there right then, Dad would let me stay the night. All his hunting friends would be there, playing poker in the tent, or telling jokes by the grill. They'd joke at me and call me Miz Camptown Girl. That was my nickname. Silly, wasn't it? They'd be drinking out of those mason jars. They could afford the best liquor, but they liked to drink moonshine out there. Some of them preferred it."

"You were talking about hydrogen," Garden said.

"Yes. I used to imagine this big mason jar, full of hydrogen, only it wasn't hydrogen, it just filtered out like that. No way to get out, but it will, and I knew everyone, everyone would know and they'd giggle over it. They finally had something on me and I decided that it wasn't going to bother me, that nothing anyone in this county thought was ever going to bother me again. Anyone in this state. You know something, Ben? It hasn't."

"Let me have your glass," Garden said. He went in and refilled her drink and took it back out to her. She was sitting on the lounge with her knees pulled up, her chin on her arms, which were folded on her knees, staring out through the screen past the palms. He put the drink down by her and put his hand on her shoulder.

"It wasn't too easy," she said, "but by the time I got back from Switzerland I'd worked it out and none of them have bothered me since then. It's just a case of not letting them get to you."

"Harper!" Garden said. He had to change the tone of her voice. He sat down on the edge of the lounge. "Take a drink!" he said.

She laughed. "I'm all right, Ben," she said, more evenly.

"I'm not so sure," he muttered, relieved.

She glanced at him. "I guess you aren't," she said. "You're not sure about me at all, are you?"

"What does that mean?" he asked. She got up abruptly and walked to the screen. He stood up and followed her, put his hands on her waist. "Harper—" he started to say.

She turned swiftly in his hands. "I wasn't ready to have you cross-examine me," she said unsteadily. Her voice shook with fury. She took a step away and he dropped his hands to his sides.

"I had to ask," he said. "I'll tell you why now."

"I don't want to hear," she said. She turned and walked a few steps and said without looking back, "I know. It was something you heard in your job. That goddamned job."

"Yes," he said.

"What a fool I was! I should have known it wouldn't work."

"Don't be foolish," he said.

She turned her head and gave him a furious look. "Foolish," she said. "I've been foolish all my life. Never more so than when I fell in love with you."

"Never more so than now," he said harshly. "Harper!"

"Get out," she said. "Go on, that's the best way, the quickest." She stared out over the inlet.

"I'm damned if I will!" he said, and started toward her. She turned back once more and gave him a look that might have been hatred. The command in it stopped him and he looked at her and said, "Damn it, you talk about being in love!"

"That might be the most foolish thing I've ever said, too," she said. "Good-bye, Ben."

He wanted to take hold of her, but her look held him and it didn't waver. He looked back at her, fascinated, and nodded slowly. "I won't take this as final. I can't."

"You'd better," she said, "for several reasons. Go on, I don't want you here."

"Can't I—"

"No!" Her voice broke raggedly and he stared and turned abruptly and went out of the room and up the hall to the front door. As he went he thought he heard her voice and he stopped and tried to decide if she was weeping and he almost went back, but then he went on, impelled by the absolute conviction that had been in her face and voice.

He drove away from the house, out of the drive onto the beach road, and turned off beside the palms above the beach. He sat there staring at the surf below him on the sand and then caught a flick of color in his rear-view mirror and glanced back to see her yellow Jag come out onto the road, the rear end slewing as she turned without slowing onto the asphalt. He twisted in the seat and watched the car hurtle toward him, and

157

flinched as it slammed past with the engine note high and harsh in a lower gear. She didn't glance aside, as far as he could tell, her face masked from him by the banner the wind made of her hair. Her car yawed into the turn down off the ridge and he flinched again as its color vanished behind sea grape. He heard the tires squall at the bottom of the turn and then the engine note peaked again, growing distant. After a moment he started his car and followed slowly after her. She was out of sight when he rounded the lower turn and he drove on up the beach.

CHAPTER 24: Pete Burke was in his office and his girl Sue smiled at Garden and gazed worriedly after him as soon as he had passed. Garden entered the inside office and Pete Burke looked up, shoving papers away, grinned at him and then stared.

"You can't have that bad a hangover," Burke said.

"All kinds of hangovers," Garden said. He sat down in front of Burke's desk and looked fixedly at him.

"What the hell?" Burke asked.

"Pete, goddam it, I could kick myself. I ought to, but I got to know, you understand that? You lived here a long time. I got to ask you about something." Burke looked at him and nodded and got up to close his office door.

"Go ahead," he said. He went back behind the desk.

"Hell," Garden said, "I feel like a fool."

"You don't sound exactly foolish," Burke said. "Angry as hell is more like it. Go ahead and ask."

158

"You know what I'm going to ask about, I suppose," Garden said.

Burke leaned back and put his feet on the desk. "Ah, hell, Ben."

"I'm not exactly a country cousin." Garden said. "But I'm beginning to feel like one."

"The Waynes can be pretty high-powered."

"All right, so you understand," Garden said. "I hope you won't— Forget that. I'm sorry."

"Won't tell people you asked," Burke said sleepily. "That's all right, Ben. Go ahead."

Garden looked at his hands, on the desk, and then raised his head. "I wasn't here," he said. "It wouldn't have mattered, I guess, if I had been. But I got to ask, about Harper. When her old man sent her overseas."

"Yeah," Burke said.

"Damn it, don't sound so smug," Garden said. "All right, you guessed, but I got to know what it was like."

"You know what it was like," Burke said, "or you wouldn't be asking."

"Pete."

"I had just started law practice a couple of years before," Burke said. "With old Judge Townsville. Wayne used to talk to the Judge on legal matters."

"All right. What you know's privileged," Garden said. "I still need to know."

"What do you need to know? You know most of it, I suppose."

"There's something," Garden said. "Something I don't understand. Something bugging her. I don't even know the questions to ask, Pete."

Burke studied the desktop. "There isn't too much to say," he said slowly. "She was sent away and you know why. Her mother was already an invalid and not too much in touch with things anymore. She died while Harper was still in Switzerland, but she hadn't been right for a long time."

"I didn't know about that," Garden said. "I knew there was something, of course."

"Yeah," Burke said. "Of course, the old man being like he was, I guess he'd been going his own way for a long time, but we're talking about Harper."

"Yes, we are," Garden said. "Was the—" He stopped and took a long breath. "Was the man from around here?"

"Ben, you ain't just trying to torture yourself?"

"Damn it, Pete—"

"All right, all right. Yeah, he was. He was some guy around town. I don't know much about him, Ben. What the hell difference does it make?"

"It makes a lot of difference!"

"All right! Calm down. All right, I guess he wasn't much, since you're asking. I think a lot of the gossip came from him. Talk that she was going to marry him."

"From him," Garden said.

"Sure, around town. All right, Ben. In the bars."

"I asked for it," Garden said.

"That doesn't make me feel any better," Burke said.

"I don't want to know who he is," Garden said.

"Doesn't make any difference," Burke said tiredly. "He's been dead a long time."

"Dead?"

"Yeah, just after Harper left, or just before, sometime in there. Got hit by a car. He was drunk, I suppose."

Garden stared at Burke.

"Out on the edge of town somewhere," Burke said. "Somebody found him the next day."

"Who hit him?" Garden asked.

"Nobody ever found out. To be honest, Ben, nobody looked too hard. He wasn't much and the story was around by then. Ben, I said I'm sorry."

160

"Yes," Garden said. He got up abruptly and went across the room. He stood looking at one of the paintings. Burke watched his back awhile and then got up and went into the side room. The refrigerator opened and closed and ice clinked. Burke came back into the room carrying two glasses.

"About time for a drink," he said.

"That seems to be the usual answer," Garden said. "Have another drink."

"Take it easy, Ben," Burke said gently.

"Hell, Pete." Garden took the drink, nodded and took a long swallow. "All right. I'll try not to be a bastard. I asked for it."

"I sort of think we ought to get drunk," Burke said.

"Maybe," Garden said, "I don't know. Was McGee sheriff then? I can't remember."

"I think he'd just made it," Burke said. "Goddam it, Ben! It's a long time ago."

"What sort of fool you think I am?" Garden asked. "You think it means a damn to me? She's the one that's up tight."

"You ain't going to help her by worrying about the past."

"You think I'd worry if I didn't have to?" Garden asked, and swallowed some more of his drink.

"I think we better get some lunch," Burke said. "If we're gonna drink this afternoon." The buzzer on his desk shrilled and he cursed and sat on the desk and reached the phone off the hook. "Yeah, Sue," he said. "Oh? Put him on. McGee," he said, aside to Garden. "Howdy, Joel, what you—" He stopped abruptly, listening.

"I'll be *damned!*" he said. "Yeah, okay. Here's Ben." He handed the phone to Garden.

"What is it?" Garden asked.

"Christ," Burke said. "Go ahead, he'll tell you. My God."

Garden stared and put the phone to his ear. "Howdy, Joel," he said. "What's up?"

"Hello, Ben," McGee said. "I done tole Howell, but I figured

161

the ex-chief would want to know. You just might be interested."
His voice had the tinny quality of a radio patch into the phone
lines.

"What the hell you talking about?" Garden asked.

"Yore buddy Ryder. You know, the people's friend."

"Him. What about him?"

"Don't you want to pay yore last respects? We got him laid
out down here on the island."

"What?"

"Yeah, deader than hell, ex-Chief. Why don't you run down
here?"

"Down where?"

"Told you, the island inside the inlet. Come on down to the
lot north of the inlet. You'll find us, I guarantee."

"How in the hell did he get over there?"

"Just floated, I reckon," McGee said. "Somebody out in a boat
spotted him and drug him up on the beach. Right interesting.
Somebody beat his head in, Ben."

"*What!*"

"Ain't that interesting? Didn't stop people gettin' killed at all,
when they fired you, did it? Come on down."

"We'll be there," Garden said, and put the phone on the
hook.

"He told me Ryder's dead," Burke said. "Murdered, I guess.
He didn't tell me any details. You going down there?"

"I guess so," Garden said.

He drove south on the highway to the south beach road and
across the narrow part of the waterway to the island and then
north to the inlet. Slumped back in the driver's seat, he felt
remote from Ryder's death. It was a hell of a thing to feel
nothing but impatience at the death of a man, but Ryder had
been a nuisance alive and he was still one, now that he was
dead. Garden felt guilty, but no less impatient.

He turned off the beach highway north of the inlet, down the steep slope to the lot. A couple of sheriff's department cars and some city cars were parked at the far end. Garden glanced up once, briefly, where the roof of Wayne's house showed through the screen of palms. He found himself hoping that Harper hadn't returned to the house, wasn't standing on the veranda watching him get out of the car and walk to where Mack leaned against the sheriff's car.

"Howdy," Mack said. "Lots of business over here lately, Chief."

"I guess," Garden said. "Where's McGee?"

"He's back on the island," Mack said. "Sheriff ain't in too good a mood."

"Why's that?"

"Well, partly because he fell in going over," Mack said, and laughed. He gestured toward the tidal run between the lot and the island. "Watch yore step! Though I guess it might put him in a better mood if someone else fell in, too."

"I'll try not to, just the same," Garden said. "Why the hell did he call me? I don't work here anymore. Howell here?"

"Howell's here," Mack said. "Go on over."

Garden managed the narrow plank above the tidal run and scuffed through the loose sand on the other side. He took one of the narrow trails through the loose brush, back under the pines, glancing aside into the brush and again thinking of Angela. Damn it, he'd forgotten to take back her statement.

He came out of the thin shade of the pines near the other end of the small island, where a group stood around a blanket-wrapped body on the sloping beach. Garden looked at it, then at the crescent of onlookers from the boats drawn up on the beach. He stood gazing past them across the shimmer of the waterway at the cumulus clouds humping up in the hot afternoon sky to the west, until Howell looked up.

"Howdy," Howell said morosely. "Come and look."

"Okay," Garden said. He went down to the group. McGee squatted soaked beside the body.

"Hey, you're sweating a lot, Joel," Garden said. "You're wet. Ryder, eh?"

"Oh, yeah," McGee said. "Take a look, you son of a bitch."

"It ain't really any of my business anymore," Garden said. He knelt and turned back the blanket. "Huh," he said. "Doc been here yet?"

"Not yet. Figure it was a tire iron, though," McGee said. "Mack'll bring Doc around in a boat when he gets here. No point in *him* falling in the goddam water."

"Doc's still pretty young and agile," Garden said. "Not like some people. I doubt he'd fall in. I don't suppose you got any useful witness?"

"Oh, hell, no," McGee said. "Way the tide sets, I suppose he went in down south of the inlet, drifted up here during the night."

"It's pretty built up, down there," Garden said.

"Still some vacant land, though," McGee said. "And he might have gone over from a boat, too. Who knows?"

"I got a car checking down there," Howell said. "They haven't called back yet."

"Nothing on him?" Garden asked. He had covered Ryder's head again, and he straightened and brushed sand from his fingers, looking away across the tidal run.

"Not much," McGee said. "Usual stuff in the pockets. Usual nothing. No sign of struggle that I can see, just the beat-in head. What's eating you, Ben?" McGee struggled to his feet, stared down at his wet front and then at Garden.

"Hell, I don't know. I told you, this is none of my business now."

"Burke's going to have you back in the job in less'n a week," McGee said. They moved a little farther from the body and the knot of deputies and cops, and Howell joined them.

164

"Is he?" Garden asked. "I saw Ryder last night, by the way, around eleven, after I left you guys."

"I thought you were headed for bed when you left us," McGee said. "Ryder? Where'd you see him?" Each time one of them mentioned the name they glanced at the bundle on the loose sand.

"I was, but I got to thinking, you know, and I went by Delmer's. Ryder was there."

"Delmer's, eh? Sure," McGee said. He nodded to Howell. "What was going on?" he asked Garden.

"Nothing I could understand," Garden said. "They'd had some fuss or another. Ryder left right after I got there. I talked to Delmer awhile and then I left. He came out of his place right after I did. Don't know where he went."

"What you talking to Delmer about?" McGee asked.

"Past history," Garden said.

"Recent past history?"

"You could say that," Garden said. "It doesn't matter, Joel. Nothing to do with Ryder."

"All right," McGee said. "You say Ryder was upset when he left?"

"Maybe. How can you tell about a guy like that? He was on his high horse about something. Maybe Delmer can tell you."

"Well, I'll sure ask," McGee said. "Rather, I'll let Howell here ask." They looked at Howell.

"Just for fun, I think I'll try to find out more about that project Ryder was working on for Delmer," Howell said.

"Good idea," Garden said. "Pete Burke said some clerk down at City Hall knows about it. You might call Pete."

"What project is that?" McGee said.

"A history of the town," Garden said. "Now don't ask me why. Delmer got a lot of stuff out of the old city files and gave it to Ryder to go through."

McGee stared at him. "He did, huh?" he said. "Damn!" He

laughed. " 'Round this town a thing like that might cause quite a stir," he said. "Especially with a nosy son of a bitch like Ryder poking around in it."

"What do you think he might have found?"

"He might have found just damned near anything," McGee said bluntly. "We had a few real swingers running things around here in the past. Hell, you know that, Ben." He glanced at Ryder. "My God!" he said. "My list of who might have wanted to slug him just went up a few names. And even then, I probably can't think of all of them."

"Well, somebody did slug him," Garden said. "You guys better look into it, then." He looked at the swirl of water going into the inlet.

CHAPTER 25: The doctor came, scorned Mack's offer of a boat and got to the island without falling in. The deputies and Howell's men shooed the onlookers farther away and Doc bent over the body and unwrapped the blanket again.

"I don't really feel like looking at that anymore," Garden said. "You want me to make a statement about seeing Ryder at Delmer's?"

"I sure as hell do," Howell said. "Could you go by and have Janet type it up? I ought to run down Burke and get some word on who at City Hall knew about that other business, too."

"Okay," Garden said. "Here comes Jimmy. Looks like he's looking for you."

Jimmy came up to them, looked indecisively between Garden and Howell and said between them, "Chief?" Garden grinned and jerked his thumb at Howell.

"Yeah?" Howell asked.

"The boys found Ryder's car," Jimmy said. "They just called. It's by the waterway, about a mile south of here."

"Anything?" Howell asked.

"It's locked. They're standing by."

"Let's go look at it," McGee said. "Nothing for us to do here."

"Suits me," Garden said. They filed back across the island and Garden waited behind and made suggestions to McGee as the sheriff again crossed the tidal creek, laughing as McGee teetered above the water.

The car was parked behind a row of pines, off an unpaved street, several blocks from any development. It was the car Garden had seen next to Delmer's Cadillac the night before. Howell peered at the window buttons without touching the handles. "Locked, all right," he said. He looked at the patrolman next to the police car. "You touch the handles?" Howell asked him.

"No," the officer said proudly. Howell grunted and went back to his car and took the microphone off the hook.

"I got some skeleton keys," McGee said. "Why don't Howell get his boys to looking for prints on those handles? Looks like it was washed and polished just recently."

Garden walked around the car, glancing through the windows. He looked at the uneven sandy ground, with the multitude of new and old tire tracks, footprints and trash left by fishermen. "Going to be hard finding anything here."

"Yeah," McGee said. They walked away from the car toward the edge of the mangrove, not twenty yards away. The green-lit heat under the mangroves and the thick tidal smell from the mud around the roots hit them. They went along the edge of the filled ground to the shallow end of a canal running out through the mangrove toward the waterway.

"Has to be out that way," Garden said. He gestured at the fill piled along one side of the canal, making an uneven trail out to the waterway. "If he'd been dumped in here he'd still be here. Had to be out there, where the tide could take him north." McGee nodded agreement and they moved into the shade of the mangrove, over the uneven footing.

A hundred yards on, the canal opened out of the dark tidal forest into the blaze of sunlight glittering on the waterway. Garden shielded his eyes and stopped where the fill under their feet spilled steeply down into the root-brown water.

"Right there!" McGee said. "See where it's scuffed up?"

"Yeah," Garden said. He moved down the slope a little, braced himself and knelt to examine the marks.

"Don't fall and wipe them out now," McGee said from above him. "Make anything out?"

"Not much," Garden said. "Enough to guess somebody fell down here recently, though, or was rolled. I reckon there'll be some of this muck and sand still in Ryder's clothes. Lord knows it's different from the beach sand up at the island."

"Can't make out anything in these tracks," McGee grumbled.

"Lots of people come out here to fish," Garden said. "Too bad there wasn't anyone last night. Or was there?"

"Let's stay off the tracks, anyway. The boys can get some pictures of them, too. I doubt it will help, but never can tell." McGee stared across the waterway. "We're just up from the town docks," he said. "Wonder if anybody there saw a light over here last night?"

"Probably not, probably didn't use one. They could have seen by the lights from over there. Enough to swing a tire iron, anyway." Garden stared into the mangrove. "I wonder if it's laying back in there somewhere?"

"If it is, we likely won't find it," McGee said. "I'll have Mack dive in the waterway out from here, just in case, but it's pretty muddy. You figure it was done right here?"

"Well, there's no marks of a body being drug out here," Garden said. "And it would have been rough carrying him, in the dark, with this footing."

"Wonder what you'd have to tell a man to get him to come into a hole like this with you," McGee asked. "In the dark. A man suspicious of everybody and everything, like Ryder was." He turned and started back.

"If we knew that, we'd probably know who did it," Garden said. He started to scramble up the bank and saw a chip of dingy white, half crushed under dirt. He picked it out and looked at it. It was a business card. He drew in a breath to call and turned the card over as he did so, then stopped abruptly. There was a license number written in ink on the other side of the card.

He must have said something, because McGee turned and looked back. "What?" the sheriff called.

Garden clambered on up the bank and walked toward McGee. "What? Nothing!" he said. "Let's get back." The card was in his pants pocket.

"Stay over to one side," McGee said impatiently. "I doubt if these tracks mean anything worth a damn, but might as well not walk all over them."

"Okay," Garden said.

Back at the car, the doors now standing open, another police car there and people sweating in the hot sunlight, Howell looked at them and said, "Nothing, not even a cigarette butt. Ryder must have been one of those guys who sweep the car out every day."

"He would have been," McGee said.

"No briefcase?" Garden asked.

"What? No, no briefcase."

"He had one with him at Delmer's," Garden said. "A dime-store-looking thing, full of papers. He got pretty huffy when Delmer suggested he leave it there overnight."

"Probably at his home," Howell said.

"His home," McGee said. "Oh, hell! Ain't there a Mrs. Ryder?"

"Yeah, there is," Howell said unhappily.

"Yeah, well, that's yore job," McGee said. "That's one I hate."

"I guess I better not leave it too long," Howell muttered.

"I'll go by there with you," Garden said. Howell stared.

"That's one part I wouldn't blame you for missing, Ben," McGee said.

"Might as well," Garden said. He put his hand in his pocket for his keys and felt the bent business card against his fingers. "You know where he lived? I'll follow you," he said to Howell. "Anything you want to start the boys on?"

"They're set," Howell said.

"I'll take care anything else comes up," McGee said. "See you all downtown."

Garden followed Howell's car out to the beach highway and south the short distance to the bridge. He saw Howell using the mike and guessed that he was getting Ryder's address. They went through town and up past Seaview and Garden nodded. Spanish Heights. Howell turned into the development and went slowly, looking for street signs, and Garden glanced at the houses as they passed.

The development had nearly doubled the population of the town. It had been one of the first huge developments in the area during the boom of the Korean War, built on what had been scrub and pineland and pastures north of town and west of the highway and the railroad tracks. A dozen builders had been involved. Several of them had gone bankrupt and their various companies had changed hands several times, in weird corporate-identity dances. Garden had been away in the Army. He had heard some of it and had gathered that no one responsible wanted to talk much about it. Then the city council had annexed the entire development, floating a bond issue to pay some mysterious complex of owners for the streets and the sewage and the water system, to the tune of much talk about "broadening the tax base." With the five-thousand-dollar homestead exemption, the homes in the Heights paid in taxes about a third the cost of the added services. The streets, like the sewers, had been redone at least twice, and every rainy season still made some of them impassible, bringing storms of protests to City Hall.

Garden couldn't remember who had been on the city council then. He thought perhaps Werner and Blough had been, but he wasn't sure. Howell pulled to a stop and Garden parked behind the police car.

Ryder's house was a rectangular box distinguishable from the others on the street only by a shiny glossiness of the paint and a cleaner sharp-edged precision of the close-cut lawn. The street was lined with clean overornamented two-bedroom houses, here in a block of retired people, one of many studding the Heights, painfully neat islands in the wider sea of bare sand lawns, paintless concrete-block fronts, and two or three old cars to each new one scattered in front of the houses. Garden walked to Howell's car.

"I hope she ain't a heart patient," Howell said. "I had one of them once. Went to tell the woman her kid had been in an accident and she went right over." They walked along the sidewalk and up the narrow concrete walk to the front of the house, being careful not to step on the manicured grass.

Howell touched the bell and bright chimes rang inside. The gray-haired woman who came to the screen door was tall, stiffly coiffured, very like Ryder. She looked through the screen at them and stiffly said, "Yes?" and even as she spoke she saw Howell's uniform and their serious faces and they saw the color drain from her face as she swayed.

Garden sighed. "Ma'am . . ." he said awkwardly.

"Is . . . an accident?" she asked, her voice old, the hauteur gone. She shoved the screen door open blindly, tottered, saying

171

thickly, "Charles didn't . . . come home. I worried, and . . ."

Garden moved inside quickly and took her arms. "Sit down, ma'am," he said gently. "Here, let me help you. Shall I get a neighbor?"

"No," she said. "No." Her voice quickened but sounded dull. "They aren't sympathetic people. Why, they'd never help Charles in his efforts . . . their behalf . . . he . . . Was it an accident?"

"I'm afraid it wasn't, ma'am," Garden said. She put her face down in her hands and Garden nodded to Howell and headed for the back of the house, looking for the kitchen and for water. And for a look at the emergency numbers in the front of the phone book, for the Ryders' doctor's phone, just in case.

He was back in a minute, a glass in one hand. He offered it to Mrs. Ryder and she took it blindly and ignored it, talking to Howell, staring past him at the wall. "It was the same up North," she said. "The neighbors weren't appreciative. The same as it was at his company. He uncovered those irregularities at the company and saw to it that the ones responsible were punished and then six months later they retired him. At only fifty-three. He knew it was because of the things he'd said to the papers. They didn't like the publicity. But a man has a right to credit for good works, doesn't he? He still has a suit pending for his full retirement pay, you know." She looked at Garden. "But they never appreciated him. He worked so hard in the neighborhood's interest, but they couldn't have cared less."

"Yes, ma'am," Howell said. "Had he told you what he was— ah—working on? Right now?"

"Terrible," she said. "Terrible. He *knew* there had been crooked work. Out-and-out stealing, he said. But it was so hard to prove. Then such good fortune, getting help like that. He even went all the way to Miami last Tuesday to check on something. Then last night he was just crushed, he was so sure that they had gotten to the one man he had been able to trust." Her

172

color was getting worse. She let the glass tip and the water ran unheeded onto the rug. Garden took the glass gently from her hand and listened to her voice, to the note in it, and went back out to the telephone.

As he dialed the doctor's number he heard her mumbled voice saying, "And he didn't know what to think when he got that phone call last night. So late. He sounded full of hope again. But he was suspicious, too. He was a careful man, you know, officer. So careful."

"Yes, ma'am. Who was the phone call from?" Howell asked.

"Oh, he didn't say. Not even to me. He was so careful. But he was concerned."

"Did he have a briefcase?" Howell asked. Garden blessed him silently.

"Oh, of course. He had all the papers in there. All the proof. Almost absolute proof, he said."

"Where is it, ma'am?" Howell asked. "The briefcase."

In her dry, agonized tone she said, "Why, he took it with him, of course. He would never let that out of his sight. My goodness, that was the most important thing in his life." Garden nodded automatically to himself, listening to the phone ring. A voice answered finally and Garden said, "Hello. Dr. Riordan's office?"

CHAPTER 26: Garden sat in the front seat of his car, heedless of the sultry heat, and Howell came wearily out of the house and down to the car.

"Well, hell," Howell said.

173

"Sure. You get anything more?"

"Nothing," Howell said. He leaned on the open door. "Nothing more than she said there at first. When she started coming apart, after the doc got here, she got suspicious. She recognized you finally. I guess you heard her."

"Oh, yeah," Garden said. "She going to be okay?"

"Riordan thinks so. She's asleep now. In spite of what she said, he found several neighbor women willing to stay with her. Guess part of it is that they're hot for any gossip they can get."

"All right," Garden said. "Don't need me anymore, do you?"

"I guess not," Howell said. "You wouldn't want to take the goddam job back, would you?" Garden laughed. "I better get back to the office," Howell said. "The boys ought to be in with whatever they found out where Ryder was killed—if they found anything. I wonder where that briefcase is."

"Would be nice to know, wouldn't it?" Garden said. "You agree with me that Delmer's the one she meant? That Delmer was the—what was it?—the one man he could trust?"

"Yeah," Howell said. "And what shook him was when you showed up at Delmer's. I guess he had you pegged for one of the bad guys."

"Yeah. I don't quite get that. But I don't know how a guy like that thinks," Garden said. "Though I sure would like to brace Delmer good and hard about what was in that briefcase."

"So would I," Howell said. "I can't see a good way to go about it, though. Not yet." He looked at Garden. "You heard about Arnold? And Delmer?"

"I've heard," Garden said.

"I hear Delmer's giving an ultimatum to the council at a special meeting tonight," Howell said. "Reinstate Arnold or they file a lawsuit."

"I wouldn't be surprised," Garden said. He reached for his car door and Howell stepped back reluctantly.

"I'll drop by in the morning," Garden said. "Give you a state-

174

ment about Delmer and Ryder last night, and one covering today. Okay?"

"Okay," Howell said. He glanced at his wristwatch, grunted, nodded and went toward his car. Garden looked after him. Howell was beginning to wear the job and wear it well. He started his own car and eased out past the police cruiser, turning to head back to the highway.

He parked and went up to his apartment. It was hot inside and he closed the windows and started the air-conditioner, then sat down at the desk, mopping his face with his hand. He pulled the dirty card from his pocket and dropped it on the desk.

The number on the back was scrawled hastily, shakily, but it was readable. There was no mistake. It was the number of the license plate on Harper's Jaguar. He turned the card over. The front said *Lawrence Ferni*. Underneath that it said *Land Investments*. There was a phone number that had a Miami exchange. The card had no address. He turned it over and looked at the license number again. Then he put it down and reached the crumpled traffic ticket out of the back of the desk and dropped it by the card.

He picked up the phone and dialed. The phone rang several times and then he heard Andros' formal voice at the other end.

"Hello, Andros," he said. "Miss Harper there?"

"No, sir," Andros said. "She has gone out."

"When do you expect her back?" he asked.

"I couldn't say, sir," Andros said.

Garden hesitated. "Mr. Wayne there?" he asked.

"No sir," Andros said. "Mr. Wayne is out of town."

"Hasn't gone down to Miami, has he?" Garden asked.

"I really couldn't say," Andros said immediately.

"Okay, Andros," Garden said. "Okay, ask Miss Harper to call me, will you? When she gets back."

"I will, sir," Andros said distantly. The phone clicked and Garden put it down slowly.

He cursed himself and picked it up again and dialed Burke's office. "Pete?" he said. "Howdy. You going to be there awhile? I need some information."

"All right," Burke said. "And I want to know about Ryder. Hell, can't I meet you somewhere? I was about to close up."

"This won't take long," Garden said. "I'll be by in a minute." Standing, he picked up the ticket and the card, shoved them into his pocket. He was at the door before he remembered and went back to the desk to get the envelope with Angela's statement in it. Downstairs he locked the envelope in his glove compartment before he started the car.

In Burke's office he spoke about Ryder's death and answered Burke's barrage of questions. Finally Burke slowed and Garden took out the dirty card and the traffic ticket and put them on the desk. Burke looked at them and raised his eyebrows. "What's all that?" he asked.

"That's what I want to find out," Garden said. He stared at Burke. "You got a lot of contacts in Miami, Pete. I need to find out some things and I need them kept quiet."

"Keep talking," Burke said. "These are personal matters, I take it?"

"That's right—otherwise I'd go to McGee."

Burke picked up the ticket and the card and examined them. "Just what *do* you want?" he asked. "Hell, Ben, this is a Miami traffic ticket, and this is a business card. What about them?" He turned the card over and examined the number written on the back and then looked back at the ticket. "Same number on both of these," he said. "From this county."

"That's right," Garden said.

Burke glanced at Garden. "All right, you sound pretty serious," he said. "What do you want to know?"

"Well, that ticket's for illegal parking. Where? Where in Miami? And the card. Who's Lawrence Ferni? It says Land

Investments. What does that mean? And no address. Where's his office? Things like that."

"I wish you'd tell me what this is all about," Burke said. "Whose car is that?"

"I'll tell you," Garden said. "Later on."

Burke groaned. "Like that, eh?" he asked. "This have any-thing to do with— Jesus, Ben!"

"I said I'll tell you later," Garden said. "Right now it's just personal business. Okay?"

"Sure," Burke said. "Ferni . . . Damn, that rings a bell, but I can't quite . . . Well, I can call a guy I know in the Miami police department. He can find out about this ticket. Although I don't see . . . And that name. Ferni. *Damn*, that name ought to mean something to me! I'll call a guy I know down there. A realtor, he knows everybody in town."

"Can you call them tonight?" Garden asked.

"Christ, Ben! Yeah, I can call them tonight. I'm sure going to be curious about this."

"Let's get something to eat," Garden said.

"I got a client coming by the house," Burke said. "Hell, I'm having to do business over dinner now, and you know what I'm doing after that, don't you?"

"I heard there's a meeting," Garden said.

"Another special meeting. I guess you heard why Delmer's calling it?"

"I heard," Garden said.

"Hell, I thought you said you could turn Delmer off from supporting Arnold," Burke said.

"I thought I could. I guess I was wrong." Garden got up. "I better not keep you," he said. "Pete, could you keep that sort of quiet?" He indicated the card and the ticket on Burke's desk.

"I wasn't planning on putting it in the papers," Burke said.

"It's sort of important to me," Garden said.

"All right! Listen, if Delmer backs the council down and makes them take Arnold back, it's going to make it damned hard to get them brave enough to rehire you. If there's anything you can give me—"

"There isn't," Garden said. "If they put that son of a bitch back on the force, I don't want the job back anyway."

"*That's* a big help!" Burke said.

"Sorry. But that's the way it is."

Garden stopped at a small restaurant where he seldom went and ordered a martini and a meal. Before his drink came he went out and found a phone booth and tried again to call Harper. Andros told him she still wasn't home.

He ate in abstraction and afterward drove slowly through town, consciously avoiding passing the police station. He went over to the beach and drove along the commercial row, past the motels and bars beginning to glitter as the daylight thinned. Past them, under the thick oaks again, he turned a block before Burke's house and went down to the beach highway. He drove south, swung up onto the higher ridge and slowed as he neared the inlet bridge.

He could see no lights at Wayne's beach house. He speeded up, drove on over the bridge and turned down the steep slope to the inlet parking lot, skirting past the parked cars near the inlet docks.

He saw another phone booth, and suddenly remembered the envelope in the glove compartment. He parked and got out and stood in the glass booth listening to the phone ring in Angela's apartment. He hung up and went back to his car.

He had crossed over the south bridge and was coming back into town before he decided to swing by. He could at least leave a note for her to call him. When he turned in at the curb in front of the old frame house he saw a light in her window. He unlocked the glove compartment and took out the envelope, got out and went toward the porch.

The curtains were pulled over the window and he rapped on the wooden door. He waited awhile and was about to knock again when the latch clacked and the door moved inward and stopped against a chain. Angela stared at him through the narrow slot of the door.

"The chief of police!" she said. "In person! Just a minute." The chain rattled and she swung the door open. She wore a red robe and she held it closed at the neck. "I just got home," she said. "Sorry for the delay, but I was about to take a shower. Step right in," she added. "I suppose I can't wait to hear what you have to say."

Garden blinked at her tone and went inside. "Don't see many door chains around here," he said, thinking about the one on Delmer's office door.

"It was Muggs' idea," Angela said. "Makes her feel more secure. She's gone on a cruise to Nassau, and she made me promise to keep using it while she was gone."

"It's a damned good idea, especially for two girls alone," Garden said. "I'm an ex-chief of police, by the way."

"But you won't be for long, will you?" she said. "Go ahead, tell me. You don't have to be apologetic."

"What are you talking about?" he asked.

"I've got a girl friend who works at City Hall," Angela said. "She heard that there was a special council meeting tonight. And what it was about. I suppose you want to get over there. So go ahead and tell me. I'll understand."

"Understand what?" he said. "And I'm not going anywhere. Here." He handed her the envelope. She took it automatically, stared at it, stared at him.

"What's wrong with you?" he asked.

"I'll be damned!" she said. She hooked a nail under the flap of the envelope, tore it, put her finger in it and ripped it open. She took out the folded sheets of paper and stood looking at them.

179

"It's there, all right," he said. "I thought just my having it would bluff Arnold. It would have, too, but I didn't figure he'd get an attorney. At least, not one ruthless enough not to give a damn. So I can't use it."

"Oh, my God, I'm sorry!" she said.

"Sorry for what? You're nutty tonight, girl, you know that?"

She looked at him and he saw she was blushing again. "I apologize," she said. "Lord, do I need to apologize! Wait until Muggs hears I was right in the first place."

"Oh!" he said, understanding. "Jesus, Angela! I told you I wouldn't use it."

"Yes, you did," she said.

"If you didn't trust me, why did you give it to me in the first place?"

She waved the papers aimlessly. The blush was still there. "I did trust you, at first, then I got to thinking. All the gossip around town about you being fired and about that cop having a lawyer. What was I to think? I *said* I'm sorry."

"Okay, okay," he said. "I guess you've been hearing about it from Muggs, too."

"Muggs worries. She's a friend and she's loyal!"

"All right! I wasn't being critical of her!" he said, grinning.

She looked at the papers in her hand. "But your *job?* What are you going to do?" she asked. "If they *do* have to take that man Arnold back—they wouldn't rehire you then, would they?"

"You're the second one's made that connection tonight," Garden said. "No, they probably won't."

"But you can't—oh, damn it! I don't want to feel guilty about this!" she said. She held the papers out toward him, suddenly. "Here, take it back."

"Now what?" he asked.

"Go on, Garden, take it back. You can use it."

"You need a keeper," Garden said. He made no move to take the statement.

"That's what Muggs says," she said and laughed.

"Angela, even if I wanted the damned job, I wouldn't want it that way. Tear it up."

"You mean that?"

"Sure. Tear it up."

"No, not that. Then you don't want the job?"

"Eh?" He thought. "Did I say that? Yeah, I guess I did. No. Hell, no! I don't want it. I was sick to death of it. I guess I haven't come right out and told anybody that until now, come to think of it. I was plenty sick of it, but I couldn't just walk out, you know."

"Why not?"

"Why not, hell! There's an implied responsibility," he said.

"Men!" she said. "Implied responsibility! You mean you've been too stubborn to admit you don't really want the job?"

"I've said—" he started to say, and then shut up.

"Yes," she said. "Why don't you want it? Go on, tell me."

"You know why not," he said. "Damned if I know how, but I'll bet you do."

"Tell me," she said.

He gestured. "Well. It's not just the nitpicking stuff. I can take that. It's a public job, you know. I *can't* just be what I want. Even people I like—hell, it's *their* idea of a chief of police, not mine. I keep getting up against that. Pete Burke—you know Pete? Well, he thinks I'm a hell of a police officer. Maybe he just *wants* to think so, but I don't know. I don't think I'm such a hell of a good police chief. Am I making any sense?"

"Sure," she said intently. "You mean, you're responsible. And you're tired of it. I hear you almost had another fight with that Arnold last night," she added.

"Now where the hell did you hear that?" he asked.

"You'd be surprised what a girl can hear around this town, if she's interested," she said. "I heard you turned around and walked away from him. Is that right?"

"That's right," he said.

"Why?" she asked curiously.

"Why? Well, hell! He'd let liquor make him brave, or reckless. Soon as he realized he was in trouble, he went sick." He shook his head. "There didn't seem to be any point in it."

"Because you knew you could whip him?"

"I *think* I could have," he said. "I didn't know for sure. No, just—there didn't seem to be any point in it." He laughed. "Funny thing. I was thinking about you at the time."

"That's not so funny," she said. She looked at him intently.

"What the hell are you looking at?" he asked, grinning at her.

"At you," she said. "Oh, damn it! Here." She stepped suddenly close to him, tossing the pages of the statement to one side. He put his hands on her shoulders, startled, and she shoved under his hands and turned her face up to him, holding him suddenly and tightly.

CHAPTER 27: "You sure as hell are strong, for such a little girl," Garden observed, after a few minutes.

She raised her head and laughed shakily. "That has got to be the damnedest observation on record. At a time like this," she said. "Let go of me for a minute." He let go and she stepped back, smoothing her red robe.

182

"It wasn't all that irrelevant an observation," he said gravely. "What brought all that on?"

"You know." She put her hands up on his shoulders, holding her arms straight. "Listen to me," she said. "You've been doing fine, so far. Don't get dishonest now, you promise?"

"I promise."

"Good! All right, then. You understand about me, don't you? I told Muggs, when you were here the first time, you've got good eyes. You see things and you understand. You understand about me, too? I have to know."

"I think so," he said seriously.

"I'm not a tramp."

"You're blushing again," he said. "I didn't think you were a tramp."

"I don't think of myself as a tramp," she said. "And I'm not a nympho, either, in case you're wondering. Some men, most men, maybe, leave me cold. But not all of them. Oh, no."

"You don't have to—" he started to say.

"I told you, be honest! Being honest is partly letting me say this and listening to me. All right?"

"I'm listening," he said.

"Good. It's only part physical. Part of it is just the way I am. I like to be touched and held. It's like a trust. It isn't that I want to be sheltered. I think I'm strong enough to take care of myself. It's, like, an affirmation, being comforted, even when I don't particularly need comfort. Am I making any sense to you?"

"Yes," he said.

"You understand, too, that I don't talk like this to everybody?"

"I kind of hope not," he said.

"I want you to know it all," she said. "So there's some more of your implied responsibility here, too." She laughed. "All right, then?"

He took a deep breath. "All right." He pulled her against him.

"Wait a minute," she said unsteadily. "Just a minute. I have to make a phone call, to break a date."

"I don't want to foul you up—" he began.

"Hush. You're not going to foul me up," she said. "Not in any way." She stopped at the door to the kitchen and frowned back at him. "Is it true, what I hear? You're engaged, aren't you?"

"I was," he said.

"God. I've got a real talent for complication," she said. "Well. Want to reconsider this responsibility? You could leave."

"What are you wearing under that robe?" he asked.

"You know very well what I'm wearing under it." She blushed again, deep and richly red, and laughed. "I'll be right in," she said, and went into the kitchen to phone. Garden walked across the living room and stood by the curtained front window. Complication, she said. Oh, yes! But he knew damned well that he wasn't going to leave.

She turned off the overhead light at the switch by the kitchen door and he turned and looked at her. The light from the kitchen outlined her. "Lock the front door," she said. "And put the chain on for Muggs." He fumbled at the door and then walked back to her and she took his arm and they went into the bedroom.

He left before daylight, at his insistence, over her complaints and amused grumbling. At that, he was considerably delayed in getting away. She finally said, "All right, then, you nut. Go stagger around all red-eyed and sleepless if you want to. I'm going to sleep until about three this afternoon."

"What're you going to do then?"

"Then I'm going to get up and have a huge breakfast and have that shower I never did get last night."

"What then?"

"Then I'm going to sit around impatiently waiting for you to

184

call," she said. "Ben, Ben." She held him violently close and kissed him, then bit his chin and then shoved him away. "You better get out of here if you're going to. In a second I'm going to pick you up and carry you back into the bedroom." Her voice changed as she said it.

"You're right," he said. "I *better* leave."

"Damn you anyway! Call by four-thirty. Ben?"

"Yes?" he asked.

"You don't have to call," she said. "You know that. But God, I hope you do."

"I'll call," he said. His own voice had thickened. He went out hastily and swung the door shut behind him. He heard the chain rattle and heard her chuckle, inside. He tiptoed across the porch and down the walk and got in his car and left as quietly as possible. The edge of the east was already light.

He ate breakfast at the all-night place in the middle of town, drank three cups of coffee and went home. It was clear light, a beautiful calm morning. He went up and unlocked his apartment. There was a note under the door and he picked it up and took it to the bright window to read, rubbing his chin.

It was from Burke. It said, *Surprise. Delmer didn't show. Nobody's seen him all day. Call me, if you don't get in too late.* Garden laughed at that and went in to shower and shave. He caught himself singing in the shower.

Later, he paused at the door of his apartment. He wasn't smiling anymore. He eyed the phone and then went out. It was barely six-thirty. He knew that if he slept at all, it would be for most of the day; and that if he ignored the prickling in his eyes he would be all right in an hour or so. Until the next day. Coffee would help, anyway. He went out.

At seven-thirty he knocked on Pete Burke's door. Harmon, Pete's houseman, opened the door and stared at Garden in amazement. Garden gave Harmon a broad cheerful grin and said, " 'Fore God, Harmon, ain't he up yet?"

185

"Just barely, Mr. Ben," Harmon said resignedly. "Just barely. He's in the study. You want some breakfast?"

"I've had breakfast," Garden said. "Just some coffee, thanks." He went inside and walked down to the study. "Howdy," he said. "You awake?"

"I hate early risers," Burke muttered. Garden went in and dropped into a chair and grinned at Burke, who looked carefully at him.

"Or *are* you an early riser?" Burke asked. "You look sort of red-eyed to me, Ben. Harmon getting you a cup?"

"Sure," Garden said. "Thanks, Harmon." He reached back and took the proffered cup and poured himself a cupful from the vacuum pot on the asbestos mat on Burke's desk. "Nothing, thanks," he said to Harmon. He sipped the strong coffee.

"God, you look cheerful!" Burke said. "People like you ought to be shot!"

"It's a beautiful morning, Pete. You ought to see it."

"I'll see it soon enough," Burke growled. He drank the last of his orange juice and eyed his ham and eggs.

"I got you some answers out of Miami," he said.

"Already? You're kidding."

"No," Burke said. "The cop I called went down and checked the central records. He was afraid that a ticket that recent wouldn't have been reported yet, but it had." He cut off a bite of ham, chewed it, swallowed. "And the realtor I know, he had a lot to say about Ferni, all right. I remembered why I ought to know the name, too."

"Let's have it," Garden said. "The ticket first."

"Sure. The car was parked on Northeast Second Avenue. Not the best part of downtown. Parked in a loading zone and sticking out into traffic. Someone had already creased it, according to what the cop said who wrote the ticket."

"How'd you know that?"

"My friend called the cop at home," Burke said. "He didn't

have to, of course. He didn't have to do anything, but he's thorough."

"Sounds like a good cop," Garden said. "Is that all?"

"That's all the cop knew. The two hundred block of Northeast Second Avenue."

"What's wrong?" Garden asked.

"I *am* going to ask some questions," Burke said. "Sooner or later, Ben. All right. Ferni, I knew I'd heard of him. He's some swinger. He's a realtor, sort of, and a lobbyist, sort of. He's got connections all over the place, in Tallahassee, on the state road board. That sort of guy. You know. If you want something to go smooth and you think you need help upstate, or if you want someone to keep other guys off your trail while you're putting in a fix, that's the kind of man you need."

"I understand," Garden said.

"Do you?" Burke asked. "Ferni has an office in a shoebox building on Northeast Second Avenue, Ben. In the two hundred block. Looks like nothing at all. He has a quarter-million-dollar home down south of Coral Gables, though."

"On Northeast Second Avenue," Garden said.

"That's right. Right in the block where Harper got a parking ticket last Monday," Burke said. Garden looked at him.

"I checked the license number, Ben. You didn't expect me not to, did you?"

"All right," Garden said. "I'll tell you about it. Go ahead."

"There isn't much else. I can give you quite a rundown on Ferni. So much that my friend left his home and called me from a pay phone to give it to me."

"Ferni ever have any dealings around here?" Garden asked.

"Some. I'm vague on it but I assume that's where I'd heard the name. He has no connection that I'm aware of with Harper's father or with Harper."

"That you're aware of," Garden said. "Is Ferni mixed up in *anything* up here, right now?"

"Not to my friend's knowledge," Burke said. "There's one other thing. Ferni's got some kind of trouble."

"What trouble?"

"Friend didn't know, but he said just this week there are whispers all over town. Whispers that Ferni's poison. Stay away from him, someone's going to get him. Someone in Tallahassee."

"Tallahassee? Where do the whispers come from?"

"Who knows? But somebody's out to get him, all right, for sure. The somebody behind the whispers. My friend said that it's quite a campaign. One day nothing and the next day, bingo! All over Miami."

"Could stuff like that hurt a man like Ferni?" Garden asked.

"Hurt him? It could kill him. He lives by whispers, by inferences. He sells shade-tree influence, puts together half-clean land deals and sells them. He's got to be a millionaire. But he's got to owe that much, too. The first day of that whispering probably cost him more business than I'll see the rest of my life."

"Harper's father had visitors from Tallahassee Tuesday," Garden said.

"Tuesday."

"The day after Harper got that ticket. In the same block as Ferni's office," Garden said. He got up.

"Well, what are you going to do?" Burke asked.

"What do you think I ought to do?"

Burke stared at him. "I once swore I'd never answer that question again," he said. "Not for any man. Hell, Ben!"

"It isn't that easy," Garden said. "And I'm not just being nosy."

"Oh?"

"Don't you want to know where I found that card? And the ticket?"

"If you want to tell me," Burke said.

"The ticket was on the floor of Harper's car. All wadded up, where she threw it. She doesn't pay tickets." He laughed, not in humor. "Would have been a hell of a marriage anyway, me a cop," he added.

Burke looked at him, his eyes narrowed. *"Would* have been?" he asked. "Where'd you find the card?"

"The card. Yeah. I found that on the ground where Ryder got laid out and tossed into the waterway."

"Jesus H. Christ!" Burke said, in a whisper.

"Yeah, Pete."

"And you didn't tell Howell or McGee? Ben, they'll have your hide! And they ought to."

"After I looked at it and saw Harper's license number on it?"

"I don't care, Ben!"

"I don't know whether I do myself," Garden said. "I'm trying to find out. You understand?"

"All right," Burke said. "You asked me what you ought to do. I take it you don't want to go to Joel McGee or to Howell?"

"Not yet," Garden said.

"Then you better haul your ass over there and find out what she was doing down there. And why her license number was written on the back of one of Ferni's business cards. And what that card might have been doing out where Ryder got beat over the head. Ryder," Burke said thoughtfully. "Ryder and Delmer. This is getting involved, you know that? I think I'll take a closer look at brother Delmer. As long as I'm not minding my own business, anyway. What did you mean, *would* have been a hell of a marriage?"

"What I said."

"You sure live a complicated life, all of a sudden," Burke said.

"You don't know the half of it," Garden said.

CHAPTER 28: Another phone call to Wayne's ranch got him a cautious maid who said she *thought* Mr. and Miss Wayne had gone to the beach house. Garden drove across the north bridge again and down to the house. He was beginning to feel wide awake.

He turned into the drive, rounded the last clump of trees and saw Wayne's old Buick, Harper's Jaguar and a new gray Cadillac parked in front of the garage. He glanced at the Cadillac when he passed it and saw that it had Tampa plates.

He knocked lightly and the door swung open immediately. Andros looked at him.

"Howdy, Andros," Garden said. "I'd like to speak to Miss Harper, please."

"I'm afraid that won't be possible, sir," Andros said formally. Garden stared at him.

"Miss Harper has asked me to tell you that she will not be able to see you," Andros said. His voice was clear and polite and remote.

"I think I'll hear that from Miss Harper," Garden said. "No offense to you," he added.

"Thank you, sir," Andros said. "But I'm afraid not. She was quite explicit, Chief Garden."

"Sorry, Andros," Garden said, surprised. He started to step forward. Andros didn't move.

"Chief Garden," he said. His voice was still quiet and polite but the note was different. Garden stopped and looked at the eyes not a foot from his.

"I see," he said.

"She said no, Chief Garden. And I am accustomed to listening to what the Waynes say to me," Andros said.

"I'm coming in, though," Garden said politely.

"No," Andros said, conversationally and courteously. "No, sir. You are not." Garden looked at Andros' hands, closed one on each side of the doorjamb. Andros was no taller than Garden. His hands were half again bigger than Garden's. His eyes were locked on Garden's and Garden suddenly understood that there was no way he could move before Andros would see the motion coming in his eyes.

"All right," old man Wayne's voice growled. "All right!" Garden's glance shifted over Andros' bulk and Andros relaxed and reluctantly moved aside.

"Come on in," Wayne said curtly. "You might as well talk." He started down the hall, leaning on a cane. Garden stepped inside and turned to look at Andros.

"I don't think I would have made it in," he said quietly to the older man.

"I know you wouldn't have, sir," Andros said distantly, looking past Garden. Garden shrugged and followed Wayne.

They passed Wayne's study and continued on to the morning room. Wayne went to one of the carved chairs by the table and sank into it, sitting straight and glaring at Garden, who sat on the foot of one of the lounges.

"Got somebody over waiting for me in the study," Wayne said unnecessarily. "I want to get back to him. Ask a man over to get his advice, you don't want to keep him setting around. So let's get this over with, Garden. I believe my daughter has broken her engagement to you. Am I right?"

"Right," Garden said.

"Let me say, I regret that. But let me also say, it's her decision. She makes them well, for a woman, and she keeps them once made. So I don't really understand what you want here."

"There are some things I have to talk to her about," Garden said. "I'm not being impolite. But they are *her* business. And I'd rather let her decide who else knows about it. Even you. May I see her?"

"I'm afraid not," Wayne said.

"I'm ready to be stubborn," Garden said.

"*Ready* to be stubborn! Garden, yore the most stubborn bastard I ever met! That's part of why I regret it. But I said, you can't see her. Not now."

"Can I ask why not?"

"Sure you can. Sure. Goddam it, I know you don't intend the humiliation. But it's one just the same. And I ain't going to forgive it," Wayne said hoarsely. He pointed, a violent gesture, and Garden turned and looked where bright sun slanted across the veranda and glittered in a nearly empty decanter on the side table.

"I don't believe that," Garden said when he understood.

"I don't myself. My daughter never has been temperate, to speak of. But not like this. When she didn't come home last night, Andros drove over here. We had worried about her, so he came in and found her. He called me. Now can I ask you to git the hell out?" He looked at Garden with tired cold hatred.

Garden got up slowly. "When will she—when can I see her?"

"She ought to be awake and sober this afternoon," Wayne said coldly. "You can see her tomorrow, if she wants. Call first. Is that all?"

"I guess," Garden said.

"Those things you had to talk to her about. Can you tell me?"

"Maybe I can find out for myself," Garden said.

"All right. Do that. Damn you, Garden, if this is the best you can take care of her, maybe it's good you broke up!"

"We neither of us have done so good," Garden said. He returned the old man's stare.

"I guess I *do* regret it," Wayne said, after a minute. "Andros will see you out."

"Thank you," Garden said.

"Go to hell," Wayne said, and Garden left the room. He passed Andros holding open the front door and looked back at him from the porch. He could see the pain in the man's face now.

"I'll come back tomorrow," Garden said to him awkwardly.

"Good-bye, Chief Garden," Andros said remotely. He closed the door and Garden went around and got into his car.

He sat in it for a minute, hands gripping the wheel. Hell and damnation, he said to himself.

He put the car in gear and turned up the winding drive. He could go south and cross at the south bridge and head down U.S. 1. Once he got on the turnpike, he could make Miami in a very short while.

He turned on the air-conditioner when he got to U.S. 1, and rolled up the window. He found that he was beginning to get angry and it was a falsely satisfying feeling, the sort of feeling he'd thought he had sworn off; that he had started walking away from the other night, with Arnold. That made him think of Angela again and he shifted uneasily behind the wheel. Complications, all right.

But the fury over Harper had shown him something, too. No matter what she said, what her father said, he wasn't through. It wasn't something he was going to be able to turn off so easily.

He thought once of calling Burke before he got on the turnpike, and then he thought, The hell with that. Burke would worry, maybe enough to call a friend in Miami, and Garden didn't want any friends dropping by Ferni's office. He picked up his ticket and drove onto the cloverleaf, looped over the turnpike and around to merge into the sparse traffic headed south. He let the Ford ease up to eighty, ten over the limit. At that, other cars passed him occasionally.

The countryside fled past him. Pines and pastures and scrub, brown-green stands of spiky sabal palms. Dark green groves and occasional ruled vegetable fields. A few miles west, the slowly churning domes of cumulus clouds grew into thunderheads out over the Everglades. Tourists talked about this straight-edged road down to Miami as though it ran across the surface of the moon; "desolate" was the kindest term they used. Garden passed a deep green pasture with Santa Gertrudis beef cattle scattered bright red across it, between the clumps of palms, and thought how beautiful it was. It would be impossible to turn off the turnpike here; you could only get off at the exits. Whether that was where you wanted to get off or not. "That's about the way it is," Garden said aloud, and grinned sourly.

He paid his toll and left the turnpike. He headed south on the expressway through heavy midafternoon traffic, the road rising and falling above the miles of shabby houses and the narrow banks of commercial buildings along the rivers of the main streets. Garden could remember when Miami was a quiet tree-shaded town. He watched the traffic, and the white rise of the downtown buildings coming closer, shining in the hard sunlight.

Driving downtown, off the expressway, was as hard as it was in any big town. Garden parked a block from Ferni's office, lucky to find a place. He got out into the furnace heat, slammed the door and squinted into the glare along the street, then walked toward the address Burke had given him.

The downstairs was as unimpressive as he had expected. There was a shabby newsstand on one side and a clothing store on the other. The stairs between were red clay tile. They went up steeply between the two stores. Garden looked up at the blank second-floor windows, eyes slitted against the glare angling along the street, and then he went up the stairs. The hall

194

upstairs was shabbily carpeted. It ran straight to a dingy window at the far end. The plastered walls were gray-brown and water-streaked. The few doors on either side were painted a dull dark brown.

The first door on the left had the name *Ferni* on it in stick-on letters. Garden looked at the door and then turned the knob. The door opened, to his surprise, and he went in.

The room was air-conditioned; not well but it was better than the dank heat in the hallway. The office looked like any good real estate office. It was a considerable improvement over the hall outside. The girl looking startled at Garden over her desk was an improvement, too. She was beautiful, with the lacquered beauty of Miami Beach. She said nasally, "Oh, hell, I forgot to lock it. We're not open. Sorry."

"You're open enough," Garden said. He smiled at her. "Ferni in?"

"He's not in today," she said. "That's why we're not open. If you could leave your name?" She smiled winningly at Garden.

He smiled back. "Ferni *is* in," he said. "You don't need to announce me." He walked past her desk toward the inner door.

"Just a minute!" she said. Her tone would have stopped most people. Garden had been expecting it. He smiled at her again and kept going. The girl pressed a button on her desk.

The inner door was locked. Garden turned and looked at her. "Let's see," he said. "You probably got a remote latch out here, right? It's that kind of operation." He walked back to the desk. The girl stared at him, the cutely made-up face under the piled hair as still as pink stone.

"Excuse me, hon," Garden said. He took hold of her secretarial chair and rolled it away from the shiny desk with her in it. He ignored her gasp while he leaned over and peered under the desk. There was a heavy button on the right side just under the center drawer. "Thought so," Garden said. He straightened, glanced with interest at the legs showing under her skirt and said, "All right, hon. Now press that button, and I'll go in and talk to Mr. Ferni."

"I'll call the cops!" she said. "Who do you think you are?"

"Who do *you* think I am?" Garden asked. "If you call, ask for Lieutenant Keefer," he improvised.

"Let me see your badge!" she said. Garden grinned at her.

"Let's save that for when it's needed, shall we?" Garden asked. "Okay. You can press that buzzer for me. Or I'll tape it down and go in anyway, and then you can worry about how many charges I can think up for you. What about it?"

"Listen, I'll lose my job!" she said. "I'm not supposed to let anybody—oh, God!"

"You sure you want this kind of job?" Garden asked. "Okay. Press the buzzer." He looked down at her for a minute, until she shifted uneasily and looked away, and then he went toward the door, feeling like a bully. The buzzer sounded as soon as he touched the knob, and he opened the door and went in.

The next room was cooler and darker, with drapes drawn at the windows. It was lushly carpeted, and it looked more like an expensive Miami Beach bar than an office. There were three people in the room. One of them was a tall blond-wigged girl who made the girl in the outer office look like a shopgirl in a cheap department store. Between the eight ounces or so of her net dress and her three-hundred-dollar wig, she had the face of a capable executive. She stood in front of what might have been a desk and might have been an expensive cocktail table, with her fists on her hips, staring at Garden in the doorway.

CHAPTER 29: "I see I'm expected," Garden said. He went in, closing the door behind him, and looked at the two men in the office.

Both of them were in their late twenties. They might have been pro football players, their faces not as yet too scarred. They wore the flashy fashionable clothes, the slightly long hair. One could have been a halfback, big enough to run inside. The other had to be a linebacker and he made the halfback look skinny.

"Neither one of you is Ferni," Garden said. "Where is he?"

"I doubt if you have an appointment," the girl said. "So how did you get in here?"

"Sheer charm," Garden said.

"So we need a new outside girl," she said. "I'll tend to that, after you leave."

"After I see Ferni," Garden said. The halfback gave a theatrical sigh.

"Don't be impatient," the girl said to Halfback. To Garden she said, "All right, mister. Don't you understand? Even if Mr. Ferni was here, he isn't taking visitors. He's busy. So buzz off."

"How come a girl with a figure like yours reminds me of an IBM salesman?" Garden asked her. "I know Ferni's busy. God knows, he's going to be busier. That's what I'm going to talk to him about." He looked at a door in the wall to his right, a slab of wood enameled Chinese red. "He in there?" he asked.

"Are you a cop?" Halfback asked. "Somehow you look like

one." Linebacker didn't say anything. He sat down in a huge curved fancy chair and stared at Garden.

"What difference does that make?" Garden asked. "I'm somebody who's going to talk to Ferni. Somebody he wants to talk to. He just doesn't know it yet."

"If he wanted to talk to you, *I'd* know it," the tall girl said. "You don't look stupid, but you're acting stupid."

"I'll say," Halfback said. The girl ignored him.

"This is about the last time I'll tell you," she said. "Out." She glanced at Halfback, who took a casual step, too casual, toward Garden. He slapped his breast pocket as for a cigarette, frowned in annoyance, looked past Garden to a ceramic cup full of long cigarettes on a low table and started toward them. Garden saw the outline of a pack of cigarettes in Halfback's breast pocket.

He took a quick step toward Halfback that was part of the same motion of his left arm snapping up, and the heel of his left hand caught Halfback between the ledge of his jaw and the cheekbone, with the weight of Garden's shoulder behind it. It took Halfback sideways and brought his hands up and Garden stepped in with his right foot, turning, and hooked Halfback low and very hard with his right fist. He kicked the man's leg out from under him as Halfback was already falling and had time to catch him across the back of the neck with his right forearm as he went thudding down into the thick rug. Garden stepped back and looked quickly at Linebacker, who hadn't moved. Garden was very careful not to breathe quickly. Halfback was absolutely still on the floor.

Linebacker blinked at Garden and said, "You move good. You're heavier than you look, too. What is it, two-ten?"

"Two-twenty," Garden said, lying by twelve pounds.

"Well, Shirley?" Linebacker said. He looked at the girl and got up, ponderous but oddly graceful.

"All right!" the girl said. "You son of a bitch!" she said to Garden, her voice rasped with emotion.

"Wouldn't it be a lot easier to let me talk to Ferni?" Garden asked, watching Linebacker.

"It might have been," the girl said furiously, "before you got rough!" She was looking down at Halfback. Garden was surprised by her tone. He saw Linebacker take a quick look at her.

"Just ask Ferni," Garden said. "What will it cost you to ask?"

"Hell with you," Shirley said viciously. "Go ahead!" she said to Linebacker. Linebacker looked at her curiously and glanced at Halfback.

"Like that, eh?" he asked. "Maybe you better ask, after all."

"What're you, afraid?" Shirley screamed.

Linebacker grinned briefly and sadly, bored. "Of our buddy here? Naw," he said. "But I just found out you ain't thinking clear. Maybe you're right and maybe not, but ask." He glanced again at Halfback, on the floor, and said regretfully, "I thought you had more sense, Shirl."

Shirley said something that made Garden blink and then she whirled away from them.

Linebacker looked at Garden. "You think I'm afraid?" he asked.

"I doubt if you are," Garden said.

"You're right. I got forty pounds on you, if you *are* two-twenty, and you ain't going to catch me by surprise like that, but I work here and I try to do things right," Linebacker said, an odd note of pride in his voice. He walked over to the slab of polished wood and felt under the far edge.

"What the hell you doing?" Shirley squalled. "I run this office!"

Linebacker looked at her flatly. "Not no more," he said. Garden couldn't hear this buzzer. Shirley turned away violently, gave Garden a look of pure hatred and went to kneel by Halfback.

The crimson door clicked and swung half open. The man in the doorway looked quickly at Garden, assessing him, and then glanced at the others in the room. He looked at Shirley kneeling by Halfback.

"Just what the hell is going on here?" he asked.

"Ask these bastards!" Shirley yelled without turning.

The man in the doorway blinked and stared at her. He was middle-aged, thin, balding, with a hawk's face above his rumpled rich clothes. He coughed into his fist.

"What the hell do I pay you for?" he asked Shirley. She didn't answer. The man stared at Garden.

"You're Ferni?" Garden asked. The man transferred his stare to Linebacker.

"What the hell *is* this?" he asked. "A tourist?"

"He wants to see you," Linebacker said mildly. "Pretty bad, I guess."

"So bad you couldn't tell him come back later? What do I pay you for?"

"You don't pay me for that," Linebacker said placidly. He nodded at Shirley. "You pay her and she told him. Only it didn't take."

"So maybe I pay you now," Ferni said after a minute. He looked at Shirley's back. "Hey, Shirley?"

"All right!" she screamed without looking around.

"All right?" Ferni said. "Okay, who're you?" he asked Garden.

"My name's Ben Garden. I'm chief of police in Easton," Garden said, "and I want to talk to you about some things that have happened up there." Ferni looked sorrowfully at Linebacker and made an extravagant gesture.

"All I need," he said. "This is *all* I need." The needling stare rested on Garden again. "You got a warrant?" he asked. "Any reason why I should talk to you?"

"No reason why I can't get one," Garden said easily. "I'm willing to do it the hard way, if you want." He glanced at Shirley and Halfback.

"Right," Ferni said, "but that don't make sense. All right.

200

Time, I haven't got it, but come on in. Maybe whatever you want, you'll find out I haven't got that, either, and you'll get out and leave me alone. That's the easy way, right?"

"Right," Garden said.

"Only remember," Ferni said, "no funny business. I got no time for funny business."

"Not since they starting leaning on you, from Tallahassee," Garden agreed gently.

Ferni stared at him with absolutely no humor. "You talk a lot," he said. "Let's see what you know." He turned and vanished inside the office and Garden nodded to Linebacker and went on inside, closing the crimson door behind him.

The inner office was as large as the two outer offices combined. The Oriental rug on the floor, twenty feet by twelve, was probably the cheapest thing in the room. Garden looked around slowly while Ferni went behind the glowing chunk of mahogany that served as a desk and lit a cigar. Then Garden went over and eased himself into the leather chair in front of the desk.

"Impressed?" Ferni asked sarcastically. He sat down behind the mahogany.

"You've got good taste," Garden said.

"Good taste. You sound like my wife." Ferni drew hard on the cigar. "What I got is money, Garden. All right, you're a cop from Easton. That crappy place. I wish I'd never heard of it. What do you want?"

"I want to know what it was Delmer screwed up so bad that you got pressure from Tallahassee," Garden said casually.

"Who's Delmer?" Ferni asked just as casually.

"Come on," Garden said. "And Ryder, how was he involved?"

"You're wasting my time," Ferni said in a bored tone.

"It could get worse than pressure from Tallahassee," Garden said. "Ryder was here Tuesday."

"I never heard of him."

"Sure, sure, and he had your card in his pocket when we fished him out of the waterway yesterday," Garden said.

Ferni stared at him.

"You hear what I said?"

"I . . . heard," Ferni said. He looked at Garden and there was thin sweat on his face.

"He was murdered, Ferni," Garden said. "And he ties right back to you, along with Delmer. Now you aren't a killer, but you sure better be a talker."

"I think I'll call my lawyer," Ferni said. He put his hand out toward the phone that was the only thing on the desk and Garden put his hand over Ferni's wrist.

"You're sweating, you know that?" Garden asked.

"You're lying to me," Ferni muttered.

"Lying, hell. Rough lines, Ferni. You always play with killers?"

"You got the wrong man. You know who I *am?*"

"Do you? You don't sound like it. Those are tough boys you got outside. Did one of them take Ryder?"

"Listen, I don't have to listen to this," Ferni said.

"You better. You're hung, Ferni. You're hung high. What was the deal in Easton?"

Ferni looked at Garden thoughtfully.

"What happened to the nerve, Ferni? You look like you're sick," Garden said.

"I don't need this," Ferni said. He leaned back to a sea-green ashtray on a table behind the desk and put the cigar down. He pressed one hand to his stomach. "I got enough to worry about, Garden. Honest to God, I don't know about this. I should have to do business this way?" He looked too steadily at Garden.

"You didn't worry about how you did business before this, near as I can tell," Garden said. "How about it? You going to talk about Delmer and Ryder or do I walk out and let it come down on you?"

"How can you stop it?" Ferni asked swiftly. "I mean, you sound like you want to deal. What you got to offer?"

"Nothing," Garden said, "nothing at all. Just your neck. You *want* to go under?"

"Sure, you're dealing," Ferni said. "But why should I want to play? Answer me that, Mr. Cop."

"I told you, I got the card. The card out of Ryder's pocket." He saw the shadow of expression cross the hawk's face and he said quickly, "And don't tell me again you never heard of Ryder. I can see."

"You can see," Ferni said. "Smart cops they got up in Easton, smart country cops. Okay, what you want?"

"I want you to cut your losses," Garden said. Ferni's eyes never left his face. "I want you to tell me what Delmer was up to. I think it's what got Tallahassee down on you. So do you. So why not tell me?"

"Why should I tell you anything?"

"What're you worried about? I can't prove anything, I ain't interested in proving anything. I just want to know what Delmer was up to. And Ryder."

"That's all."

"What you got to lose?" Garden asked. Ferni laughed briefly. "Whatever the business was with Delmer, I'd guess you've lost that already," Garden said.

"Put it another way. What have I got to gain?"

"Just this. You tell me what I want to know and I'll try to take the pressure off you. I think I can. I think so, because when the man pressuring you understands that you're not dealing with Delmer anymore, it won't be worth his while."

"Tell me more," Ferni said.

"Okay," Garden said. "I got nothing to promise, but I'll try.

You know a man named Wayne?"

Ferni laughed long and contemptuously and thinly. "You're wasting my time, after all," he said. He picked up his cigar.

"So you know him."

"You think I'm a fool? Of course I knew he owned— Yeah, I remember him, from a deal a few years ago, but he only had a little of that." Ferni stared blankly at Garden. "Next you're going to tell me Wayne is the man that put the pressure on me. Big news!"

"So you know," Garden said. "All right, then I'll tell you again. I might be able to get him to take it off."

Ferni laughed in his face. "So tell me how," he said.

"What did you start to say? Wayne owned what?"

"Maybe we're through talking," Ferni said.

"Sure," Garden said. "You think I can't smell it, smell you sweating? Ferni, you're dead, you know it. You're panicked over how many others might know it. I told you. Give me a good reason and I can get Wayne off you."

"Who're you?" Ferni asked. He relaxed and puffed on his cigar.

"I'm marrying his daughter," Garden said.

"His daughter," Ferni said.

"You've heard of her?" Garden asked grimly.

Ferni nodded and stared at him. "That's how they were going to—" He stopped abruptly.

"Going to what?"

"That Ryder, sure."

"What about Ryder?"

"That sly crap he kept talking." Ferni shook his head.

"He kept what? Talking about her, about Wayne's daughter?"

"That stupid bastard," Ferni muttered.

"Wayne or Ryder?"

"Neither. Delmer, taking in that Ryder. Letting Ryder talk

him into coming here. Ryder, a *nothing*. I should work with a man hires a dog like that? I ought to have my head examined. Ryder, he couldn't stop talking about the Waynes. What's Wayne? So he's going to sell a beach house. What's to be so hipped up about?"

"Yeah," Garden said. "All right, so Delmer is going to buy Wayne's beach house? In a pig's eye! Wayne would never sell."

"Delmer's problem," Ferni said. "He knew. Get it on paper, then come back and see me, I told him."

"Go on," Garden said.

CHAPTER 30: "You understand that I'm completely out of the deal, as of now?" Ferni asked.

"I hear you," Garden said. "What deal?"

Ferni stared thoughtfully at him.

"I guess I'm nuts," he said, "but what difference? I'll say that before you can say it, okay? It was a straightforward thing, a condominium. Choice beach property. Delmer could pick up the property, strictly not for sale, you understand." Ferni grinned. "Everything is for sale and Delmer said he has the right price. So who was I to object?"

"Beach property? Wayne's beach house? He'd never sell that," Garden said again.

"No?" Ferni asked. He shrugged.

"I don't think he could," Garden said. "There's a convenant, isn't there?"

"Don't make me laugh," Ferni said.

"What did Delmer want with you, financing?"

"Right! Right, what else? Plus, just in case there was any trouble from other property owners in the area, a little legal work upstate, you understand. Besides, he wanted a front. He's the smooth local boy, he can't be a villain, he has to hang onto votes." Ferni grinned. "He didn't say all this so plain, you know. But that's the way it was."

"And it was worth all this?" Garden asked.

Ferni looked at him scornfully. "Say a million," he said. "Say a little over, a little under, whatever, and don't worry about any goddam zoning, okay?"

"What did he say he was going to use to push Wayne into selling?" Garden asked.

Ferni looked at him opaquely. "That I don't know," he said. "I wasn't interested. You get a paper, mister, I told him, and come see me. Then we'll deal."

"Don't you see?" Garden asked him. "That's why Wayne lowered the boom on you. What they were levering him with—"

"I don't want to talk about that," Ferni said casually. "That was none of my business. You go and talk to Mr. Delmer about that, right? As of now, I'm out. You can tell Wayne that."

"I don't think I've found out all I want to know," Garden said. "What were they pushing Wayne with?"

Ferni looked at him carefully, coldly. "You're pretty interested," he said finally.

"I'm listening," Garden said. "You were thinking about it, just now."

Ferni took a slow rich drag at his cigar. "I guess I don't want to go into that," he said.

"I'm still waiting," Garden said. He was trying not to let the strain show.

"You've found out all you're going to," Ferni said. "What else I got to tell you? I made a deal—a tentative deal—with a man

206

who hired some kind of fool. He made some fuss, I don't know what kind, with Wayne, so I'm out of it." Ferni looked at Garden narrowly. "That Ryder's really dead?"

"Really," Garden said.

"It figures," Ferni said.

"Don't get ideas," Garden told him. "There's no profit in it."

Ferni looked at him contemptuously. "You got what you wanted?" he asked.

"All I'm going to get, I guess," Garden said.

"Sure," Ferni said. "Garden, I've talked to lots of cops. Cops don't come in dealing, not when they're being cop. At first I thought you had your hand out, then I knew better. You sap! You didn't find out a damned thing you didn't know when you walked in here. All you did was talk to yourself. Was all that crap necessary?"

"I thought so," Garden said.

"It might cost you," Ferni said. "I don't like to be shoved. I can't afford to get shoved. And I got an office to run."

"All right."

Ferni grinned thinly. "And maybe I'll enjoy it," he said. "I been taking enough crap lately. I didn't really enjoy taking it from you, even for a little while. You ready to leave?"

"Yeah," Garden said.

"Good! Please go out that way." Ferni gestured toward another door, in the far wall. "I got enough uproar in the outer office, thanks to you," he added.

Garden got up and let Ferni escort him to the far door. He stopped, holding the knob in his hand, and looked at the hawk-faced man. "When they were here the other day," he said, "Ryder and Delmer, did either of them say anything about— about somebody following them? Or somebody they saw?"

"Now why do you ask that?"

"Come on," Garden said.

"Maybe they did, maybe they didn't. You know that bastard

Ryder, he talked a lot. How should I remember all he said?"

"So you didn't hear anything?"

Ferni's look was still opaque. Garden wished he could read it. "No," Ferni said. "Listen, I'm busy. Don't come back. And tell Wayne I'm out. I had nothing to do with it, with whatever. Get him off my back, if you want to do something useful."

"You think I can do that in time?" Garden asked. He looked curiously at Ferni.

The look Ferni gave him was contemptuous. "Maybe not," Ferni said. "Maybe not. Maybe you won't try, eh? Well, I made it once, I can make it again. I don't ask for favors, not from punks like you."

"I don't offer them," Garden said, "but I'll talk to Wayne. I guess I owe you that."

"Yeah! Thanks!" Ferni said. "Good-bye, Mr. Cop."

Garden turned the knob and opened the door and went through it. It swung shut behind him and he was in the dingy hall again, at the end away from the stairs. He looked back at the dark brown unlegended door behind him and at the dirty fire door at the other end of the hall and turned and went toward the stairs to the street.

He was nearly to the door that opened to Ferni's outer office when it was pulled open and Halfback stepped quickly into the hall in front of him. Garden stopped.

Halfback didn't look good. He looked hurt and furious and nowhere near as sleek as he had looked before. "All right," he said to Garden. "All right, goddam it!" He closed the door behind him. Traffic sounds came up the stairs into the dim hot hallway.

"What you got in mind?" Garden asked wearily.

"What you think, you bastard? I'm out a job and Shirley's out a job. You think I'm going to thank you and kiss your butt? You got something coming."

"I thought we'd gone the route," Garden said. "Why don't

you just let it go?" Goddam Ferni, he thought.

"In a pig's ass," Halfback said. He eased toward Garden.

Garden sighed. "This isn't going to be too easy, you know," he said. He could hear his own voice. There was a dead note in it that bothered him. He knew Halfback could hear it, too, and that it was encouraging him.

"I don't want it easy," Halfback said grimly.

"Forget it, buddy," Garden said.

"Sure," Halfback said. He took another easy sliding step nearer Garden.

Garden took a long jolting breath. He felt the anger. It used to be a warm satisfying half-guilty glow that would carry him through the violence. It didn't seem to work anymore. He thought fleetingly of Angela. It wasn't really her fault. Or her credit, for that matter. He stepped toward Halfback and Halfback stopped abruptly.

"If that's how you want it," Garden said. He heard the dead note still there.

Halfback's face was in the shadow. The stairwell was behind him and that might help, but so was the light and that didn't.

"I'm gonna—" Halfback started to say, and Garden moved. He jumped, bringing his feet up in front of him, and snapped his legs out toward Halfback's upper body. If it had worked just right, he would have kicked Halfback into the stairwell and that would have been that, but it didn't.

Halfback twisted convulsively and Garden's feet only grazed his chest. It was enough to throw Halfback against the wall, drawing a coughing grunt from him; but it turned Garden off balance in the air and he hit hard on his hip and one hand, trying to draw his feet under him as he landed, spinning on the floor before he had his balance—too late as he ducked, turning.

Halfback's kick caught him on the shoulder, near the neck. Garden went over with it, twisting, banging into the far wall, getting his feet under him as fast as he could. He got far enough up to throw himself back against the wall and catch Halfback's next kick with his hands, shoving up, trying to throw the leg upward. Halfback overbalanced and went over backward. He hit hard and twisted convulsively away. If Garden could have followed, he would have caught him on the floor, but the effort of the throw brought feeling roaring into his shocked shoulder and he fell against the wall. Halfback somersaulted backward to his feet and now Garden's back was to the stairwell. He had the light, but it was awfully close behind him.

"Want to go downstairs?" Halfback asked, and laughed harshly. He didn't sound short of breath. He leaned toward Garden, feinting with his hands.

"Yeah!" Garden said. He stepped quickly into Halfback's dodging hands and hit the man with a short hard left, full in the face. It snapped Halfback's head backward and dropped his hands, and his knee skidded off outside Garden's thigh without damage and Garden twisted and drove his left elbow into Halfback's head and continued swinging his body to the right, bringing his left leg up and out stiffly, ramming his sole into Halfback's groin, catching his own weight against the wall with his right palm. As Halfback doubled forward, Garden shoved off the wall and twisted back the other way, grunting with the effort, and brought his right arm around like a club. The edge of his hand caught Halfback on the thick muscle between the ear and the shoulder and he went sideways. Garden grabbed Halfback's sport coat over the shoulder and continued his swing, hauling Halfback around and forward. Garden shoved and teetered on the top of the stairs, then caught himself. Halfback made sodden thumping noises, shockingly loud, going down the steep stairs. He sprawled loosely through the opening and passersby broke and swerved away from him as he slumped out onto the sidewalk.

Something like a bright bomb, completely and terribly painful, exploded in Garden's back. He fell forward into the stairwell, grabbing desperately at the rail, caught his stumbling descent and turned himself, his weight on his arms, to crash into the side of the well. He hung onto the rail and looked numbly up at Linebacker standing at the head of the steps.

"Nothing personal," Linebacker said to him slowly, "but you ought not to be able to do that, you understand, even if he's fired."

Garden's back throbbed. He said, "I get you," through clenched teeth and hung onto the railing.

Linebacker took one easy massive step down onto the first step of the stairs. He watched Garden carefully. Behind him Garden saw Shirley's ravaged face peering down, glancing at him and then staring down to where Halfback sprawled on the sidewalk.

"He got fancy, didn't he?" Linebacker asked. He shook his head, looking down at Garden. "He always gets too fancy," he said. "Now me, I'm a plain man. No fancy stuff."

"Wait." Garden said with difficulty. "You taking up his mistakes? Wait a minute."

"I'll make my own mistakes," Linebacker said. He leaned toward Garden and hit him. It didn't seem to be a hard blow, but it broke Garden loose from his grasp on the railing and tossed him swerving down the stairs. He caught at the railing partway down and saved himself from the complete plunge.

He careened out the doorway, his knees buckling as he hit the level sidewalk, tripped over Halfback's legs and slammed into the side of a car parked at the curb. He rested for a few seconds and then pushed himself painfully half erect, turning, and leaned against the car. The sidewalk was deserted, except for Halfback's limp sprawled bulk. Faces flickered from storefront shelter, watching avidly.

"Going to be cops here soon," Garden said to Linebacker, who stood just inside the stair opening, out of sight of the hungry faces. "Ain't you had enough?"

"What's the matter?" Linebacker asked. "You hurting?"

"Damned right," Garden said. "I'm serious, you bastard, this is enough. What do you owe him, anyway?"

"Owe who?" Linebacker asked pleasantly. "Maybe this was all for myself. Well, okay. Don't come back, friend."

Garden didn't answer.

He watched Linebacker turn and climb the stairs, unhurried, his bulk making him waddle like a bear going up the steep slope. Above, Garden caught the faint shape of Shirley standing unmoving at the head of the steps, waiting for Linebacker.

Garden shoved himself upright from the car and turned, avoiding Halfback. He walked very carefully, ignoring the interested and furtive looks he got from the shopfronts. He sweated a lot, getting back to his car. Once inside it he sat for what seemed a long time, gripping the wheel. No police car came down the street. After a while he started the engine. Backing out of the parking place and turning into traffic was difficult. He wasn't inclined to twist around in the seat to look at traffic.

"And I still don't know," he muttered to himself, driving. "Nothing more than I did. I guess I can lean on Delmer. I guess I got to lean on Delmer."

Getting onto the expressway was a nightmare and he was sick and dizzy by the time he reached the entrance to the turnpike. He drove north in a painful haze. By the time he reached the Pompano plaza, with the gas station and the restaurant, he felt unable to drive any farther. He angled off the turnpike and parked away from the buildings and got out of his car. He went unsteadily into the restaurant and found the washroom and was sick.

Afterward he washed his face and went out into the late afternoon breeze. He found some shade and sat down for a while. Then he went back into the restaurant and had a couple

212

of hamburgers and drank a milkshake. People stared at his bruised face. He ignored them. He still felt ravenously hungry, in spite of the faint sick ache that filled him whenever he moved. Recognizing the symptoms, he returned to the counter and bought a bar of milk chocolate and ate it slowly and methodically outside, standing in the shade. The cloying sweetness made him want a stiff drink, but he knew the sugar would help. He went to the washroom and rinsed out his mouth and looked at his wristwatch. It was well into the afternoon. He tried not to think about how far it still was to Easton.

CHAPTER 31: Garden unlocked the door to his apartment and went inside, closing the door behind him. He stripped in the dim living room, dropping his clothes on the floor, went through the bedroom and walked into the shower. He twisted on the cold water, taking a jolting deep breath against the shock, then soaped himself gingerly.The old jock-strap instinct, he told himself. Take a shower when the action's over. He dried off and padded naked into his bedroom.

Then he made the mistake of looking at the bed. He went over and sat down for a minute. Just for a minute, he said to himself. Later he dimly remembered lying back across the bed.

He came awake with a start and lay still, looking up at the ceiling.The light in the room was clear and pale. He smelled tobacco smoke and turned his head. Angela sat in the chair by his desk. She smiled at him. "Hi," she said. "Awake now?"

"Where the hell'd you come from?" Garden mumbled.

"Want a cigarette?" she asked.

"No," Garden said. He yawned rackingly. "My God, what time is it?"

"Nearly eight."

"Christ," he muttered. He sat up with difficulty, wincing at the stab of pain through his stiff back. She came over to the bed, looking concerned.

"You've been bleeding," she said. "What happened to you, Ben?"

"I had a rough day," he said. He grinned at her.

"It must have been quite a fight."

"Oh, no. Not like it could have been," he said. "Hell, I'm hardly marked."

"Just a minute," she said. She went into the bathroom and ran water. She came out with a washcloth and a towel and bathed the side of his face where Linebacker had hit him. He let her do it.

"How long have you been here?" he asked.

"Well, you were going to call at four-thirty, so by six I was climbing the wall. I told myself I wouldn't call, but at least I could look up your address and drive by. I saw your car out front, and I didn't see any yellow Jaguar."

"How the hell did you—"

"I told you there's a lot of gossip, if you listen." She looked at him, a level look, and then turned her head. "Anyway, I finally came up. You hadn't locked the door. . . . I like what you wear to bed, Ben."

He glanced down at himself. "Oh! Oh, yeah," he said. "You nut. Listen, are you hungry?"

"My God, I'm starving," she said. "Put some pants on, if you must, and let's go eat. Ben?"

"Yeah?"

"Are you all right?"

214

"What the hell kind of question is that?" he asked. "Hell, girl, give me one of those cigarettes."

"You don't smoke," she said, smiling. "Here." She handed him a cigarette, fumbled getting him a light.

"You're teaching me bad habits," he said. He drew on the cigarette, coughed and got up, walking stiffly away from her across the room. It didn't hurt too much, after the first effort to stand. While he was dressing he glanced at her and then looked away from her level stare.

Outside he took her arm and asked, "Where do you want to eat? The Cattle Car?"

"Let's go somewhere out of the way," she said.

"The hell with that."

"Ben," she said, "I don't want to make any difficulty."

"I promise you won't," he said. "Okay, where, then?"

"It's too bad Devlin's is closed," she said. "All those private rooms. That's where couples like us used to go."

"That's enough of that."

"All right," she said. "Yes, I like the Cattle Car. You'd be surprised how much steak I can eat."

"No I wouldn't." They went down the steps to his car.

In the restaurant several people nodded to him and looked speculatively at her. She looked over at him and said, "See?"

"See what?"

"I tried to talk you into going somewhere more private," she said resignedly, mischievously, "but no, right out in the open. Flaunting me, sort of. Good thing you aren't a public servant anymore, sir."

"Keep it up. I may yet paddle your ass right out here in public, too. Dessert?"

"Lord, no," she said, "and get fat? Fatter. But I'll have coffee. Ben, you don't have that look anymore. Like you're about to fall in on yourself. You must have had a hell of a day."

"Your fault," he said. "I sort of started out with no resources this morning. Yeah, I had quite a day, hon." He said the "hon" automatically and she started to put her hand over his and then pulled it back to her coffee cup and looked around for their waitress. "I met a bunch of funny people," he said. "Some of them are people with a lot of trouble."

"Tell me about them," she said.

"I will," he promised, "but not right now. It isn't really a very good story." The waitress came over and poured their coffee. When she went away Garden said, "You know I feel pretty good now? I really think I'll live."

"I wasn't in much doubt," she said. "But you've got your strength back? How about that!"

"That isn't the most ladylike tone of voice I ever heard," Garden said. "Not exactly."

"It's the steak," Angela said, grinning. "All that *protein.*"

"Where the hell is the check?" he said, looking for the waitress.

"Aren't you sleepy?" she asked. "Really, Ben."

"Sure I am," he said. "I'm going to sleep for about twelve hours. Later. Much later."

"Braggart," she said happily. When he looked away her face changed and she glanced down at her coffee cup, then she quickly composed her face and smiled brightly and wickedly for him.

They left the Cattle Car and he glanced at his watch and said, "Hell, it's early."

"Not too early," she said.

"Yeah. Want to stop in at Smitty's?"

"Why, sure," she said, "of course."

"What's wrong?"

"Aren't you overdoing the hell-with-them attitude?"

He laughed and took her arm. "Don't worry about that," he said. "Come on, girl! No, I just want to see what's going on. You know how it is."

216

"You aren't chief of police anymore," she said. "You don't have to worry."

"Everybody tells me that," he said.

"Okay, then," she said resignedly, "let's go to Smitty's." He helped her into his car.

Smitty's was almost full and the jukebox was working full time. A score of people looked around through the dim roaring room as Garden wedged the door open and let Angela walk in. They found two empty seats at the end of the bar away from the door, Garden nodding and speaking to people and ignoring their furtive looks. He ordered from Devlin, who glowered at him and went back down the bar.

"You certainly are getting lots of attention," Angela murmured. "Ben, you sure this is what you wanted to do?"

"I expect so," he said placidly. She squeezed his arm and then took her hand away.

He nodded to Issac, just down the bar from them. "Howdy," he said.

"Well, hello," Issac said jovially. He peered past Garden at Angela.

"Mr. Issac, Miss Lang," Garden said, leaning back.

"Pleasure," Issac said.

"You still on vacation?" Garden asked.

"You bet," Issac said. "Hey, that woman."

"What woman?"

"Right over there," Issac said. He inclined his head a little. "What?"

"That girl. The one I saw with your man, the mate. That got kilt. Remember, in the car, out at that bar?"

Garden stared across the dark bar, caught a glint of copper hair. "Oh, yeah," he said.

"You don't sound too excited," Issac said in disappointment.

"I already knew," Garden said. "Sorry, and thank you."

"Oh, well," Issac said grumpily, and turned back to his beer

217

with a last sidelong glance across Garden at Angela's legs.

"I don't come in here very often," Angela said. "Is it always this loud?"

"What?" he asked. "Oh, yeah. Yeah, it's pretty noisy."

"All right," she asked. "What's the big attraction?" She turned and looked down and across the bar.

"Hell, I'm sorry," he said, "but I really got to go see about that. I wouldn't have believed it. That dumb son of a—"

"What're you talking about?" she asked. He motioned to Sharkey and put a bill on the bar, taking the drinks.

"I'm sorry," he said. He took a sip from his drink. "I'll be right back, hon, I promise."

"All right," she said. He put his glass down and squeezed past the backs at the bar and she smoothed her hair and looked fixedly at the mirror behind the bottles across from her.

Garden went around the looping end of the bar, nodding to people and slapping shoulders lightly, and came around to Tommy Kelley on the far side of the bar.

"Howdy, Ben!" Kelley said loudly and jovially. "Where in hell'd you get that purty girl? Bring her around here."

"Hello, you stupid bastard," Garden said quietly. "What the hell you think you're doing?"

"Howdy, Mr. Policeman," Delmer's wife said. She twisted on the stool next to Kelley and looked at Garden, flushed and defiant. She had one hand on Kelley's arm. Next to her, the gaunt Martin slipped his arm around her waist and nodded at Garden.

" 'Lo, Ben," he said. "Want a drink?"

"I got one, Martin, thank you," Garden said.

"You know Lorna, here, don't you, Ben?" Kelley asked. He put his arm around Delmer's wife's shoulders, expansively hugging her above Martin's arm. She sat back between the two big men and sipped at her drink and looked sullenly at Garden. Garden glanced briefly at her legs under the very short skirt.

218

"Sure I do," he said. "How are you, Mrs. Delmer? How's Johnny?"

"Fine, I reckon," she said sourly.

"He in town right now?" Garden asked.

She shrugged and glared at him. "Why don't you call his office and find out? I ain't—I'm not his secretary. Jes' call up the office like I do. Till I got tared of it."

"They aren't open right now," Garden said gently. "Was he home today?"

She shrugged. "Maybe," she said remotely. "Honey, my drink's gone," she said, wide-eyed, to Kelley. "All gone! What you gone do about that?"

Kelley turned his head and bellowed, "Sharkey! Damn yore eyes, where you when a lady wants a drink?" Lorna giggled and Martin chortled with her, rocking her on her bar stool.

"Okay," Garden said to Kelley, "I reckon you know what you're doing."

Kelley glanced swiftly at the girl next to him. She was leaning forward out of his arm's grasp, talking to someone on the other side of Martin. "Oh, I reckon," Kelley said softly to Garden. "Don't worry, Ben."

"Worry!" Garden said. "No, I won't. Don't you worry, you hear?"

"We just having a little fun," Kelley said cheerily. He looked at Garden with no humor at all. "Just having fun, Ben," he said. "And maybe doing a little serious talking, when we get around to that—but we gonna have fun first. Hey?" He pulled at the woman's shoulders and she swayed back upright between Kelley and Martin, looking around.

"Aw right," she said smolderingly; not too drunk, not really very drunk at all. She gave Garden a challenging look. "This policeman don't look like he approves," she said to Kelley. "Looks pretty snotty, don't he? You gone stand for that, Tommy?"

219

"Aw, don't worry," Kelley said. He squeezed her shoulders. "Have that drink, then you and me and Martin'll go for that boat ride we been talking about. How you like that?"

"I like that fine," she said, staring at Garden.

"Have fun," Garden said to Kelley. He nodded at Mrs. Delmer.

Kelley laughed loudly and winked at Garden. "I reckon we will, Ben," he said. "I reckon!"

Garden swung up on the stool next to Angela and said, "Hi. Here I am, back the same night."

"Hi," she said. "You sound grim."

"Damned fools," he said. "How you doing on that drink?"

"I don't want another one," she said. "What damned fools?"

"Some people," he said. "Sharkey! Hi!"

Angela looked casually down and across the bar. "Those people, the ones you were talking to?" she asked. The trio had turned to face the bar again, the men crowding the redhead just a bit closer, chortling loudly over a joke while she laughed between them, tossing her hair back and looking over her glass at the others across the bar.

"Yeah," Garden said. "That damned fool Kelley. He's getting her drunk. I guess he thinks he knows what he's doing."

"She's not drunk," Angela said, not looking at Mrs. Delmer. "No?"

"I don't think so and I think she knows what she's doing, what she wants."

"Well, you're probably right there," Garden said.

"Could we go now, Ben?"

"Sure," Garden said. "Something wrong?"

Angela got down from the bar stool. "Probably not," she said. "Just—well, all right, Ben. There, but for the grace of God—"

"Oh, knock it off!" Garden said. He took her arm, dropped a bill on the bar and moved her through the narrow passage behind the backs.

"You don't like that?" Angela asked him. "I'm sorry, Ben."

"Nothing like!" Garden said, shoving the street door open.

"No?" she asked. "All right, Ben." She went out into the street and took his arm and they went toward the car. She pressed his arm and he scowled, thinking about Kelley.

CHAPTER 32: In the morning, Garden sank into the chair across from the chief's desk and looked at Howell, at Burke. "Okay," he said, "so I'm up and I'm down here. What's the rush?"

Howell handed him a cup of coffee and he accepted it eagerly.

"Well, you're in again," Burke said.

"What?"

"Here," Burke said. He handed a letter over to Garden.

"What's that?"

"That's a letter from the council, offering you your job back," Burke said. "Here, take this, too." He handed Garden his badge.

Garden looked at Howell. "Hell," he said.

"Ah, take it easy," Howell said. He hid any disappointment well. "Put your badge on, Chief," he said.

Garden made no move to pin on the badge. He looked at the letter. "I don't see but one signature on here," he said.

"Right," Burke said, "mine. But we voted and the minutes will show it."

"How'd the vote go?"

"Frieden and me for. Werner wanted to vote against, then

221

wanted to abstain and then gave in and made it unanimous."

"How about Blough and Delmer?"

"No Delmer. He's clean out of sight still, and Blough, last I heard he was still on a drunk. A real one."

"Right," Howell said. "One of my—one of the boys got a call down to a joint way at the end of town last night. Blough'd been there all day, drinking in the morning, passed out all afternoon, in a back room. The bartender got shook up finally and called us, figured he might be dying."

"What'd they do?"

"Ran him home. Before they got back to town he was sitting up wanting a drink. They carried him into his house and let his wife have him."

Garden shook his head. "You trying to tell me I'm legally chief, eh?" he asked.

"As legal as anything else this council has done," Burke said with resignation. "Put on the damned badge."

"Here," Howell said. He got up from behind the desk. "Come on around here and sit down."

"Howell, goddam it—" Garden started to say. He looked down at the badge in his hand. "What about Delmer?" he asked slowly.

"What about Delmer?" Burke asked. "Evidently he didn't show up at his law office all day, nor yesterday either. His secretary is about up the wall."

"He's around," Howell said, "but he's laying low."

"What's his wife say?" Garden asked casually.

"No answer at his house," Burke said. He eyed Garden. "You sound sort of cagey. What is it you know?"

Garden reached up and pinned the badge on his shirt front. Howell sat down in a chair next to Burke and Garden got up and sat on the desk.

"You ain't gonna ask where I was yesterday?" he asked.

"I noticed the bruises," Burke said. "So where were you?"

Garden told them. Howell and Burke listened with concentration. Garden said nothing about Harper. He didn't name Wayne. He described the property Delmer had been negotiating for only as a piece of choice beach land and he was aware of Burke's narrow stare.

When Garden finished talking and leaned back to stretch, Howell stared at him and shook his head. "What's the matter?" Garden asked.

"Ben, you didn't have to go to all that," Howell said. "We could have had somebody down there question this Ferni about his business with Delmer."

"Sure," Garden said.

"All right, maybe we wouldn't have gotten anything that way," Howell said. "But what we got your way?" He looked at Burke. "Legally, that is."

"Nothing," Burke said, nodding. "Coffee, Ben?"

"Thanks," Garden said. He yawned. "Damn, I'm still sleepy," he said.

"Nothing," Burke said again, handing Garden a cup of coffee. "Nothing for court. Of course, outside of court . . ."

"Like maybe we ought to spring a few things on Delmer?" Howell asked.

"Yeah. If we can find him."

"He's in town," Howell said. "One of the boys saw him driving in from the country this morning. I asked them to keep an eye out after you talked to me," he added to Burke.

"That won't get around?" Garden asked.

"I doubt if it makes much difference," Burke said. He rubbed his forehead. "Howell's been looking at brother Delmer, Ben. I been helping. Right interesting."

"I'll bet," Garden said.

"You know, you try to mind your own business around town. You might get ideas that somebody's not so good a risk anymore, but ordinarily you don't pry any. Unless you got to do business with him, of course. Mostly you try to mind your own business, and then, too, politics. . . ."

"Okay, okay," Garden said. "What about Delmer?"

"Ben, he's right up the wall," Burke said. "It's not like he was trying to keep up with the Joneses. It's like he was trying to *be* Jones. Either he was figuring there was no tomorrow, or he was sure he was about to have the world by the tail."

"Figure on that last idea," Garden said. "How deep is he in?"

"Like a few days ago he got rid of his wife's little car and got a Cadillac for her. Conned one of the guys at the Cadillac place into giving him enough credit that they look pretty serious down there. He hasn't made a payment on the other Cadillac in three months, either. And he gave one of Werner's salesmen a token deposit on a piece of ranch land, the old Danton place, remember? Now that's a good piece of pasture. So he's got to come up with a third in ninety days; that's over a hundred thousand bucks all by itself. Meanwhile it has to be off the market. Werner fired his salesman, and that's one of the reasons Werner swung around. And there's other things. Little things, like his wife's unpaid clothes bill over on the Beach. I hear that's several thousand bucks. And the liquor store bills."

"What do they say at the bank?" Garden asked.

"What you reckon they say at the bank?" Burke asked. "Not much. They just looked at me and sweated. Delmer's into them pretty deep on the house alone and he's got nothing in savings."

"It ain't too original a picture," Garden said. "Lots of that sort of thing around here. But not many of them are as smart as we thought Delmer was. So what do you think?"

"He thought he was going to get money," Howell said.

"Sure. And a lot of it, and pretty quick."

"Sure! And then his fast deal fell apart. No wonder he's been out of touch. It's a wonder he hasn't jumped the state," Howell said.

"And this about his wife," Burke said. He looked speculatively at Garden. "She *was* Carter's girl?"

"One of them. Or he was one of her men," Garden said.

"And Delmer knew it. One more thing for him to worry about. The last thing of all, maybe."

"It figures," Howell said. Burke nodded.

"I don't know," Garden said harshly, "but I guess it's time we went and talked to Delmer."

"Where you want to start?" Howell asked.

"How about his home?"

"Nobody answers the phone," Burke said.

"What's that prove? Let's go out and take a look, Howell. Pete, you going to come along?"

"Oh, hell, yes," Burke said.

"All right, then," Garden said.

They started for the door and Howell glanced at Garden casually. "Ain't you going to wear a gun, Chief?" he asked. He laughed. "You got out of the habit pretty quick, didn't you?"

Garden hesitated and then said, "The hell with it." He felt Burke's glance again and went out.

It was already hot and Howell rolled up the windows of the sedan assigned to the chief and turned on the air-conditioner. Then he glanced over at Garden, getting in the other side, and said, "You want to drive?"

"Get on with it," Garden said.

"Suppose Delmer isn't home?" Burke asked from the back seat.

"Then we put a man watching the house and we go look somewhere else," Howell said.

"Yeah," Garden said. "Howell, what we going to say if Delmer is home and asks to see our warrant?"

"We show it to him," Howell said. "It's in the glove compartment."

"I'll be damned," Garden said.

"I told you. We been looking pretty hard at Delmer," Howell said.

"So you were going out there this morning, whether I was back in or not?"

"That's right," Howell said.

"Good," Garden said, grinning. Howell drove out of the parking lot and down U.S. 1 through the bright morning. The traffic was already heavy and Garden was glad Howell was driving. It gave him time to think.

They parked in front of Delmer's and stared at the house. "Nobody cut that grass in a while, have they?" Howell said. "Or watered it."

"I sort of think they're past worrying about things like that around here," Garden said. He got out of the car.

"Might as well go up and ring the bell," Howell said, getting out the other side. Burke joined them and they looked at the house for a minute.

"I'll get the warrant," Howell said. "I see her car's gone, but his is here." He nodded toward the carport.

"Well, let's go see," Garden said. They went up the walk toward the house. Garden watched the windows, but saw no one. Howell rang the bell and they waited, sweating in the heat. They could hear the air-conditioner droning around the corner of the house. Howell leaned on the bell again.

They waited and Howell looked at Garden and raised his eyebrows. "Walk around back?" he asked.

"Sure," Garden said. He nodded to the left. "You two go that way," he said, "I'll go by the carport." He let them move away and then he went to the right, looking back until they went out of sight. Then he returned very quickly to the front door and carefully tried the latch. It was locked after all and he muttered to himself and went rapidly around to the carport and eased through it. He felt the hood of the scuffed dark-red Cadillac. It was cold. He grunted and went to the door in the back of the carport.

He heard the scurry of feet inside and jerked back against the wall next to the door. It opened and Delmer came through it, looking around warily. He saw Garden and Garden smiled at him and took hold of the door, just in case Delmer wanted to close it again. He looked at the car keys in Delmer's hand.

"You going somewhere?" he asked.

It was a visible effort for Delmer to get words out. "What business of yours is it?" His voice rasped and his face was haggard and vicious.

"In a bad way, aren't you?" Garden asked. "Let's go in and visit awhile."

"You go to hell," Delmer said more shrilly. "Get out of here. Get off my property."

"Now just take it easy," Garden said. "Don't you see? We're going to *have* to talk sooner or later. I been down to see Ferni, Delmer. It's all over, you know that?"

"I don't know what you're talking about," Delmer said. He looked desperately past Garden at the maroon Cadillac.

"I expect the Cadillac place'll send somebody by to pick up that car in a little while," Garden said conversationally. "It's all played out, isn't it? Let's have that talk." Out of the corner of his eye he saw Howell and Burke come around the carport from behind the house. Delmer glanced swiftly past Garden at the two of them and his shoulders sagged. He blinked at the others, then at Garden.

"That's a warrant Howell's carrying," Garden said easily. "And I reckon you see I'm wearing a badge again? You see we're coming in to talk, don't you?" Delmer looked at him, his face slack, heavy with sweat.

"Just take it easy," Garden said.

"All right," Delmer said. He cleared his throat. "All right. I don't know anything—I don't know what you want, what you think you're after, but we're ready to cooperate. Naturally, I—"

"Shut that up!" someone snarled.

Garden turned his head quickly toward the open door. "Well," he said. "Well, surprise! What you doing here, Arnold?"

Arnold moved closer to the door, looking suspiciously at Garden, glancing quickly toward Delmer. "None of yore business," he said to Garden. "Cooperate?" he said to Delmer. "Cooperate! What the hell cooperating you gone do, you bastard? That ain't how you talked before."

"Now take it easy," Garden said. He looked at Delmer. He was glad that Burke and Howell had stopped out of Arnold's sight. "Mr. Delmer, I told you I've talked to Ferni. I know about your deal with Ryder. Sounds like a sort of explosive deal and I guess it was. You ready to talk about it?"

Delmer opened his mouth and Arnold hissed, "You shut up!"

"What's eating you?" Garden asked him.

"Garden, before God—" Delmer blurted thickly. He swallowed. "I didn't have anything to do with it!" he said suddenly. "I didn't tell him to pull anything like that. He went crazy, that's all."

"What you talking about?" Garden said swiftly.

"Shut up!" Arnold yelled. He stared wide-eyed at Delmer. He was sweating worse than Delmer was. "You shut up! You—big shot! Gone to run this town, you said! Look at you, shitting yore pants. Shut up now!" Delmer backed farther into the carport, away from Arnold.

"Anything like what?" Garden asked clearly and loudly. "What did he do, Delmer? He kill Ryder?"

"Garden—" Arnold's voice cracked.

"At your suggestion, Delmer?" Garden asked.

Delmer flinched. "No," he said. "No. I just told him, quiet him down. I meant talk to him, scare him maybe. Ryder came out when I called, out to the beach, and Arnold went over. Talk to him, I told him, that's all, but he wasn't supposed to get rough.

Not like that, not like that, you fool!" he said to Arnold. "Not kill him!"

"All right!" Arnold said. "All right, you punk!" He reached back to his hip and brought the .38 forward into sight and Delmer tumbled back against the front of the Cadillac, staring.

CHAPTER 33: "Put that goddam thing up!" Garden said. He took a step back into the carport.

Arnold followed the step. He was still inside the door, though. "Yeah!" he said. He was white, palsied. "Yeah, all you big shots, all alike. Gone to make me chief of police, wasn't he? Too scairt to go out of this house last night, too scairt to move. What we gone do, he asked me, what we gone do? I show you what we gone do!" The sweat poured off him.

"You shaking too hard, Arnold," Garden said. His stomach twinged when the muzzle of the pistol swung toward it. "Easy now," he said loudly.

"Easy now! I hear you, Chief of Police!" Arnold said. "I'll show you easy now, both of you big shots. I'm gone get out of here. Too bad you ain't gone to stop me, ain't it?" He licked his lips, moved slowly into the doorway, holding the gun more steadily now, aimed at Garden. Garden took another step backward, hoping to pull Arnold on through the door. He prayed that Delmer wouldn't look toward Burke and Howell and he fought to keep himself from looking at them.

"Come on out, Arnold," Garden said contemptuously. "You mighty big with a gun, aren't you? Always was your problem.

A gun or a badge, anything you felt gave you an edge. Without it you're nothing."

"I ain't taking nothing anymore," Arnold said raggedly. He took another step toward the door.

"Yeah? You'll take anything I want to give you," Garden said loudly. "Step on out here, you silly son of a bitch. You ain't got guts enough to get close, have you? Got to stand back in there. How'd you get poor little Ryder to make it easy for you? You wouldn't have done it if it was hard. Not enough guts."

"Garden! You, Garden, here. Here!" Arnold said wildly. He stepped through the door into the carport. "Here!" he said, raising the gun. Howell's gun slammed shockingly loud under the roof of the carport and Arnold lurched aside and crumpled forward. His gun bounced on the concrete and Garden flinched away from it and then jumped toward it. Arnold hugged his arm to his upper body, half turned toward Garden and tried to speak, and then sagged unconscious. Delmer slumped against the nose of the Cadillac, gray and shaking. Burke swore to himself in a low voice, coming up beside Garden, staring. Howell grinned in satisfaction, shoving his pistol back in its holster.

"Pete," Garden said, "go inside and call. Get an ambulance here, and some cars." Burke vanished and Garden took a deep breath that somehow wasn't deep enough. "Howell, I thank you, I do thank you. Here, hang onto this one." He picked up Arnold's .38, automatically taking a pencil out of his shirt pocket and inserting it into the muzzle. "Delmer, you just stay still, okay?" He knelt over Arnold.

"How's he?" Howell asked.

"Shock. Not too much blood. I think you got him a little low, though."

"I didn't know how close he was to squeezing it off," Howell said. "I wanted it to hit solid."

"Oh, I ain't complaining," Garden said. Burke came out and joined them, nodding to Garden. Delmer slid down to sit on the concrete floor in front of the Cadillac.

Garden eyed him. "Come on, Mr. Delmer." He went over and helped him up. "Let's go inside and talk a little," he said. "Howell, Pete, you guys keep a lookout and get the ambulance around here as soon as it comes."

Howell looked at Delmer. "You need a witness, Chief?" Delmer was gray, staring.

"I don't think so," Garden said easily. "Just getting this one inside before he keels over. Come on, Delmer." He held the door for the man and they went through the kitchen and into the dining room. Delmer dropped heavily into a chair and put his face in his hands.

"Okay," Garden said harshly. "Where's Ryder's briefcase?"

"What?" Delmer asked dully.

"You heard me. Ryder's briefcase. That he had all his notes in. Where is it?"

Delmer raised his face and looked at him. "You and that bitch," he said. "Yeah."

"Make sense. Where's the briefcase?"

"Ryder thought that was her, took down the number—saw her on the turnpike north of West Palm Beach, saw her fall in behind us, then saw that yellow car again, parked. One more thing, one more wild hair. After he'd pissed Ferni off, maybe scared him out of the deal. What a fool! But who else did I have to work with? Who else would go through all that crap down at City Hall? Who else could have found what he found in all that junk?"

"I don't believe Wayne would leave anything incriminating lying around City Hall," Garden said. He watched Delmer carefully.

"Wayne. Wayne, hell! Hell, no—his errand boy. Found enough on him to make him spill his guts. Used to be a big shot around town, too. Just an old drunk now. Talks pretty good, when you get him sober enough to be scared, not sober enough

231

to be careful." Delmer was beginning to recover, to sober out of hysteria. He closed his mouth and stared at Garden.

"Who're you talking about?" Garden asked. He tried to hold Delmer's eye. "Hell, you mean Blough?"

"I don't have to talk to you," Delmer muttered.

"No, sure you don't! I got you good for accomplice in Ryder's death. After the fact. Let's hear more about Blough."

"You don't want to hear it," Delmer said. "Take my word, you don't. Cut it out, Garden. You ain't taking me in on Ryder. You'll deal."

"Deal, hell. Deal for what?" Garden asked.

Delmer laughed shrilly. "Kilt the whole thing," he said. "That fool Ryder. He had to talk to them, I guess. Had to call her up. And then Arnold. If I just had somebody smart to work with! Arnold was supposed to scare Ryder, but they both wanted to be heroes. Ain't that a laugh!"

"I'd like to have it straight," Garden said softly. "I'm going to get it straight, you hear?"

"The hell you want it straight," Delmer said. "You want it hushed up, like all of them. Okay, you're boss. You'll get what you want. But don't push me no more."

"You—" Garden started to say, and then heard the screech of tires in the drive. He looked up frowning as a heavy car door slammed.

"Who the hell's that?" he muttered. Delmer stared at the table.

Garden got up and started through the dining room. He was nearly to the living room when he heard the key grating in the front door lock. He stood still and waited. It took a while, but finally the front lock clicked open and the door pushed wide.

Garden stepped to the side, so he could see into the entrance. "Well, well," he said.

Lorna Delmer stopped inside the entrance and looked at Garden. She swayed a little.

"What'n hell you doin' here?" she asked.

"You feel all right, ma'am?" Garden asked.

"Feel all right? That a hell of a question, Mr. Cop. Sure I feel all right." She walked toward him, not the steadiest walk in the world. Her clothes weren't disarrayed, they just looked that way. Her hair was a tangled mess, recklessly shoved back from her face in wanton bright waves. Her face had the stiff blurred intense look that lots of sex, lots of liquor and lots of rage can all produce. She gripped a large purse, swaying a little.

"Where is he?" she asked muzzily. Garden looked at her, trying to decide if she was about to pass out or about to break into hysterics.

"Lorna?" Delmer said behind Garden. "Lorna, where the hell you been?"

She looked through Garden, moved aside, went past him with her drunken walk. "There," she said. "There you are, you son of a bitch!"

"You—you—where you been?" he asked again.

"Where I been? I been out, you bastard. Out gitting something you ain't been giving me, right?" She giggled unexpectedly, spitefully. "And I been hearing things, oh, yeah, you big shot. Gone run things, gone make me rich. Oh, that's mighty fine and all the time Lorna do this, Lorna don't do that, Lorna take all this shit and like it, Lorna be a lady. Lady, hell!" She glared at him, ignoring Garden.

"Shut up! Shut up. You sound like—" Delmer shrilled and she cut him off.

"Sound like—sure I sound like—sound like a slut, you gone say. You said it enough. Well, screw you, little Johnny. Little Johnny, you up the creek without a paddle now and I heard, I heard, all right." She was weeping now. "You kilt him, kilt Billy Carter. You think I wouldn't find out? They told me, Kelley and Martin, those bastards! They ought to have told me something, after they screwed me all night. And I liked it, you hear, I liked it. How you like that? Only not as much as I liked it with Billy, you son of a bitch. I loved him and you *kilt* him—"

"Wait a minute!" Garden yelled. She moved toward the table, still unsteady, but her hand was quick coming out of the purse with the flat glint of a gun and Garden was just too late, the gun cracking twice before he had her wrist and snatched it up and back, twisting the gun away, spinning her into a lounge at the side of the dining room in a loose flurry of tossed red hair and yellow cloth, a wild huddled hysterical pile.

Over the noise she was making, Garden yelled, "Delmer!"

Delmer stared blankly ahead. His arms were still folded on the dining table. His eyes changed. Dullness came up over them and then the color went out of his face, very quickly. The wound under his eye showed blue against the new pallor. His head dropped over into his arms and some imbalance took him, slid him gently down out of the chair into the thick synthetic rug, a series of tumblings and dull thudding falls. Garden went around the table and looked down at Delmer. He looked as dead as anybody Garden had ever seen. Garden looked stunned at the .25 in his hand. Lorna twisted and screamed on the lounge.

Burke and Howell burst in through the kitchen and stopped short just inside the room.

Garden looked at Burke. "I guess I got what I wanted," he said. He wasn't sure Burke heard him. He thought that was just as well.

The uproar never quite seemed to die down. It ebbed and swelled again. Finally, when the long vehicles with the flashing lights thickened in the drive, an ebb came. They gave Lorna a shot and led her to a car, with Howell beside her holding a notebook. Someone had put a blanket over Johnny Delmer. When the white-clad boys came in to get him with their stretcher, Garden went into the pale kitchen.

He stood by the screen door to the carport, breathing deeply.

It could be in the bedroom. But would he leave it there where Lorna would be? He looked out through the screen. No, it would be somewhere Lorna might not look, and in the house. He looked slowly from side to side, thinking. He knew he'd find it, but it might be a long day.

CHAPTER 34: "All right," Burke said. Garden looked down at his desk.

"Arnold'll live," Burke went on, "and he's broke all apart. It was all Delmer, he says. Not much to that Arnold, was there?"

"There never is," Garden said.

"No. So that was Ryder. And not much trace on the real estate deal. You know about Blough, of course."

"No," Garden said. "What about Blough?"

"Well, it isn't much, either. Just an ordinary stroke. I hear he'll recover, some. Not all the way."

Garden looked up from the desk, from the scuffed briefcase he'd dug out from under a pile of old magazines in Delmer's utility room. "When was that?" he finally asked.

"When? Sometime last night, I reckon," Burke said impatiently. "I heard this morning. He's over in the hospital. The way he was drinking . . ."

"Yeah," Garden said.

"And of course your friend in Miami, Ferni, he ain't going to talk."

"What you trying to say, Pete?" Garden asked.

"Me! Nothing, Ben, you've got it wrapped up. You got Arnold

for Ryder. He doesn't know why, nothing like that. Delmer led him astray, he says, and he wants a good lawyer. Nobody's going to get much out of Lorna Delmer. I don't think. *She'll* get a lawyer; not me, but someone will take it for the peanuts she's got left, or for the notoriety, and she'll get second-degree somehow. Maybe even a suspended sentence."

"That's all right with me," Garden said.

Burke looked at him. "Is it?" he asked. "Okay. And then there's Billy Carter."

Garden leaned back in his swivel chair and looked past Burke, out the window. It was beginning to cloud up, that early in the morning, going to storm.

"I guess it's going to be that Delmer killed Billy Carter," Burke said. "Is that it?"

"That's what Lorna says," Garden said.

"And that's what might get her the way out, in spite of common sense," Burke said. "Okay, you tell me, Ben. Did Delmer kill him?"

"Oh, yeah," Garden said.

"Shit, Ben!" Burke said.

"In a way he did," Garden said. "Pete?"

"No," Burke said. "No, Ben, not no more."

Garden grinned sadly at Burke. "Christ, Pete," he said. "Religion?"

"No. What do you think I am? Okay, a police buff. Playboy lawyer, likes to play cop, likes to play councilman, right? We been friends a long time, too, but there comes a time to stop playing, even with friends."

"What do you want?" Garden asked.

"I want to know what's in that briefcase," Burke said, "Ryder's briefcase. We play these games, Ben. We run the town, okay. I think we do a better job than just any jerk might do, but we get all wrapped up in keeping things looking good. Me, I'm no better than the rest. Hell, I don't want to be any better than

236

the rest. I want to keep things looking good, too. But Ben, there's a limit."

"Well, I'll be damned!" Garden said.

Burke was getting angry. "Goddam it, level with me!" he said. "What do you intend to do?"

Garden got up and went away from Burke and looked out the window.

"I ain't going to ask you if you're engaged again," Burke said quietly.

Garden stood still for a minute. "That's good, Pete," he said mildly, at last. "That you aren't going to ask me."

"That's Ryder's briefcase?" Burke asked.

"Oh, yeah," Garden said. "To listen to you you'd think I'd hid it out."

"Okay," Burke said.

"That's all right, Pete," Garden said. He looked down at the briefcase. "You were awful near right, you know?"

"Goddam it, Ben!"

"Yeah," Garden said. "Keep things looking good and tell yourself that's best. Best for everybody, and keep rearranging what good means, eh? Sure!"

"I don't mean—" Burke started to say.

"Sure you do," Garden said.

"Okay," Burke said. "Get mad if you want to."

"I ain't mad," Garden said. "I had a talk about it with Angela this morning."

"Angela? Oh, yes," Burke said.

"Oh, yes." Garden mimicked him. "Come on, Pete, you know all about that by now. She's quite a kid."

"What did she say?" Burke asked.

"She told me to let things slide," Garden said. "To let things blow over. So I asked her if she'd still want to see me, if I did that. So she got mad as hell, said of course she did, what did I think she was?"

"So what are you going to do?" Burke asked. He kept his voice casual.

Garden looked at him angrily. "Goddam it, Pete!" he said. He rose and picked up the briefcase.

"I don't like this any better than you do," Burke said.

"Want to bet?"

"But I'm not stupid, Ben. I know a lot about what went on around here and I think I understand."

"All right," Garden said. He walked out of the office and Burke followed him. Howell, in the outer office, stood up.

"Get the car," Garden said harshly. Howell went out and Garden followed him, swinging the briefcase in his hand. Burke was behind Garden.

They drove across the bridge to the beach and Garden said, "Let's go down to Wayne's place, Howell."

Howell nodded and turned south.

"How do you know they'll be there?" Burke asked.

"Because I called Wayne this morning," Garden said.

"Ben . . ."

"All right," Garden said. "You figure pretty good, Pete. How do you figure it?"

"Nothing Ryder could pick out of the City Hall files would bother Wayne very much," Burke said. "He should worry about gossip? And any funny business Ryder managed to piece out would be under the statute of limitations. So that couldn't have been anything to use for a lever on Wayne, to make him sell that property."

"Keep on," Garden said.

"But not everybody's as tough as Wayne is, as secure. Maybe Blough wasn't?"

"Maybe, hell," Garden said. "Okay." He tapped the briefcase, twisted around to look over the seat back at Burke. "Right," he said tiredly. "Ryder's notes are in here. That son of a bitch must have been a good accountant, you know that? He followed the thing down through a whole handful of contractor's reports, as near as I can tell. Of course, it was Spanish Heights. Blough was on the council then and he must have got a pretty good payoff. Right good business. Werner was just beginning to crowd him a little and I guess he needed a big deal about then."

"You got that out of Ryder's notes?" Burke asked. "And what does that mean?"

"Not one damned thing, I'd guess," Garden said. "After fifteen years? So they'd bribed people right and left? Who could make a case now? But what looks like sense to you and me might not make sense to an old man with the d.t.'s, eh? And they weren't after Blough, they were after Wayne."

"Ah," Burke said, leaning forward.

"Yeah," Garden said emptily. "Wayne. I guess Delmer and Ryder got Blough just coming out of a drunk, and really put it to him. Delmer probably had the old sot convinced they were going to send him up to Raiford Prison, because the way Ryder's notes read, he really spilled. He told them just what they wanted to hear. What Delmer wanted to hear, anyway."

"And what was that?" Burke asked reluctantly. Howell was silent, listening as he drove.

"Wayne's been pensioning Blough for fourteen years," Garden said.

"I wondered," Burke said.

"Been paying him steady," Garden said. "Enough so that he didn't have to sweat the real estate business. Enough so that he could relax and live it up. Of course, it wasn't enough that he could *really* do without the business. Though I'd guess he didn't figure on that. When it started pinching he probably started to drink a little harder, and he didn't have to worry much about money, so he probably didn't worry at all, eh? Until it was sort of late to worry."

"Yeah," Burke said. They turned up onto the ridge, above the glittering morning sea.

"Well," Garden said.

"You want to go on?" Burke asked.

"Oh, hell, Pete!" Garden said. "You probably can guess. Anyway, it's in there." He nodded down at the briefcase. "Turn in here, Howell," he added.

"I know," Howell said. They turned, dipped down toward the waterway, swung around and stopped outside the garage. Garden glanced at the yellow Jag, at the old Buick.

"I got to go inside," he said. "Have a little talk."

"You want me to go in with you?" Howell asked.

"No," Garden said. "This is my party. You guys take it easy. I'll be back in a while." He got out of the car, looked in at them. Burke got out the other side, walked around and leaned against the fender.

"All right!" Garden said to Burke. He turned and made his way to the front steps, up to the veranda and the front door. It opened as he approached it, and Wayne looked at him.

"I see you're wearing that badge again," he said.

"You answering your own door today?" Garden asked. "Yes, sir, I'm wearing that badge again. May I come in?"

"All right," Wayne said. "Come on in." He turned and Garden went in and followed the stooped old man down the hall and into the study.

Wayne went around behind the desk and slumped into his chair and then looked up at Garden. The cold bright glare belied his tired posture. "All right," he said. "Why you here?"

"You know, don't you, really?"

"I don't feel like guessing games. Suppose you tell me."

"I had to run all around hell," Garden said, "but I ran. And I found out things. Delmer was pushing you to sell this place, wasn't he?"

"Delmer? He's that punk kid on the council, from over in the 'Glades?"

"Don't give me that shit!" Garden said. "I told you, I found out. He was pushing you and you wouldn't sell, of course, so he got dirty. Pretty stupid of him, but he did."

Wayne looked unwinkingly at Garden. "You got any more wild ideas?" he asked.

"Lots," Garden said. "He had that guy, Ryder. Sick, but good at his business. He was an accountant. Delmer got him some foolish stuff out of the city files and Ryder put two and two together and they came out five and they pointed back to Blough."

"What the hell is this all about?" Wayne asked.

"Can't you understand I'm not bluffing you?" Garden asked. He swallowed. "Goddam it! Least you could do is help me out some."

Wayne's face was stony. "What am I supposed to have to do with anything this Ryder got out of city files, or with this Delmer? Or with John Blough?"

"That last one is one question too many," Garden said. "You been paying Blough's bar bill for fourteen years and Delmer found out why."

"You could leave now," Wayne said.

"No, of course you ain't tied into anything with the city. It was Spanish Heights, wasn't it? I guess you sold the land in the first place, but you didn't show up anywhere. Nothing to tie you to fraud."

"Or anybody else," Wayne said. "At least, I doubt."

"I guess not, too," Garden said, "but Blough, drunk and punchy as he is? Probably wasn't too hard for Delmer to convince him they had him by the balls. Once they figured out he *must* have something on you, why, then he was worth their while."

"You seem to know more than I want to know," Wayne said. "Git out of here, will you?"

"No," Garden said. "Yeah, I know a lot. More than I wanted to. I been reading Ryder's notes. Do I have to talk about what they pounded out of poor old Blough?"

"I don't want to talk about Blough," Wayne said hoarsely. "I gave up on that son of a bitch years ago. And this Ryder, why should I be interested in a sad bastard like him?"

"Oh, come on," Garden said raggedly. "When somebody took a shot at him from up here, coming in the inlet on Tommy Kelley's boat, and missed him and hit Billy Carter? Poor Billy. Old fisherman like him, he deserved better luck. I told you, I read Ryder's notes. And the shot *had* to come from up here."

"I'm going to take you on this," Wayne said. His voice was almost calm, but not quite. "You're making a bad mistake, Ben, bad."

"No mistake. None at all. I tell you, I *know*, Mr. Wayne. You think this is easy for me? Think again. But I know."

"You can't—"

"Prove it? I can make a case. It was always plain, always. I tried like hell not to see it. But the shot *couldn't* have come from nowhere else. And I got what Ryder wrote out. I guess he called, didn't he? The slimy little son of a bitch. Delmer complained about Ryder fouling him up. Delmer was after money. Ryder was after fun, his kind of fun."

"Delmer's dead, I hear," Wayne said. "Ryder's dead."

"Right. But Blough isn't, not yet. And I got Ryder's notes. Ain't you going to help me at all?"

"What do you want?" Wayne asked distantly.

"I want a way out of this. I can't see any. I can't let it go. Don't you see that? I tried to—God almighty how I tried to! But I just can't."

"All right," Wayne said. He sounded far away. "I guess I knew. Hell of a thing, when a man can't protect his family. That bastard. What did you call him, slimy? That doesn't say it, Garden. A man like that, he can't expect to be let alone!"

"Can't he?" Garden said. "You want me to believe *you* shot at him? You wouldn't be so stupid. And you wouldn't miss."

242

"I told you," Wayne said harshly, remotely. "I told you. What more do you want?"

"I want out of this," Garden said. "But I'm not going to get out, am I?"

"Git out of here!" Wayne said desperately.

"All right," Garden said. He went out into the hall, leaving the old man looking down at the cluttered desk.

In the hall, Andros looked somberly at Garden. "I heard," he said.

"All right!" Garden said. "What have *you* got to say?"

"You can't believe Mr. Wayne fired that shot," Andros said. "As you said, he would not be so stupid."

"Okay, I'm listening," Garden said. He felt the desire to laugh building within him, knowing exactly what Andros was going to say.

"Chief Garden, I shot at that little man, that bastard."

"No shit!" Garden said.

"I tell you, I overheard the phone call. I listened then after I had seen how Miss Wayne acted, after the first call. That was an evil man, a vicious man. He wanted to pull everyone down, to hurt everyone. Not for any good, just to hurt. I knew he had to be stopped and you do not stop a sick man like that short of killing him, so when the boat went out I saw him aboard and I got the rifle. When the boat came back in at noon, I fired at him. I am sorry I missed, and sorry, too, that I killed the mate."

"I hear you."

"I am ready to go with you," Andros said.

"Goddam it, Andros!" Garden muttered. He walked away, down the hall. He stopped and looked back.

Andros stood looking after him. His eyes glittered even in the dim light.

"I will wait by the door," Andros said courteously.

"Don't bother," Garden said wearily. He went into the morning room.

"It's about time!" Harper said, her voice gay and glassy.

"Yes," Garden said. "About time."

"I heard some of what Andros was saying in the hall," she said. "Enough to understand. Well, Ben, here we are, eh?" She picked up her glass and sighed at him through the amber glow. "Of course, you know Andros didn't do it."

"Of course," Garden said.

"And I suppose you want to know all about it."

"Want to! No, not really."

"That phone call. Ryder. God, what a voice! *There* was a man who'd found his mission in life. Ben, you should have heard it. He knew everything and, God, was he happy about it! He practically *oozed* triumph. What makes people like that, anyway?"

"Damned if I know," Garden said. "Damned if I know anything."

"Well, anyway"—she took a long swallow—"as I say, he knew it all." Her laugh rang like thin silver. Garden shifted uneasily. "Oh, he left no doubt about that. John Blough must have fallen all apart. I guess you know it all, don't you?"

"No," Garden said. "Damn it, Harper!"

"I really don't think I meant to do it. You know the funny thing, the really funny thing? I went out there that night thinking he'd marry me. I was *happy*, Ben! Isn't that funny? I remember how happy I was. I thought, I'll tell him how it is with me and he'll want to marry me after all. All this misunderstanding will be over with. Isn't that funny?" She drained the glass. "I was just nineteen," she added.

"Not very funny," Garden said.

"So then I found out different and when he got out of the car laughing at me and started to walk away—"

"All right!" Garden said.

"Blough was the one Dad called. Blough was very good. I couldn't stand him. He saw to it that everything was kept quiet, and he got rid of my car and paid off the deputy who found the body. Very clever, wasn't it, Ben? Good business for John Blough, too, until just recently. You know, I can't remember what he looked like, not at all."

"Listen," Garden said. "Oh, Harper, listen to me—"

"No, Ben," she said. "Too late to listen." She poured herself another drink and Garden walked up close to her and looked at her hands.

"I didn't understand how you could do it," he said. "How you could be so calm, so easy. But you weren't, were you?" He watched the gentle tremor of her hands. "Ah, God, Harper, how long have you been like that?"

"A long time," she whispered, "a long time, Ben." She raised her glass.

Garden looked at her and took the long breath. All right, he thought hopelessly, and then the shot slammed through the house, through the hall behind them, shocking the words from him.

She turned slowly, her face fragile, her eyes huge, and looked at him; not out into the hall, but at Garden.

"Oh, God!" he said stupidly.

"Oh, yes," she said distantly. "Yes. That's all I need."

"Harper!" he said. He reached for her. She pulled away stiffly, looking at him furiously, slyly.

"Oh, no!" she said. "No!" She lifted the glass in both hands, looking over the glass at him. "No!" she said again. "Don't you see? No, not ever. Go on, now."

"Oh, God," he said again. He turned and went into the hall. Andros stood by the door to the study, looking at him with no expression. Garden went swiftly up the hall and brushed past Andros, opening the door to the study. He stopped just inside, staring at the desk.

He turned and went out into the hall again and looked at Andros. "He sure as God did it right," he said emptily. "I guess there'll be a note there, too. Sure."

"I'll call your police, sir," Andros said woodenly. He looked through Garden while he spoke.

"Don't bother," Garden said. "They're just outside." He went past Andros and out across the veranda, down the steps and around the brick walk. He met Burke and Howell halfway around.

"What was that, Ben?" Howell asked. "A shot, wasn't it?"

Garden grunted. He pulled his badge loose from his shirt. "Here," he said to Howell. "That? Oh, yeah. You got another dead one inside. A confession, sort of. I doubt if you'll be able to shake it."

"What?" Howell asked. "What? Hell, Ben!"

"Here," Garden said again, shoving his badge at Howell. "Here. You're chief again. I've had it. Here, take it! I'll be in the car," he said to Burke. Howell automatically took the badge, stared down at it.

"Ben!" Burke said.

"Go on inside!" Garden said. "You're the police buff, ain't you?" He pushed past them and went on along the brick path, under the gently moving palms, toward the car; free, and breathing deeply, trying to get enough air.